Moss Hysteria

A Flower Shop Mystery

Kate Collins

AN OBSIDIAN MYSTERY

OBSIDIAN
Published by New American Library,
an imprint of Penguin Random House LLC
375 Hudson Street, New York, New York 10014

This book is an original publication of New American Library.

First Printing, April 2016

For more information about Penguin Random House, visit penguin.com.

ISBN 978-0-451-47344-8

Printed in the United States of America
10 9 8 7 6 5 4 3 2 1

Penguin
Random
House

PRAISE FOR THE *NEW YORK TIMES* BESTSELLING FLOWER SHOP MYSTERIES

"One of my favorite mystery series."
—Kate Carlisle, *New York Times* bestselling author
of the Bibliophile Mysteries

"The Flower Shop Mystery series stays fresh and keeps getting better." —*RT Book Reviews*

"Kate Collins never fails to deliver a spectacular story."
—Lorna Barrett, *New York Times* bestselling author
of the Booktown Mysteries

"A nimble, well-crafted plot with forget-me-not characters."
—Laura Childs, *New York Times* bestselling author
of the Tea Shop Mysteries

"Kate Collins has played a major role in shaping the off-shoot of the 'cozy' mystery into a growing entity of its own, the romantic mystery. I, for one, am grateful."
—Once Upon a Romance

"Colorful characters, a sharp and funny heroine, and a sexy hunk boyfriend."
—Maggie Sefton, national bestselling author
of the Knitting Mysteries

"Always an autobuy for me!"
—Julie Hyzy, *New York Times* bestselling author
of the White House Chef Mysteries

"A clever, fast-moving plot and distinctive characters."
—JoAnna Carl, national bestselling author
of the Chocoholic Mysteries

"As fresh as a daisy, with a bouquet of irresistible characters."
—Elaine Viets, national bestselling author
of the Dead-End Job Mysteries

Other Flower Shop Mysteries

To all of us who suffer adversity and, like Abby Knight, rise from the ashes and forge on.

To all of us dreamers who, like Abby Knight, believe in our visions and see them come to be.

To all of us romantics who, like Abby Knight, really do find our heroes.

As always, to my soul mate, Jim, whose love reaches through all eternity.

Moss Hysteria

CHAPTER ONE

Sunday

"Marco, would you get the door, please?"

I waited for a response, but my request was met by silence. The doorbell pealed again, so I stopped unwrapping our mismatched wineglasses to call, "Marco? Where'd you go?"

He didn't answer—he was probably taking our dog, Seedy, to the backyard—so I stepped around the pile of crumpled newspaper in the kitchen and hurried to the front hallway. It was currently the only area in our brand-new two-bedroom ranch that wasn't cluttered with boxes. My nose itched from chemical overload—new carpet fibers, wood floor stain, paint, and draperies—so I paused to give it a good rub.

I opened the door to find nine women on my porch. They were lined up like bowling pins, the ones in front bearing casserole dishes, the ones in the rear leaning out for a better look. The kingpin of this merry band was forty-five-ish, with long blond hair that swept over one eye and fell in bouncy curls past her shoulders. She wore an off-the-shoulder white pullover with a tight gold miniskirt and knee-high white boots, an outfit that would better suit my fourteen-year-old niece, Tara. Heavy gold hoops swung from her ears as she tossed her hair away from her eyes.

"Hi, I'm Mitzi Kole," she said in a perky soprano. "We're the Brandywine Babes Book Club, more commonly known as the Bees. We all want to say"—she inhaled loudly and then the whole group chorused with her—"welcome to Brandywine."

"Wow. Thank you." I pushed back the sleeves of my paint-splattered yellow sweatshirt and stretched out my hands to accept Mitzi's dish, only then noticing the black newsprint on my fingers that was undoubtedly all over my nose.

"We also want to invite you to our book . . ." Mitzi stopped, her fake black eyelashes fluttering madly as she focused on something behind me. Her fellow ninepins leaned out farther.

I glanced around to see Marco coming toward the door wiping his perspiring face with a towel, ruffling his wavy dark hair in the process. We'd been unpacking since early morning and he hadn't shaved, a look I found sexy. Judging by the ogling going on, as nine pairs of eyes swept down his well-muscled torso, taking in his short-sleeved navy T-shirt and snug-fitting blue jeans, so did the Bees.

"As I was saying," Mitzi said, having suddenly developed a throaty alto, "we'd like to invite you *and* your husband to our book club Wednesday evening." She reached around me to offer a dainty hand to Marco. "Hi, I'm Mitzi Kole, the president of the club. I live two doors down." She tossed her hair. "Our backyards nearly *touch*."

Marco wiped his hands on the towel then gave her hand a polite shake. "Marco Salvare. Nice to meet you." He nodded at the rest of the group. "Ladies."

Sidestepping me, Mitzi moved in front of him and said in a sultry voice, "I *do* hope you'll come Wednesday, Marco. We'd *love* for you to try us on for size."

More like try *her* on for size.

"That's Abby's department," Marco said. "She's the social director."

Mitzi swung around to size me up. "Well, then I'll just have to convince *her.*"

I gave her a polite smile.

"We'll let you get back to unpacking," Mitzi said to Marco. "It's been a pleasure meeting you—both." She did an about-face, raised her hand, and on cue the Bees deposited their dishes in my front hall and swarmed back up the sidewalk behind her, buzzing excitedly.

As I turned to go, I noticed my next-door neighbor Theda Coros clipping back the winter-dead branches on her rosebushes. She smiled at me and shook her head as though she found the Bees silly.

"Nice neighbors," Marco said as we toted casserole dishes to the kitchen. He put his dish in the refrigerator then turned to take mine but instead used the towel he'd thrown over his shoulder to wipe the smudges off my upper lip. "Nice mustache, too, Groucho. Any interest in going to their meeting?"

"I'm thinking about it." Actually I was thinking about how Mitzi's lascivious glances in my husband's direction would have made me furious when Marco and I were dating. But I knew without a doubt he wouldn't do anything to jeopardize the love and trust we had for each other, so I blew them off. "Where's Seedy?"

"In the backyard. She loves watching the neighbor kids play."

We'd rescued our little dog the previous fall after I

learned she was to be euthanized. No one had wanted Seedy, who aptly fit her name. She was a small, ugly mutt with brown, black, and white fur; an underbite; large butterfly wing ears with tufts on top; and only three legs, but she had the sweetest nature and most loving personality I'd ever encountered.

Before my second visit was over, I had fallen hopelessly in love with her. Seedy had proved to be a wonderful pet and had even kept me from certain death just weeks earlier when Marco and I were tracking down a killer. I couldn't imagine life without her.

We'd barely stuffed the last casserole into the fridge when the doorbell rang again. "I'll get it," Marco said and strode off.

I opened a box marked *Kitchen* and found it filled with shoes, so I trotted off to our bedroom with it. Both bedrooms and a guest bathroom were off a hallway that ran to the back of the house, with the master at the far end. I put the box on the floor and glanced around, trying to visualize how the room would look when everything had been stowed.

On my way back to the kitchen I stopped to consider the hallway and decided the long expanse of off-white drywall would be the perfect place for our family photos.

"Abby, would you come here, please?"

At the door was a new group of women, this time bearing pies, cakes, cookies, and a bottle of wine. We'd had the Bees. Were these the Birds?

"This is Reagan," Marco said, introducing the leader of the pack, a pleasant-looking thirty-ish woman. Her conservative navy jacket, jeans, and gym shoes were a sharp contrast to Mitzi Kole's 1980s sex kitten outfit. "Reagan, this is my wife, Abby."

"Everyone here knows Abby," Reagan said with a bright smile, "and you, too, Marco. You're the Brandywine celebrities."

I liked Reagan right off the bat.

"Reagan and her group have a book club, too," Marco told me, his eyes brimming with amusement. "Books and Bottles."

"Bottles as in wine," Reagan said, presenting me with a bottle of red. "I'm sure you and Marco are overwhelmed with all the unpacking, but because you've already been accosted by the Bees, we felt it important that we stop by to welcome you and invite you to *our* meeting. It's Thursday at my place. I live right around the curve in the road, the white house with the yellow shutters."

Yellow. My favorite color. Another plus in Reagan's column.

"So here." She took a foil-covered pie from the woman beside her and placed it in Marco's hands. "Think of us when you're having dessert tonight." As they trooped back up our sidewalk, Reagan called, "Thursday at seven. We serve appetizers and desserts."

"You should join one of the clubs," Marco said, as I tried to make room on the crowded kitchen counter for all the sweets. "You're always looking for something to do in the evenings."

"We'll see."

"We got lucky deciding to build in this development, Abby."

I grunted. I was still digesting Mitzi's outrageous come-on toward my husband.

Marco was about to bite into an oatmeal cookie but paused to give me a skeptical look. "You don't agree?"

"I think one of the *Bees* is hoping to get lucky."

"What are you talking about?"

"Queen bee, Marco: Mitzi Kole. I was appalled by how blatantly she was hitting on you. I hope that's not a sign of things to come. I'd hate to start out life here avoiding a neighbor."

"Come on, babe, she was just being friendly."

"Seriously, Marco? Did you just arrive on this planet?"

He pulled me into his arms. "I'm teasing, Sunshine. I've met many Mitzis, and trust me, I know how to deal with them. *Motto*. Be polite and keep my distance. What do you say we take a break? We've been unpacking since five a.m. Let's heat up one of the casseroles and open that bottle of wine."

I was too exhausted to argue, and it really was nice to have food already prepared. But I'd already made up my mind. If I joined a club, it would not be the Bees.

The weather that April day was mild, so after dinner we took our wine and went outside to sit on the front porch swing. Seedy sat on the porch's top step, one eye on us, one eye on the cars going by. I'd always dreamed of having a cozy little house with a front porch swing and Marco had surprised me by installing one that morning. Now my new husband and I sat side by side, rocking gently, enjoying the stillness of the spring evening.

The chance to be together for an entire weekend was rare, as Marco usually had duties at Down the Hatch Bar and Grill in the evenings. He also owned the Salvare Detective Agency, something he'd dreamed of establishing since his Army Ranger days. But this weekend was special. We'd finally moved out of my parents' house and into our very own honeymoon cottage.

We'd met nearly two years ago, shortly after I'd bought Bloomers Flower Shop, when Marco helped me track down the hit-and-run driver who'd smashed my newly refurbished 1960 yellow Corvette convertible. That case turned out to be connected to a homicide, and after we worked together to pinpoint the killer, my second career was launched. Now I was Marco's partner not only in life but also in his PI business. He liked to call us Team Salvare.

"Am I interrupting?" our next-door neighbor called from her front porch.

"Come over, Theda," I said. "Have a glass of wine with us."

Theda had been a great help as our house was going up. Because she'd lived in the development for more than a year and had been one of the first to move in, she knew the ins and outs of the building process and had kept us from making costly mistakes.

In her late sixties, Theda had the strong profile and striking good looks of her Greek heritage. She was a tall woman, large-boned and thick-bodied but not obese, with curly dark hair sprinkled with gray and shrewd brown eyes that didn't miss a detail. She had been widowed a decade ago and had a man friend she saw occasionally.

"I was just about to take my evening stroll," Theda said. "If you'd like to join me, I'll show you around the neighborhood. We can have that glass of wine afterward if the offer is still open."

I glanced at Marco. "Want to go?"

"I'll get our jackets."

We hadn't really had an opportunity to see much of the Brandywine community. Because of our dual occupations, plus the brutal winter snows that had hung on through March, we'd only driven through it. The sub-division was a community of ranch homes developed by Brandon Emmett Thorne. Its streets looped around the park and a large man-made pond before circling back to the main entrance.

All three streets were named after Brandon—Brandonbury, Emmett Lane, and Thorneapple, which Theda said was just one example of Brandon's pomposity. We had met the developer only once, at our closing, but Theda assured me I would reach the same conclusion once I got to know him better.

With Seedy on her leash, we accompanied Theda around the curve of our street to the clubhouse situated near the main entrance to the subdivision. After pointing out various features Theda said, "You've probably seen the park, so let's walk the length of the pond before the sun sets."

From the clubhouse we followed a path down to the south end of the pond then walked in the grass at the water's edge as we headed north toward our house. The pond was about a city block long, a quarter of that in width and fifteen feet at its deepest point. The pond ended behind her lot, giving her a view of both the water and the park.

"You've got the best location in the neighborhood," I said, holding tight as Seedy strained on her leash. She'd seen something interesting and seemed determined to explore it. "No, Seedy," I said, pulling back on the leash. "Too damp and mossy there."

"You're right about that," Theda said, stepping down to the shore to prod a mossy section with the toe of her shoe. "We have a problem with it on both ends of the pond, but this end is much worse. The moss was supposed to have been treated last fall, but no one has ever come out to deal with it. Now it's spreading into my lawn.

"And yet I love living here," she continued. "It's a great community. In fact, sometimes I feel like I live on a movie set. Neatly tended houses, well-kept lawns, our own park, a clubhouse with a fitness center . . ." She paused to stare at something in the water and gave a shuddering gasp. "Oh, my—and a body floating in the pond."

CHAPTER TWO

As Marco called 911, Seedy lifted her nose and began to howl, so I took her back to our house and tied her up to the post Marco had installed near the sliding door. But as I returned to the pond, she started howling again.

"He's Brandon Thorne's construction superintendent," Theda was telling Marco. "We were supposed to have a meeting Friday evening about the moss situation, but he never showed up. Now I know why."

"What's his name?" I asked.

"Dirk Singletary." Theda kept shaking her head as she stared at the bloated face just visible about six feet from shore. "He must have slipped under the water and drowned."

"It doesn't look deep enough," Marco said.

"You can drown in a teaspoon of water," Theda said. "And really, how else would you explain it?"

The most obvious explanation made me glance at Marco and shake my head in disbelief. "We've been here one day, Marco. One day."

He put his arm around me and pulled me close. "There are other possibilities, Sunshine."

Over Seedy's howling I heard sirens approaching. "The police will be here soon. I'd better put Seedy inside."

Our little rescue dog had a fear of most men stemming from the abuse she'd suffered at a previous owner's hands. Seeing a swarm of them in uniform would be too much for her, so I let her in the house, petted her until she'd calmed down, and came back to find a police officer talking to Marco and Theda, two more officers getting ready to tape off the land abutting the pond, and a crime scene photographer preparing to take photos.

The lead officer was Sergeant Sean Reilly, our buddy on the New Chapel, Indiana, force. Reilly was a good-hearted, nice-looking guy in his forties. He had helped us on many of the cases we'd solved.

"How's it going, Sarge?" I asked as I joined Marco.

"Fine until Marco's call came in." He pushed back his cap with his thumb and shook his head at me. "How do you do it? How do you manage to find dead bodies everywhere?"

"I don't *do* anything, Reilly. It's not a talent."

"Like a cosmic trouble magnet," he said to Marco.

"If anyone's to blame, it's me," Theda said. "I noticed the body first."

"I'll need to get statements from all of you," Reilly said. "How about if I take them in your respective houses so we can get out of the way here? Ma'am, I'd like to start with you."

"Of course, Officer," Theda said. "Come this way."

As they headed toward her back door, a pair of EMTs wheeled a mobile stretcher between our houses. I glanced around to see a handful of neighbors gathered on the sidewalk in front, a few of them I recognized from the book clubs.

Noticeably absent was Mitzi Kole. But then I looked past Theda's backyard and saw her standing outside her back door waiting while a small fluffy white dog did her business on her lawn. Mitzi saw me, lifted her hand in a quick greeting, grabbed the dog, and darted back inside.

Marco stayed to watch the police work, but I went back to my unpacking, making good headway in the kitchen until Marco brought Reilly in. Then, over coffee and one of the tins of cookies, we sat at the card table, which served as our makeshift dining table, and told our side of the story. That took all of two minutes.

"I talked to the coroner after I left Mrs. Coros's house," Reilly said. "He found evidence of a severe blow to the back of the victim's head leaving a deep impression. He was guessing it was from a heavy tool of some kind. It's still preliminary, but he's calling it a homicide. He won't have more information until he performs the autopsy tomorrow."

I sighed and plunked my chin on my hand. "One day. We've been here *one day*."

"Did Theda have any leads for you?" Marco asked.

Reilly reached for another cookie. "She gave me a few names."

"Any of our neighbors?" I asked.

Reilly rubbed his nose. "You know I can't discuss an ongoing investigation with you."

That was his way of saying yes.

"Great," I said. "A body on our first day *and* a murderer in the neighborhood."

"Don't jump to conclusions," Reilly said. "Only one of the names is a neigh . . ." He caught himself. "Anyway, according to Mrs. Coros, this guy Dirk wasn't well regarded here. Some of your neighbors have reported jewelry missing, and Mrs. Coros believes Dirk was responsible. Apparently he had access to many of the homes through a set of master keys kept in the developer's office at the clubhouse. She informed the developer, but he hasn't done anything yet about securing the keys."

I glanced at Marco. "Did Dirk have access to our house?"

"I had our locks changed right after closing." It was one of the many details he'd handled because I'd been so swamped with work.

"Is there any proof that Dirk was the thief?" I asked.

"You'd have to ask Lisa Wells," Reilly said. "She's the detective working that case. She'll probably be given this investigation, too."

Detective Wells had been the detective assigned to my case when I'd had my identity, and nearly my life, stolen by a young woman who wanted to be me. Fortunately, Marco helped me prove my innocence, and the detective had worked with us to clear my name.

Reilly drained his cup and rose to leave. "Gotta go. Good luck with the unpacking." He paused at the door to look around our house. "Nice place."

"Thanks, Reilly." I shut the door and turned back to Marco. "I *thought* we had a nice neighborhood, too. Now I'm not so sure."

Monday

Marco brought the newspaper into the bathroom, where I was putting on my mascara. Other than a moisturizer, light blush, mascara, and lip gloss, I didn't do much to my face. It would've taken too many layers to hide my freckles, and besides, Marco thought they were cute.

He held up the paper so I could see it in the mirror.

MAN DROWNS IN POND: MURDER SUSPECTED

I put away my makeup kit and tried to tug a comb through the tangled mess of red hair. What did I do in my sleep to cause such snarls? Headstands? "Is there any new information?"

"Not much. Dirk was thirty-six, married, with a wife and two boys aged eight and ten. He moved here from Colorado six months ago. As Brandon Thorne's superintendent, he was in charge of new construction, coordinating subcontractors, and arranging warranty work on existing homes. Originally from Wilmington, Delaware."

"His poor wife." I gazed at my hunky hubby in the mirror and sighed morosely. "I can only imagine what she's going through right now—or those poor little boys."

Marco was still reading the article. "This isn't good. Theda's mentioned."

"Because she found the body?"

"No, because, as your reporter friend Connor MacKay put it, she was the last one to see Dirk alive."

Connor MacKay was not my friend and never had been, but I let that pass. "Why would he write that? Theda said Dirk never made it to her appointment." I took the newspaper from Marco and skimmed the article. "It doesn't say Dirk never made the appointment. Why doesn't it say that?"

"Let's hope it's a misprint."

Marco let Seedy and me off in front of Bloomers then drove away to find a parking spot for my old Corvette. We were still carpooling as a result of two factors: Marco's Prius being totaled by a murderer, and a decision not to replace it in order to save money for the house. I was determined to change that.

The truth was, I missed driving my refurbished 1960 bright yellow 'Vette. I missed the independence it gave me. With the flower shop now operating in the black and Marco's bar doing well, the money we made from our private investigations could go toward a car for my beloved's use. Simply put, I wanted my baby back.

My stomach rumbled, causing Seedy to glance up at me as though I had growled at her. "Don't judge me," I told her. "You got to eat. I didn't."

I paused outside the three-story redbrick building that housed my floral business to gaze up at the sign above me: BLOOMERS FLOWER SHOP, ABBY KNIGHT, PROPRIETOR.

One day I'd have to remember to get that sign redone. It should read: Abby Knight *Salvare*, Proprietor.

Bloomers Flower Shop sat on Franklin Street, one of four streets that made up New Chapel, Indiana's, town square, facing the east side of the big four-story limestone courthouse that sat squarely in the middle of a wide expanse of lawn. All around the square were restaurants, banks, law offices, and other shops that were thriving now after a few rough years of barely scraping by.

Not many people were out at this time of the morning, but once Bloomers opened, we'd get a lot of traffic in our coffee-and-tea parlor from people who worked in the courthouse and other businesses on the square.

I checked to make sure the big red-and-white striped awning over our two bay windows was in good shape then unlocked the yellow-frame door with the beveled glass center and went inside. I shut the door behind Seedy and we both sniffed the air. "*Ahh*. Do you smell that, Seedy? That's breakfast cooking."

Former owner Lottie Dombowski's delicious scrambled egg skillet was a Monday-morning tradition at Bloomers. With our new house in its current state of chaos, I was looking forward to relaxing over her breakfast even more than usual. I paused to glance around my cozy shop, with its old-fashioned cash register at the counter near the door, the big open armoire filled with crystal and ceramic gifts, silk arrangements, and candlesticks, the round oak table in the center that held lovely floral arrangements, the wicker settee in a back corner with a huge Dieffenbachia plant behind it, and the glass-fronted case that held a plethora of ready-to-buy fresh flowers.

My stomach growled again—it got angry when it wasn't fed on time—so I set off for the purple curtain that separated the shop from my nirvana—the workroom—and beyond that, the kitchen, where my meal awaited.

"Abby, love," Grace whispered, motioning to me from the doorway that led to our coffee-and-tea parlor, "a moment, please."

Grace Bingham was the sixty-something British expat who ran the parlor I'd added after taking over the shop from Lottie. It had been intended as a way to draw in more business for the floral side, but Grace's homemade scones—a different flavor every day—her gourmet blends of coffee, and her expertly brewed teas were almost more popular than my arrangements.

Grace kept glancing toward the curtain as she waited for me, as though afraid someone would overhear. She was a slender woman with short, stylish silver hair who always dressed in a sweater set and matching skirt with flats. Her hands were clasped at her waist as though about to deliver a speech, a sure sign a quote was forthcoming.

She had one for every occasion; still, I couldn't imagine needing one for breakfast.

"What is it, Grace?"

"A word of caution before you proceed."

That was never a good way to start the day.

"I'd like you to keep in mind these words from William Shakespeare. 'There is nothing either good or bad, but thinking makes it so.'"

"I have no idea what that means, Grace."

"*Hola*, Abby!"

But I had a sudden feeling I knew who it was about. I turned toward the curtain as my new employee, Rosa Marin, emerged.

"Just keep what I said in mind," Grace whispered quickly, then ducked back inside the parlor.

A midthirties woman of Colombian decent, Rosa Marisol Katarina Marin was a bombshell, with luxurious dark hair, prominent cheekbones, smooth skin, dark eyes, a wide smile, and abundant curves. Today she had on a patterned V-neck blouse in sky blue and pink with a tight white skirt and mile-high blue heels. Around her neck was her trademark lightning bolt pendant, a gift from her recently departed husband.

I'd met Rosa when she enlisted Marco and me to find out who had attempted to kill her husband. She had loved the flower shop atmosphere so much that she'd offered to help when we were shorthanded. And after discovering Rosa had a natural talent for arranging flowers and working with customers, Lottie and Grace had pressed me to hire her.

I hated to admit it, but I was a tad envious of Rosa. Everything I'd struggled to achieve came easily to her, and it was tough to watch my staff and family fawn over her every accomplishment. But I couldn't justify not hiring her because of a little pettiness on my part, and our need for an extra hand kept growing, so a month ago we'd made her a full-time employee.

"Come see what I made you for breakfast!" Rosa said, looping her arm through mine. She tended to talk excitedly and loudly, something everyone but me found endearing.

"What *you* made?"

"*Sí,*" she said proudly. "Huevos Marisol, my beloved *abuelita*'s recipe. My middle name—Marisol—is in her honor. Come!" She opened the curtain so I could walk through. "You don't want it to get cold."

I didn't want it, period. I wanted Lottie's egg skillet. Why had Lottie let Rosa take over breakfast? She had already invaded my workspace and become Lottie's and Grace's darling. Now this?

"You'll love my *huevos,*" Rosa was saying as she led the way. "I use a special blend of chili peppers, onions, and tomatoes."

"They're not hot chili peppers, are they?" I asked.

"Of course they are hot," Rosa replied. "I just cooked them."

Lottie was already seated at the narrow counter we'd attached to the back wall, forking the egg dish into her mouth. "Sorry to start without you," she mumbled. "Rosa said I had to eat them before they cooled."

Rosa patted the wooden stool beside Lottie's, then placed a full plate in front of me. Grace came in with a tray of coffee, cream, and sugar and began to pass out cups.

I sniffed the food on my plate, then took a small bite. It tasted good—at first. And then I swallowed and the burning began.

"Hot peppers," I rasped. "Water!"

"No water," Rosa said, putting a piece of toast in my hand. "Bread."

I stuffed a huge chunk in my mouth and waited for my vision to clear.

"I didn't think they were that hot," Lottie said.

"They have a little heat," Rosa said, "but you'll get used to it. Next time I'll use a different kind of pepper."

There would be a next time? I wanted to push my plate away, but my stomach was so empty that I had to eat. I took a bite of toast with every mouthful of *huevos*, and, as Rosa had promised, I got used to it.

"So?" she asked when I'd finished, draping her arms over my shoulders. "What do you think?"

"To be honest, Rosa—"

"Stop," she cried. "Nothing good ever comes after 'To be honest.'"

In the background I could see Grace and Lottie warning me to be kind.

I took a deep breath and pasted on a smile. I was not a good liar. "I was going to say I liked them, but less heat would be better."

She clapped and then threw her arms around my neck again and hugged me. I glanced at Grace and she gave me a nod. Lottie gave me a thumbs-up.

With breakfast over, we had a meeting in the coffee-and-tea parlor to discuss business matters, and then they wanted to know about the tragedy that had occurred in my new neighborhood. They'd all read Connor Mac-Kay's account in the morning paper.

"The article made it sound as though your neighbor Theda Coros may be a suspect," Lottie said, pouring herself another cup of coffee.

"Connor MacKay got it wrong," I said. "He loves to sensationalize his stories. Theda had an appointment with the man, but he never showed up."

"He was dead in the water," Rosa said. "How could he show up?"

"Exactly," I said.

"I know Theda from my bowling league," Grace said. "She has an interesting history. When we have time, I'll share it with you. But right now, we have fifteen minutes before we open. Spit spot, everyone."

At that, we went our separate ways, Grace to ready her coffee machines and set her water on to heat, Lottie to restock the glass-fronted case and open the cash register, me to check our flower stock and place orders, and Rosa to start on the tickets waiting on the spindle.

Although the workroom was windowless, the colorful blossoms and heady fragrances made it feel like a tropical garden. Vases of all sizes and containers of dried flowers filled shelves above the counters along two walls. A large slate-covered worktable occupied the middle of the room, two big walk-in coolers took up one side, and a desk holding my computer equipment and telephone filled the other side. Beneath the table were huge bags of potting soil, wet foam, and a plastic-lined trash can.

In the short hallway beyond the workroom were a tiny bathroom and the galley kitchen where we'd had breakfast. At the very back of the building was the exit into the alley.

An hour later I was at the computer, filling out an order form, and Rosa was behind me, seated on a stool at the table humming as she worked. She paused to ask, "Did you talk to your mother this morning?"

"No."

"You didn't talk to your mother this morning? Don't you talk to her every morning?"

I had to stop thinking about the order I was placing and replay her question in my mind before I could answer. "No."

"Abby, one day you will lose her and then you will regret not talking to her every day. I phone my mother every morning as soon as I get up just to tell her I love her."

"Good for you." I was trying to concentrate. Rosa was not making it easy.

"So your mother didn't tell you about her new art project?"

I stopped again. "My mother doesn't do art anymore. She's writing children's books now."

"Abby, when you are an artist, you never give up art."

Well, there you go. My mother wasn't an artist. She may have thought she was. She may have produced a variety of horrendous art projects, such as her giant bowling pin hat rack with Homer Simpson's face painted on it, her Dancing Naked Monkey Table, her beaded jackets made with one-inch wooden beads, her colored feather hats that left dye all over their wearers' heads, or her sea glass sunglasses debacle, all of which she had expected me to sell at my shop. But she was not, in the least sense of the word, an artist. She was a weekend hobbyist—or rather, she had been. Now, besides teaching kindergarten, she wrote children's mysteries, and quite well, too. She'd found her forte at last.

"If you had talked to your mother," Rosa continued, "you would have heard that we are now collaborating on her newest art project."

I hit *Enter* by mistake and lost the entire screen. Gone.

Just like I wished Rosa was at that moment. I turned to face her. "You're working on an art project *together*?"

"*Sí.*"

"She loves writing her children's books. Why would she stop?"

"She is going to do both: write books *and* create art. But because her time is more limited, I am helping her with her new project, and it is not ready yet. That is all I am going to say. If you want to know more, you will have to call her—or maybe she will call you."

My cell phone rang, and I gave a start. But then Marco's face popped up on the screen, and that was also a surprise. He rarely phoned during the morning because it was our busiest time. I took the phone into the kitchen to talk in private. "What's up?"

"Reilly just called to let me know that the coroner has officially ruled the death a homicide. The police are opening a criminal investigation and detectives brought Theda down to the station for an interview early this morning. He said she's still there."

I glanced at my watch. "It's after ten, Marco. There's no reason for her to be questioned that long, especially since she already gave a statement—unless they've drawn a target on her back. They're not calling her a person of interest, are they?"

"Reilly didn't come out and say that, but I doubt he would have called otherwise. I got the distinct impression his call was intended as a warning."

"A warning for what?"

"To be cautious. We could be living next door to a murderer."

CHAPTER THREE

"Theda is not a killer, Marco. My inner radar would be dinging furiously if she was. Will the cops let her answer her phone? I want to text her and tell her to ask for a lawyer."

"They can't stop her from answering the phone if she hasn't been charged with anything. Hold on. I'm getting a message from Reilly." Marco put me on hold and then returned moments later. "It's okay. She's been released. They must have cleared her."

"Thank God."

"I'll let you get back to work and see you at home later. I'll bring dinner."

I ended the call and reached for a ticket on the spindle, thinking about how lucky I was. I ran the business of my dreams, had married the man of my dreams, and had built the house of my dreams.

And as an added bonus, our next-door neighbor was not a killer.

When I returned to my desk, Rosa made no further reference to the art project, but at least now I was braced for Mom's impending arrival. Monday afternoon was her designated drop-off day for her artwork. Surprisingly, she didn't appear at three thirty as she usually did.

As Lottie, Rosa, and I took time out for our midafternoon tea break, Lottie brought it up. "Your mom is late," she said, glancing at the clock on the wall. "Oh, wait. She's a writer now. I keep forgetting she gave up art."

"An artist never gives up art," Rosa said, then took a drink of tea.

"So she's back to creating?" Lottie asked.

Rosa merely smiled mysteriously, so I said, "Apparently she and Rosa are working on something."

Rosa pretended to lock her lips, then winked at Lottie. "It's a secret."

And hopefully it would stay that way.

Marco brought home a container of white bean chicken chili, two garden salads, and half a loaf of garlic bread. I had set the card table with white soup bowls, colorful paper napkins, and bright orange candles in a pair of white ceramic candlesticks. I even had wine poured. Having dinner in our very own home felt like a celebration.

We toasted our new house, each other, and Seedy, whom we could see across the room sitting on an upholstered chair watching out the front window. Then we chatted about our day as we polished off the food.

Our living room, dining area, and kitchen ran from front to back as one giant room. It had nine-foot ceilings that made the space feel larger, a set of three double-hung windows in the front facing the street and a sliding glass door on the rear wall of the dining area. A granite-topped island separated the dining area from the kitchen.

The walls were painted a basic white because I didn't know what my color scheme was going to be. I needed to tap my cousin Jillian, a fashion consultant, for decorating advice.

In the meantime, we were living with odds and ends—Marco's oak bedroom set, a scarred, red vinyl–topped card table and chairs, a worn tan sofa we'd borrowed from my parents' basement, and Marco's beat-up black leather recliner. I'd had nothing to contribute, having gone from my parents' home to college, to my best friend Nikki's apartment, to Marco's bachelor pad, and back to my parents' home while our house was being built.

"When we buy a new living room set," I said, watching Seedy circle the chair a few times before settling down, "and we need to do that soon, by the way, we're going to have to train her to stay off the furniture."

"Good luck with that." Marco clinked his glass to mine.

"I can do it. I watch *The Dog Whisperer.* Let's go furniture shopping Saturday. It's my weekend off and our neighborhood open house is in two weeks."

"Shouldn't the neighbors be throwing a welcoming party for us?"

"It'll be fun, Marco. A great way to meet everyone here. We've got that beautiful patio and a big backyard, so we might as well put them to use. So Saturday is okay?"

"As long as we're back by six. We're meeting my mom at Café Venezia's, remember?"

"I still don't understand why she won't tell us what it's for."

"She likes surprises. I'm just glad *Mama* has her own place now." Marco often fell into a dialect when he referred to his mother, who still had traces of Italian in her talk. "Living with my sister and her two kids was wearing her down."

I laughed. "*Your* mother was worn down?"

"She *is* getting older, babe."

"She's not even sixty yet, Marco. She has more energy than I do."

The doorbell rang and Marco went to answer it while I cleared the table.

"I hope I'm not interrupting," Theda said, stepping inside.

"We just finished dinner," I said. "Come back to the kitchen and talk to me."

She twisted her fingers together nervously. "Actually, I'd like to talk to you both."

I sat at the card table with Theda while Marco poured her a glass of red wine. "What's the problem?" he asked, sitting down across from her.

She turned her wineglass back and forth on its base. "I had to talk to the detectives this morning. They sent a squad car to collect me. They said it was just to gather more information, but the way they questioned me, I know they think I had something to do with Dirk's death."

"What did they ask?" Marco said.

"Was I positive Dirk hadn't shown up at my house? Was I angry about the moss problem? Did I have trouble dealing with Dirk in the past? Was I afraid to tell them that Dirk really had shown up? Over and over, as though they were trying to catch me in a lie. First a young woman talked to me—Detective Wells was her name—and then she left and a Detective Corbison came in to ask the same questions."

I glanced at Marco. Al Corbison had tried to pin a murder on me in similar circumstances, except I really had been the last one to see the victim alive. I'd delivered flowers to the man's office.

"Detective Corbison was very rude," Theda continued. "He kept interrupting me and asking me if I was sure that was my final answer, hinting that he had evidence to the contrary. He was obviously trying to get me to change my answer. I told him again and again I did not meet with Dirk Singletary, because he never showed up."

"But the police did let you go," Marco said. "That's good."

"With a caveat not to leave town," Theda added. "Detective Wells said they'd have to find an alibi witness who could verify my story. I told her I live alone with just my foster cat for company. She said in that case she'd have to find a neighbor. Detective Wells at least was polite."

"So what can we help you with?" Marco asked.

"I haven't used a lawyer in a decade or longer. If the detectives want to question me again, I wouldn't know whom to call."

"I'll give you Dave Hammond's phone number," I told her. "I clerked for him when I was in law school. He's the best you can get. You won't find anyone more conscientious, I guarantee."

"You went to law school?" Theda asked.

I glanced at Marco and smiled. "Briefly."

"Abby was destined to be a florist," Marco said, putting his hand over mine, "and my life partner."

"Someday I'll tell you the story, Theda." I pulled up Dave's number on my cell phone and let her type it into her phone. "Call for an appointment tomorrow morning and tell his secretary that I referred you and why. I'm sure Dave will see you as soon as he can. And then if you do get another call from the detectives, Dave can meet you at the police station."

Theda heaved a sigh of relief. "Thank you. I've never been in this kind of situation before. I volunteer at a cat rescue facility. I'm just an elderly woman who loves animals."

"Out of curiosity," I said, "do you know if Dirk had any enemies in the neighborhood?"

"Well," she said hesitantly, "I wouldn't call them enemies. Let's just say he was widely disliked. He had a smug attitude that people found irritating and condescending. And then there was the missing jewelry, costly pieces that started disappearing not long after Dirk began working at Brandywine.

"First, an elderly couple, dear friends of mine, were robbed of all their gold jewelry while they were out of town on vacation. Police found a window unlocked, so they suspected that one of the construction workers had noticed the house vacant and slipped in after dark. But I questioned that. Thieves take electronics, grab-and-go things. They don't take time to pick through jewelry boxes.

"Then two months ago another friend, a widow on the other side of the park, reported the theft of her diamond necklace and bracelet and blamed the plumbers who'd been working in her house. Because she had a doctor's appointment, Dirk was supposed to let the plumbers in and keep an eye on them. But no evidence was found that pointed to the plumbers, and they passed polygraph tests, so the case was dropped."

"Was Dirk questioned?" I asked.

"Yes. He said he let the men in and left, which, if true, was wrong of him. He was supposed to stay there until the plumbers were finished."

"And the police took him at his word?" I asked.

"Yes, they did. Dirk was simply not on the police's radar, so the incident passed. A week later, another neighbor reported her diamond wedding ring missing. Dirk and his assistant had been in her house to patch some nail pops that day, so both men were questioned and released. The police decided she'd lost it. But she knew better. It had been sitting on her dresser and then after Dirk and Rye left, it was gone.

"Then about ten days ago Mitzi Kole told me she was missing an heirloom ring worth twenty thousand dollars in addition to a diamond pendant valued at ten thousand. I asked her if Dirk had been inside her house recently, and she claimed he hadn't. However, I saw him enter via her front door twice that week. When I reminded her of that, she got snippy with me and said he'd just dropped off some information on a security system.

"I didn't contradict her, but I know for a fact that Dirk had been inside her house for at least an hour on each occasion, and those weren't the first times. I know this because the chair I sit in to watch TV faces a window that looks out on her front porch. So why was she lying to me about him being there?"

"Were they having an affair?" I asked.

Theda shrugged. "All I can say is that he wasn't there to repair anything unless the repair required a bottle of wine and box of candy."

"Did anyone in Brandywine besides you suspect Dirk?" Marco asked.

"Many, and I have a strong hunch that Dirk's assistant does, too, although you'll never get him to say so. You may have met him while your house was under construction. Rye Bishop? Wears his baseball caps backward? Has a little Southern twang in his talk? When something outside warranty work needs repairing, Rye is the guy to fix it. Everyone here loves Rye, by the way. I should say everyone but Dirk."

"Why?" I asked.

"I don't know," Theda said. "All I know is that he took perverse pleasure in humiliating Rye, scolding him over some trivial thing or another and making it seem like Rye didn't know what he was doing. It was terrible to witness. I stepped up to his defense once, but Rye later asked me not to. He said it made the situation worse."

"What was Rye's reaction to Dirk's behavior?" Marco asked.

"He'd just walk away, shaking his head. I think it kept him from punching Dirk in the face."

"Why wasn't Dirk fired?" I asked. "Surely the residents complained."

"You bet we complained, straight to the top—Brandon Thorne. But for some odd reason, Brandon ignored our complaints. At our monthly association meetings Dirk was so condescending to Brandon that he almost seemed to be mocking him at times. You'd think for that reason alone Brandon would've fired him. So why didn't he?"

"What's the purpose of the monthly meetings?" Marco asked.

"Connie should've explained that to you. It's our chance to air complaints. Dirk was supposed to log everything we brought up at the meeting and then see that they were fixed. Unfortunately, it was a rare day when he followed up on anything."

"How often is Brandon here?" Marco asked.

"He's usually at each meeting. He was here last Friday, in fact."

Theda pushed back the folding chair and rose. "I won't take up any more of your evening. Thank you for your advice and for Mr. Hammond's phone number."

"Be sure to tell Dave everything you told us when you meet with him," I said.

"I'll call him first thing in the morning—unless I'm in jail."

"Don't joke about that," I said as I walked her to the door. "It happened to me."

At Theda's shocked look I said, "It was a case of mistaken identity. And Dave was there immediately to straighten it out."

"If the cops do phone or come to your door before you see Dave," Marco said, "don't answer. Call us immediately."

"Now you're frightening me," Theda said.

I put my arm around her. "We have a lot of experience with these situations, Theda. We're here for you."

I closed the door and leaned against it, watching Marco take the wineglasses to the kitchen counter. "What do you think?"

"If there was solid evidence tying her to Dirk's murder, they wouldn't have let her go." Marco took my hand and led me toward the bedroom. "Know what else I think?"

"Tell me."

"That since I rarely get to spend an evening at home with my wife during the week, we need to celebrate."

"And how might we celebrate, Mr. Salvare?"

Seedy ran to the front door and scratched it with her paw, whining.

"I guess that's our answer," I said.

"Not so fast," Marco said, pulling me into his arms. "We'll take her for a walk, then pour a little more wine and retire to our new boudoir."

Pleasurable tingles ran up my spine and I snuggled closer, wrapping my arms around his ribs. "You're sexy when you use words like *boudoir*."

"Baby, I've got sexier words than that, but I'll save them for later."

Tuesday

"We got a second notice about the Midwest Regional Flower Show, sweetie," Lottie said, showing me the leaflet that had come in the morning mail. "The deadline for entering the competition is coming up."

I put a bouquet I'd just made into the second of our two walk-in coolers and stepped out to see Lottie standing at my desk shuffling through the stack of envelopes our postal carrier had delivered. She swiveled toward me. "You're gonna compete this year, aren't you? We have a championship title to uphold."

Lottie Dombowski had owned Bloomers before I rescued her from certain bankruptcy by assuming the mortgage. Lucky for us both, I'd had enough left of the money my grandpa had left me for college to satisfy the bank, or neither one of us would be where we were now. I had just been booted out of law school and dumped by my then-fiancé Pryce Osborne II, and Lottie's husband, Herman, had gone through open-heart surgery, which had resulted in loss of employment and sky-high medical bills. Bloomers had been our lifeline.

Lottie was in her midforties, a large-boned woman

with a hearty laugh, quick wit, and short brassy curls worn Shirley Temple style. Her trademark was the color pink—from the barrettes that held her curls off her face, the T-shirt she wore with white jeans, down to the ruffled socks she wore with her hot pink tennis shoes. She said all that pink helped balance life with a husband and "the quads"—her four teenage sons.

"What is the competition for?" Rosa asked. She was lining a deep pot with wet foam.

"The one I've always entered is for the best floral arrangement using live flowers," Lottie said.

"Did you ever win?" Rosa asked.

"Twice. Have you seen the Silver Rose trophy in the display case up front? Abby won that last year, and guess who presented it to her? Me. The past winner always presents it to the new winner."

"If Abby wins again," Rosa said, "will she have to give it to herself?"

Lottie laughed. "Something like that."

"Why don't you enter, Lottie?" Rosa asked.

"Because I did it for years, and now I've passed that baton on to Abby. It's hers to win or lose."

"Then you must enter again," Rosa said to me. "You don't want to lose the trophy."

"I feel bad saying this, but I really don't have time," I said. "It takes a lot of preparation to plan a trophy-worthy arrangement, and then I'd have to give up an entire day to attend the flower show. With Bloomers' business booming and our private investigation business growing, and all the work involved in moving into a new house, I'm stretched to the limit."

Lottie put her arm around my shoulders. "It's okay, sweetie. We'll win it back next year."

I hoped so because I did feel guilty, just not enough to add that stress to my already burdened shoulders.

I plucked an order and went into the first walk-in cooler to pull my stems. The arrangement was for a baby shower being held at a local restaurant. The colors they wanted were purple, pink, and yellow, but they didn't want to break the bank for it. So I used a white tin toy baby carriage about half a foot long, put a tiny pink stuffed bear in it, and arranged yellow, purple and white tulips to look like the bear was holding a bountiful bouquet.

"That is *precioso*," Rosa said when she saw me wrapping it. "And the anniversary arrangement you made before is *inspriado.* I was just looking at it in the cooler and thinking what a shame it is that you will not be entering the flower contest. Are you sure you don't have time?"

"I'm positive. I just can't afford to stress myself out. I have too much to do."

Rosa sighed sadly. *"Qué lástima!"*

"I don't know what that means."

"What a shame," Grace translated, bringing in our midmorning tea. Grace had spent a year in Spain as a young woman. She called it her year of living dangerously. "I agree, Rosa. Abby is quite creative with her arrangements. But *lo que será, será.*"

"Sí." Rosa looked at me sadly and shook her head.

"Again," I said, "I don't know what that means."

"Whatever will be, will be," Grace said. "Or in the modern vernacular, it is what it is. Speaking of which, I heard that Theda spent over two hours with detectives yesterday morning. Don't tell me she's a suspect."

"Not as of yesterday evening, but I gave her Dave Hammond's name and told her to go see him ASAP."

Grace heaved a sigh of relief. "Good. Theda doesn't need more of that kind of trouble."

"She's been a suspect before?"

"Yes, in her first husband's death. It happened somewhere in Illinois, if I remember correctly. He drowned in their swimming pool and she was the one who found him. There was never any evidence to charge her with murder, so she was released. But those detectives put her through the wringer, let me tell you."

"This story came out while you were bowling?" I asked.

"Oh, heavens, no, love. It was during the rounds of beer afterward."

"And now the poor woman has found another man dead in the water?" Rosa made the sign of the cross. *"Dios mio. Qué mala suerte."*

"Bad luck indeed," Grace said. "But she wasn't left poor by any means. That was what made her such a perfect suspect."

I returned to my work, but my thoughts were still on Grace's story. What were the odds of one person finding two bodies the same way? And why had Theda said she'd never been in a situation like that? If I wasn't so sure of my gut instincts, I might admit to being a bit suspicious of her. I just hoped the detectives hadn't unearthed that information, too.

CHAPTER FOUR

Marco had to work that evening, so Seedy and I met him at the bar for dinner and then we went home. As Seedy and I were returning from our evening walk, I saw Theda about to enter her house and called hello.

She turned and smiled. "Hello to you, too. Are you busy? Come have a glass of wine with me."

I checked my watch and decided I could spare half an hour before tackling the stacks of boxes in our bedroom. "I'll take Seedy home first," I called.

"No, bring her. There's someone I want her to meet."

The *someone* turned out to be a beautiful male Russian Blue feline Theda was fostering. I hesitated to bring Seedy inside, fearing the cat would attack her, but Theda assured me the friendly fellow loved dogs. Nevertheless, I sat at one end of the blue sofa with Seedy at my feet and Theda sat at the other with the cat in her lap.

"I haven't named him," Theda said, stroking the animal's silver-blue fur. "I'll leave that up to his forever family. But he answers to Kitty. Poor thing was abandoned, starving, and in very bad shape when we picked him up. I've nursed him back to health, but he still has a problem with some men—very distrustful of them. When he senses something amiss, he hisses and snaps."

"Seedy is distrustful of most men, too, but she doesn't snap. She hides."

"Not Kitty. Once, when I had him outside on a harness, a man going door to door through the neighborhood approached me about a magazine subscription. For some reason Kitty leaped on his back, clawing the man and biting his ears until he fled. Later I read in the paper that the man was arrested after breaking into a home in another neighborhood."

"Kitty was protecting you."

Theda snuggled the cat against her. "Yes, he was. He's a big sweetie, very affectionate and playful. Blues are known for their loyalty and intelligence."

Kitty wiggled to get down, so Theda set him on the rug. A large feline, Kitty had several inches in height on Seedy, so I gathered my dog in my arms just to be on the safe side. But Kitty came up to the sofa and put his paws on it so he could sniff Seedy. And my little mutt responded by wagging her tail and giving a friendly yip. I finally set the dog on the floor, and the cat head-butted her affectionately.

"Kitty even plays fetch." Theda picked up a cat toy and tossed it across the room. Kitty dashed over to get it, grabbed the toy, and brought it back just like a dog, with Seedy hobbling along after him.

I watched the two play while Theda went to her kitchen and returned with glasses of red wine. "Thank you for your referral to Attorney Hammond," she said, handing me a glass. "I have an appointment to see him in the morning."

"No further calls from the detectives?" I asked.

"None. Fingers crossed that this is over."

Wednesday

Crossing my fingers never worked for me, and apparently it wasn't working for Theda, either. She phoned me at Bloomers around noon to say that Dave Hammond was going with her to the police station to meet with detectives later that afternoon. I was angered but not surprised by the detectives' actions, and so after delivering flowers to the New Chapel Savings Bank, I walked around the corner and up the block to the police station to have a talk with Lisa Wells to see why she was so focused on Theda.

"Detective Wells is still at lunch," the officer behind the security window said. "Leave your name and number and I can have her call you."

"That's okay. I was in the neighborhood and thought I'd say hi. We worked on a case together once."

"Maraville PD?" he asked, squinting at me as though he should recognize me.

"Salvare Detective Agency," I said. "Have a nice day."

I walked outside and looked around for a place to wait. With any luck, Lisa was at one of the eateries in town, and I could catch her upon her return. I noticed the used car lot on the opposite side of the street, so I crossed over and wandered through the rows of automobiles, keeping one eye on the police station. I saw one car with a big sign in the front window that said HYBRID, so I stopped to look at it.

"Got your eye on that silver beauty, I see," a salesman called, coming out of the building at the rear of the lot, wiping his mouth with a napkin. By the glob of mustard on the front of his white shirt, I was betting he'd seen me and hastily stuffed the rest of his lunch into his mouth.

"We just got this one in two days ago." He walked

up to me and extended his hand. "My name's Randy. And yours is?"

"Abby Knight . . . Salvare." I always forgot to add my new last name.

"Salvare. Salvare." He rubbed his chin. "Where have I heard that?"

"My husband owns Down the Hatch."

"Yep. That's where I've heard it." He opened the driver's-side door. "Slip inside this baby and see how immaculate it is."

I stuck my head inside and glanced at the interior. It really was in excellent condition, and I liked the color. Silver was easy to hide in traffic, just the kind of vehicle Marco would want.

"This is a Lexus RX four-fifty H," Randy said. "The H stands for hybrid."

I slid in behind the steering wheel and checked it out. "How much?"

He gave me a price, and I blanched. "Sorry. We can't afford it. We just built a house and we're kind of stretched to the limit."

"Then let's talk a price you can afford. You're a local. We'll work with you. We like to take care of our own."

"Okay. Cut off five thousand and then we'll talk."

It was his turn to blanch. "Five thousand! That's a little extreme. Can we meet somewhere in the middle?"

I adjusted the rearview mirror, checked the side-view mirrors and the console controls, then got out of the car. "Forget it. This isn't the right vehicle for my husband. If he had to evade a killer, his back view is impeded because of that rear slant, and the controls are too busy. He'd have to take his eye off the road to use the mouse, and in a dangerous situation, it could cost Marco his life."

Randy was staring at me as though I were talking in a foreign tongue.

"What he needs is a Prius, or something of similar design." At that moment I saw Lisa Wells striding toward the police station, so I said, "Sorry, but I have to go. Thanks for your help," and hurried toward her.

"Wait," Randy called. "Let me see what I can find. I'm sure we can come up with something your husband will like."

"Lisa!" I used her first name, acting as though she was an old friend I hadn't seen in ages.

A classy-looking woman in her late thirties, Lisa had on her customary black pantsuit, today with a mint green blouse and black flats. Her thick golden hair was held in a loose bun by a pair of decorative black-and-gold chopsticks, and she wore her black leather cross-body bag so that it rested on one hip.

She stopped and put her hand over her eyes so she could see me. "Abby?" She smiled as she put out her hand to shake mine. "Good to see you. I read about you in the papers all the time, Ms. Private Eye. How are you?"

"Doing well. Bloomers is busier than ever, and I got married a few months back."

"Then congratulations are in order. To Marco, right?"

"You remembered! How have *you* been?"

"Oh, you know. A cop's life." She knew my dad had been a New Chapel police sergeant. She checked her watch, ready to move on.

Before she could make an excuse to leave, I said, "Hey, you'll never guess where Marco and I moved. Brandywine."

"Brandywine," she said, as though trying to place it. I had a feeling she knew exactly what I was talking about, but still I said, "Where they just found the body in the pond. We moved in this past Saturday. Great way to start life there, right? In fact, Marco and my next-door neighbor Theda Coros and I were the ones who discovered the body."

"Theda Coros is your neighbor?"

"Yes," I said, and then hesitated. Did I want her to know how much I knew? I shouldn't trust any detective one hundred percent, but I did like Lisa. I would have to play this one by ear. "I'm surprised Theda didn't mention our names."

"She did, but she said Mr. and Mrs. Salvare. I didn't make the connection." Lisa checked her watch again. "Do you have time to talk?"

I took a seat in front of a cluttered desk in the cramped detectives' quarters on the second floor of the police station. Lisa got us coffees in cardboard cups then sat at her desk and picked up her pen, ready to get on with business. "I'm glad you stopped me. I need to find an alibi witness for your neighbor and was going to have to canvass your neighborhood."

"Great timing," I said. "Odd how the universe works, isn't it? Has the coroner made a determination yet on whether you've got a murder case?"

"He's calling it a homicide, but I think he'll be changing it to criminal homicide soon." She clicked her pen impatiently. "So give me your version of finding the body."

"Sure. We found it sometime after supper on Sunday. Marco and I hadn't seen all the neighborhood amenities, so Theda gave us a tour. Our last stop was the pond, and we had just reached the south end of it when we spotted a body in the water. Actually, my dog saw it first. I mean *him* first. Marco called the cops and we gave statements. End of story. So why do you need an alibi witness for Theda?"

"She was the last one to see the victim alive."

I smiled. "Well, no, she wasn't, as I'm sure she told you. She had scheduled an appointment with Dirk, I mean the victim, to take a look at the moss problem behind her house, but he didn't show up."

"When did you move in again?"

"Saturday."

"And how is it you know he didn't show up Friday evening?"

She had me there, and by the tilt of her eyebrow, she knew it. "Look, Lisa, you've met Theda. She's what, seventy-ish? Works at a cat rescue shelter? Kind as can be and so helpful to us when our house was under construction. Believe me—she's not the killer type."

"So you're saying there's a type?"

Lisa had the annoying habit of answering with a question. "Well, no, not a single type. What I'm saying is that there are other people you should be investigating. For instance, the neighbor on the other side of Theda by the name of Mitzi Kole. And the developer, Brandon Thorne, and the handyman—"

"Let me stop you for a moment, Abby. Where did you get these names?"

Once again, Lisa had me. "From Theda."

Lisa smiled knowingly, clicking her pen. "Of course."

"You say *of course* like Theda is some kind of murdering mastermind."

Lisa leaned her chin on her fist. "You met her how long ago? Do you *really* know Theda Coros, Abby?"

I wondered if Lisa was referring to the suspicions around Theda's first husband's death, but I wasn't about to mention it. "Would you at least take a look at these other people?"

She studied me a moment and then, either taking me seriously or merely trying to appease me so I'd leave, pulled her yellow legal pad closer. "Okay, give me the names again."

"First, Mitzi Kole. She had expensive jewelry stolen by Dirk—the victim."

"*Allegedly* stolen. It hasn't been proven."

"Okay. Also Mitzi was probably—allegedly—having an affair with Dirk, I mean the victim."

"You can say Dirk. Next name, please."

"Brandon Thorne, the developer."

"Go ahead."

"Dirk's assistant, Rye Bishop."

"Uh-huh."

"That's all."

She finished writing, clicked her pen off, and stood up, reaching out to shake my hand again. "Thanks for your help, Abby."

I rose. "You'll check those people out?"

She sat back down and began to write, saying with very little conviction, "Sure."

"She won't, Marco. I could tell by the way she answered me. Lisa is going to pursue Theda before she looks at anyone else."

We were sitting in the last booth at Marco's bar having dinner. I called it "our booth" because that was where much of our courtship dining had occurred. Seedy was under the table, gnawing contentedly on a beef bone.

Down the Hatch Bar and Grill was New Chapel's favorite watering hole, a gathering place for the attorneys and judges from the courthouse, as well as college kids from New Chapel University. Like my shop, the bar was housed in an old brick building, but unlike Bloomers, its charm had been buried behind dark wood paneling and a suspended ceiling popular in the 1960s.

Even the décor was outdated, with a giant carp mounted above the long, dark wood bar, a bright blue plastic anchor on the wall above the row of orange booths opposite the bar, a big brass bell hanging from a post near the cash register, and a fishing net suspended from the beamed ceiling. I constantly urged Marco to give the bar a much-needed remodel, but he wouldn't hear of it, claiming his clientele would revolt if he changed a thing.

"Give Lisa the benefit of the doubt, Abby. She's a smart woman. She has to be curious about the names you gave her."

"Were the detectives curious about anyone else when you were accused of murdering a clown? Or when they thought I killed my former professor?"

Marco stuck a french fry in ketchup and ate it, studying me. "You want to investigate, don't you?"

"I don't *want* to, Marco. I've got a lot on my plate, and so do you. I feel like we *have* to for Theda's sake. She's been so good to us, and I'd hate for her to be put through the wringer a second time."

"Whoa. Back up. What second time?"

"Didn't I tell you what Grace told me?"

He leaned toward me. "Does this look like the face of someone in the know?"

I reached over and wiped a trace of ketchup off his upper lip. "It looks like the face of someone I love."

He grabbed my hand and brought it to his lips,

kissing my fingertips. "If you think that lets you off the hook, Mrs. S., you're wrong. Explain, please."

"I don't really have much to tell. All Grace said was that Theda's first husband drowned in their swimming pool, and she found him."

"That doesn't explain why she was a suspect."

"Grace said something about a suspicion of foul play, but there was no evidence to charge her."

"Ah, now we're getting somewhere. Lisa Wells probably did an Internet search and uncovered a newspaper account. Naturally that would raise her suspicions. It raises mine."

"To the point where you would ignore other potential suspects? You know that's what'll happen, Marco."

"Are you *that* sure of our neighbor's innocence? We've met her only about half a dozen times."

"I trust my gut instinct, Marco. You know that. And how many times has it been wrong?"

Marco studied me as he finished off his beer. "So here's how this will go. I'll tell you to wait and see what happens with the police. You'll ignore my advice and begin your own investigation until you've collected enough proof to convince me to get involved. So let's skip to the chase. Who's on your suspect list? Just the three Theda mentioned?"

I smiled as I pulled out the small notebook I always carried in my purse. No argument this time! "Yes, just three people. Brandon Thorne, Rye Bishop, and Mitzi Kole."

"Add Dirk's wife and Mitzi's husband to the list."

"I should've thought of that. So how do you want to proceed?"

"I'll find out what day Brandon Thorne will be at

Brandywine and set up an appointment. You make arrangements to go to Mitzi's book club meeting tonight and get Dirk's home address and phone number from the clubhouse directory so we can set up a meeting with his wife on Saturday if possible. I'll take care of Mr. Kole."

"We're going furniture shopping Saturday—don't forget."

"And meeting my mom for dinner. It'll be a busy day. What else?"

"We can interview Rye Bishop when he comes to look at our wood floor tomorrow."

"Is something wrong with the floor?"

"Remember I pointed out how rippled it looks by the sliding glass door?"

"Right."

He didn't remember.

"Rye said he'd stop by over the noon hour, so we can talk to him then." I wrote everything down and then put my chin on my fist and gazed at my handsome hubby. "Thanks for making this easy, Marco."

He reached across the table for my hand and traced a circle in my palm. "If you really want to thank me . . ." His low, sexy voice trailed off suggestively, sending shivers of delight up my spine.

"What do you have in mind?"

Gert, the waitress who'd worked at Down the Hatch since long before I was born, passed by, carrying two bowls of ice cream topped with strawberries and whipped cream. Marco looked at me and raised his eyebrow. "Let's just say it involves you and me and strawberries and whipped cream."

"Yum. Dessert."

He smiled playfully. "Yes . . . dessert."

*   *   *

"Have more dessert, Abby. It's fat-free."

All eight women laughed as Mitzi Kole tried to serve me a second helping of strawberry cheesecake with whipped cream on top. It was not the dessert either Marco or I had in mind, but as we were finishing dinner I'd remembered that the Brandywine Babes' Book Club was that evening. If I'd missed it, I'd have had to wait a week for another such opportunity.

Mitzi had been clearly disappointed that I'd come solo, but none of the others had seemed fazed. In fact, Marco would've been the only male in attendance, and that would have been awkward for both of us.

Now, at eight o'clock, I'd already consumed a handful of chocolate-covered strawberries, a sliver of strawberry pie, and a tiny square of strawberry-covered cheesecake. If I had to even look at another strawberry I would be ill. I hoped Marco would understand.

Who could have guessed tonight's dessert theme would be strawberries? It had been chosen to go along with their book selection for the month, an erotic novel that somehow involved them. After hearing their discussion, I was glad I hadn't read it. I might never have eaten those plump, juicy berries again.

We were seated in a living room decorated with a pair of bright white leather sofas accented with pink-and-white striped pillows, and two navy blue armchairs. The walls were bright white with one glossy navy accent wall. A pair of neon pink art deco floor lamps provided the only light.

Mitzi had even coordinated her outfit to match her décor, with tight-fitting navy slacks, a white V-neck sweater, huge pink chandelier earrings, a matching cuff bracelet, and high-heeled pink mules. Lottie would have felt right at home.

The other women wore casual but expensive clothing. I recognized some of the pieces from Windows on the Square's display mannequins. I was the only one under-dressed, still wearing my white button-down shirt and blue jeans from work. The combination sounded dull, but under the yellow bib apron with the bright Bloomers logo on the front, it worked well.

The book discussion, when it finally got under way, was over in ten minutes, and then the gossip session began, most of it involving Dirk Singletary's death—exactly what I'd hoped for. What I wasn't prepared for were the jokes at his expense, with several of the women teasing Mitzi about having had a hand in his demise. Rather than tak-ing offense, however, she joined in the laughter.

"Someone does you wrong," said a woman named Carol, "give Mitzi a call."

"Sheriff Kole on patrol," said Dara, another mem-ber, pretending to aim a gun.

Mitzi put her finger to her cherry pink lips. "Sh-h-h! Abby might get a nasty impression of me."

Carol put her hand to the side of her mouth and said in a stage whisper, "You mean like the nasty *impres-sion* Dirk left on your new down comforter?"

The women tittered.

"You are so bad!" Mitzi squealed, and everyone hooted with laughter.

I leaned toward Ann, a young woman about my age who was seated beside me, and whispered, "Were Dirk and Mitzi having an affair?"

Ann shrugged and with a coy smile whispered back, "We have a *Don't ask, don't tell* policy here." She reached for a chocolate-covered berry and popped it in her mouth, still grinning.

"Seriously, though, Mitz," said a woman named Sarah, "what did Brandon's insurance agent tell you about your loss?"

Mitzi pulled an angry face. "He offered me a lousy ten thousand. Can you believe that? I told him he'd be hearing from my lawyer. Ten thousand, my ass!"

"I still can't believe that jeweler in Maraville sold off your jewelry the next day," Dara said. "He had to know it was hot. A guy like Dirk comes in with expensive pieces three, four, five times, and Mr. Jeweler doesn't suspect something's wrong?"

"Maybe they were working together," Carol said. "Maybe the jeweler was a fence."

"Look out, Mr. Jeweler Man," Sarah said in a sinister voice, "or you'll be the next one to go."

"Yeah, don't go near the water, Mr. Jeweler Man," another said.

"There's no way anyone's going to lure that jeweler down to the water," said Dara. "He's way too shrewd."

"I'll bet Mitzi could do it," Carol said, and the others laughed.

"Yeah, Mitz. Show us how it's done," Dara called.

"Like this," Mitzi replied. She stood up with her back to us, hands on her hips, glanced over her shoulder to give us a provocative come-hither look, then sashayed toward the kitchen, stopping to beckon by crooking her finger. It was quite an act, and all the Bees laughed.

Ann leaned close to say quietly, "They're just kidding, you know."

I gave her the same coy smile she'd used on me earlier. "Right."

CHAPTER FIVE

"How was the meeting?" Marco asked. He was reading a manual on crime scene investigations, leaning against pillows propped up on the wicker headboard. Seedy, curled in her bed in a corner of the room, lifted her head to greet me with a tail wag.

"It was fascinating. A study in narcissism."

"The book?"

"No, Mitzi Kole." I walked over to scratch Seedy's head. "I think she killed Dirk."

Marco put the book down. "Based on what?"

"The way she and her friends joked about his death. The hints they tossed out about Mitzi and Dirk having an affair. Her anger at him stealing her jewelry. And my gut feeling that she did it."

"Not a lot of hard evidence there, Sunshine."

"Not yet." I unbuttoned my shirt and tossed it into the laundry basket in our closet. "I need to question her without the other women present. Or you."

"You don't want me there?"

"If you're there, Mitzi will play the vixen, and it'll be impossible to get serious answers from her. I saw her in action tonight." I slipped out of my jeans and turned my back on him, twisting around to imitate Mitzi's come-hither look, finger crooking and all. "That's supposedly her way of luring a man to his doom. It's not going to be how she lures you to yours."

Marco tossed back the covers and came after me, sweeping me up in his arms and carrying me to the bed. "You're the only one who's going to lure me to my doom, Fireball."

Thursday

"Now that most of the boxes are unpacked," I told Marco over breakfast the next morning, "I'm going to ask Jillian to come over and give me some decorating advice."

He didn't say anything for a moment, possibly because hearing Jillian's name typically made his brain freeze. "I think we're capable of making those decisions."

"We can make *decisions*, sure, but I want our house to look like a professional did it. I've always dreamed of having a beautiful home, Marco, and I really want it to be perfect. Our open house will be here before we know it."

He rinsed his oatmeal bowl, stuck it in the dishwasher, then came to the table, where I was finishing my coffee, and put his arms around me. "You, me, and Seedy. It's already perfect, sweetheart. But I want you to be happy, so go ahead, call Jillian."

I turned to smile up at him, putting my hands over his. "Thank you, Marco. I appreciate that."

He leaned over and kissed me. "Just don't plan on me being here."

I didn't blame him for feeling that way. My cousin Jillian wasn't the easiest person to be around. But she was an expert at pulling pieces together to make terrific outfits because of her background in fashion design. She had used that talent to turn an ordinary three-bedroom apartment into a showplace.

Unfortunately, as a child Jillian had been coddled by her parents because of her severe scoliosis. By the time she hit her teens, the scoliosis had been fixed but nothing could undo the spoiling. Even her husband, Claymore, was perfectly happy catering to her.

Two months ago, she'd had an adorable baby girl named Harper Abigail Lynne Osborne, whose initials by no coincidence spelled HALO. Harper was Jillian's little angel. Add to that a pampered Boston terrier she'd adopted the same time we'd taken Seedy into our family, and I could understand Marco's reasons for wanting to be scarce.

But rather than driving him away from his own home, I had a solution. "I've decided to hire Tara to babysit at Jillian's house so Jillian can come alone."

"Last time you asked your niece to babysit, she refused, remember?"

"I'll bribe her. Don't worry, Marco. I'll make it work."

"We'll see. If you're meeting in the evening, I'll probably be at the bar anyway."

I glanced at my watch. "Speaking of that, it's time to go to work. Aren't you going to shave?"

"Seedy and I are staying home this morning. I want to get my exercise equipment out of the garage and installed downstairs. Down the Hatch doesn't open until eleven anyway, and Rafe said he'd cover the lunch hour for me."

"That works. If I'm late getting home, you can show Rye Bishop the damaged floor."

*   *   *

It wasn't Rye keeping my husband company when I returned home for lunch. It was Mitzi Kole. When I pulled into the driveway, the garage door was up, and Marco and Mitzi were inside, half of an elliptical machine on the floor nearby. Marco had on black workout pants and a T-shirt that showed off his well-muscled torso. Mitzi was wearing a white leather jacket and a short, tight navy skirt with high-heeled navy ankle boots. She was standing with one hip cocked, her back to me, and I saw her toss her mane of blond hair then reach out to lay her hand on Marco's biceps.

I gunned the motor with visions of running her down. But that was the old Abby. The new Abby was older and wiser and didn't want to spend her life in prison because some pathetic, oversexed older woman was flirting with her husband.

Both turned as I pulled to a stop a mere two yards away. Marco lifted his hand in greeting, and Mitzi opened her mouth in surprise. Clearly she hadn't been expecting me to come home in the middle of the day. That was undoubtedly the reason the red satin blouse under her jacket had a V-neck that opened almost to her waist, revealing that she wasn't wearing a bra.

I got out of the 'Vette and shut the door with a bang.

"Oh, here's Abby now," Mitzi called. "Hi!" She waved as though delighted to see me. "You're just the person I wanted to talk to."

"Perfect timing, then." I stopped in front of her with a smile that said, *I know what you're up to.*

Mitzi's own smile faltered. "As I was just telling Marco, I think the Bees gave you the wrong impression last night. I want to correct that."

"I'll let you ladies talk," Marco said. He lifted his eyebrows at me.

Mitzi turned to watch him carry the half-assembled machine through the door connecting our garage to the house and then turned back. "He's so cute."

I smiled politely. "Thank you. What kind of impression do you think you left last night?"

"That I may have had something to do with Dirk's death." She shrugged, palms up. "We joke a lot at book club. You'll see when you start coming to meetings regularly."

Like that was going to happen. "No, I understood that everyone was joking."

She fanned her face. "Whew! I don't want to get off on the wrong foot or anything. I mean, Dirk *was* a bastard, but that's no reason to kill him. Not that I *could* kill anyone." She flexed her biceps as though I could see through leather. "Try these muscles. Try them!" She took my hand and placed it on her upper arm. "Would I have the strength to hold someone underwater? Not likely!"

Interesting. The newspaper article hadn't mentioned that Dirk had been held underwater. Yet since he was found in the pond, I couldn't say it wouldn't be a normal assumption for someone to make. But did Mitzi really believe I'd fall for her *His being a bastard is no reason to kill him* story?

To make it clear that I wasn't buying it, I said, "How awful that he robbed you of such valuable jewelry. Theda mentioned that one piece alone was worth twenty thousand dollars."

"At least that much. All told, I lost over thirty thousand. And Brandon Thorne thinks I'll settle for ten grand? No frigging way. He's just as big a bastard as

Dirk was. Do you know what I learned through all of this? Brandon doesn't vet his employees or even bond them. In this day and age, who doesn't do background checks?" She shook her head in disbelief.

Clever how she tried to divert the subject onto Thorne. "Are you absolutely sure Dirk was the one who took your jewelry?"

"Of course I'm sure. No one else was in my house that week but him."

"Not even your husband?"

"Frank's home just on weekends. He travels for business. Dirk was there on that Tuesday to, um, patch some nail holes, and I discovered my jewelry missing on Wednesday. I know it happened that week because I'd worn them to dinner the previous Sunday evening."

"Was Rye working with Dirk that day?"

"No, Rye didn't come with him."

"That's rather unusual, isn't it? I thought they worked together."

Mitzi twisted a lock of hair around her fingers and shrugged.

"Were you there while Dirk was working inside your house?"

"I had a hair appointment."

"But you let him in."

"Actually, he used the master key from the office. But that was common practice around Brandywine. When a worker needed access to someone's house, Dirk would let them in and stay around to supervise. Who would've dreamed there would be a reason to distrust Dirk?" She huffed angrily. "Of course, if Brandon Thorne had done a background check on Dirk, he never would've been employed."

"How do you know?"

"Detective Wells told me when she was investigating my theft."

"Was Dirk still there when you got home from your appointment?"

She waved her hand, flashing her long, polished fingernails. "Long gone."

"Then how do you know Rye didn't come with him?"

"I asked. When I found my jewels missing, I wanted to know who had been in my house."

"Whom did you ask?"

"Brandon Thorne's saleswoman, Connie. She, Rye, and Dirk share an office at the clubhouse. She knows their comings and goings by their appointment calendar."

"So you called the police to report your missing jewelry, and I'm assuming they talked to Dirk."

"For the third time. He'd already been questioned two months earlier when some of the other residents here were robbed. But Dirk swore he didn't take my jewelry and there wasn't any evidence to prove he did, so they had to let him go."

"Wasn't there something in his records to indicate a criminal history? You mentioned that he wouldn't have been hired because of a background check."

"All allegations, nothing ever proved." Mitzi sighed morosely. "To think I trusted that bastard. And to think it could've been avoided if Brandon wasn't such a cheap ass."

"Last night the women were talking about a Maraville jeweler. Was there evidence this jeweler was involved in the theft?"

"No. He claims he purchased my jewelry from someone matching Dirk's description." She scowled. "Dirk was sly. He used a fake ID. And I'm positive he was behind the other thefts in the neighborhood for these reasons." She enumerated on her fingers. "He had access to the homes that were robbed. He had excuses for being in the houses. He knew when people weren't home."

"Sounds plausible."

"That's what Detective Wells said, but she couldn't tie Dirk to the thefts. He didn't leave any fingerprints, and no one witnessed him taking anything."

"I'm shocked that the jeweler didn't have security cameras."

"Oh, he had them, but here's where Dirk was cunning. He wore baggy jeans, dirty white athletic shoes, and a gray hoodie with the hood pulled up and a black baseball cap underneath, just like Rye does. Detective Wells said she couldn't get a clear enough image of the man's face to make an ID. Rye was interviewed, but again, there was nothing to prove either one had taken the jewelry."

"Could Rye be the thief?"

"How could he be? He wasn't in my house that week."

"But he had access to the master key, too, didn't he?"

"It wasn't Rye," she said firmly.

Mitzi wouldn't elaborate, so I asked, "How did Dirk get along with Rye?"

"Dirk was awful to him, just cruel, and for no apparent reason. Have you met Rye? He's a sweetheart."

I looked at my watch, prompting Mitzi to do the same. "Actually, Rye's due here any minute."

"And I need to run." She wiggled her fingers. "Mani/pedi time." She glanced at my short, bare fingernails and said, "My beauty salon could help you with those. Call La De Da and ask for Sonja. She's the best nail tech ever. She's my hairstylist, too."

"I'll keep that in mind. And very quickly, where were you last Friday evening?"

She put a fingertip to her puffed-up lip, thinking. "Where was I? Oh, right! I was at La De Da. I gave myself a spa evening—total body and scalp massage, waxing, mani/pedi—the works. It was pure heaven."

Why was she having a manicure and pedicure just a few days later?

As she started backing away, I said, "If you had to choose someone from the neighborhood with a strong reason to want Dirk dead, who would it be?"

She paused to nibble her lower lip. "Well, there was no love lost between Dirk and Brandon Thorne—that's for sure—or between Dirk and Rye, for that matter."

"But you said Rye was a sweetheart."

"Sure, to all of us in Brandywine. That doesn't mean Dirk didn't push Rye until he snapped. We all have our breaking points, right?" She glanced over her shoulder at Theda's house. "But there's the person I'd watch."

"Theda?"

Mitzi nodded. "She may seem harmless, but don't be fooled by her act."

"What act is that?"

A pickup truck turned into the driveway. Mitzi waved to the driver then said, "Just be careful. Don't believe everything Theda says." Then she trotted up to the truck to give Rye a hug and kiss on the cheek before hurrying up the sidewalk toward her house.

I glanced back at Theda's window and saw the curtain drop.

"Afternoon, Mrs. Salvare." Rye gave me a sheepish

smile as he ran his palm over his cheek. "Mitzi always does that. If I forget to wipe off the lipstick, my wife gets all bent out of shape."

I detected that twang Theda had mentioned. "Mitzi certainly is friendly," I said.

He gave a light laugh. "Yes, ma'am. You could say that."

Rye Bishop was a stocky younger man of average height. As Mitzi had described, he wore a gray hooded sweatshirt, baggy jeans, and dirty white sneakers. Today the hood was down and a black White Sox baseball cap was on his head backward.

"This may seem like an odd question," I said, "but is that always how you wear your cap?"

He looked up, then felt his head and removed his cap, revealing a thatch of short brown hair underneath. "I'm sorry. My mama taught me to take off my hat in the presence of a lady."

"No, that's fine. I just wondered if you always wear it backward."

"Just sometimes," he said. "I can turn it around if you find it offensive."

"No, please. I don't mind."

Holding his cap, he said, "I understand your floor is damaged."

"I'm afraid it is. Come inside and see."

I called down to Marco in the basement to let him know Rye was there, then took Rye to the dining room and showed him the floor in front of the sliding glass door. He got down on his knees to examine it, then used a screwdriver to take off the metal threshold and look beneath. "You've got water damage," he said, as

Marco joined us. "Looks like your door might have been standing open during a storm."

"That doesn't make sense," Marco said. "Wouldn't the workmen notice?"

"If they were here when the rain started," Rye said. "My guess is that it was open when they quit and the rain came in later."

My floor was damaged because of a worker's carelessness? That started my temper rising. "Shouldn't someone check the houses at the end of the day?"

Rye put the threshold back and stood up. "Yep."

Marco was annoyed now. "Then why wasn't it checked?"

Rye twisted his cap in his hands. "I can't say for sure."

"Whose responsibility is it?" I asked.

"When your house was built, it was Dirk's. Now it's mine."

"I hope you're doing a better job than he was," I said.

"Yes, ma'am. I check every house under construction before I leave for the day."

"What can be done about the damage here?" said Marco.

"This whole section around the door will have to be removed and new wood put in, maybe the subfloor, too, depending on how far down the water traveled. If you want my opinion, I'd ask for a whole new floor. You'll never get a perfect match to this floor color otherwise."

"Will you relay that to Thorne for us?" Marco asked.

Rye used his thumb to scratch his head, looking doubtful. "I sure will try."

"You don't sound too confident," I said.

He gave us an apologetic look. "I know from experience Mr. Thorne is just gonna tell me to have the flooring contractor replace this area only. A whole new floor would cost him a lot of money."

"I understand, but unfortunately, that's his problem," Marco said. "Tell Thorne we expect a new floor."

"Yes, sir, I'll tell him what you said first thing in the morning when I report in. Is there anything else you need while I'm here?"

"Yes, there is," I said. "We want to pick your brain about something. Would you like a beer or an iced tea?"

"A glass of sweet tea, if you'd be so kind."

I headed toward the kitchen. "Have a seat. I was about to have lunch, so would you like a sandwich? We have turkey and cheese."

"No, thank you, ma'am. I already ate. But you both go ahead. I know you've got businesses to get back to."

I poured glasses for all of us, found some sugar packets for Rye, and put everything on the table.

"What can I do for you?" Rye asked, placing his baseball cap in his lap.

"We're investigating Dirk Singletary's death," Marco said. "We'd like to get your input on it."

His friendly smile dissolved, his expression turning guarded. "I'm afraid I can't help you there. I don't know anything except what I read in the newspaper."

"That's okay," Marco said, folding his hands on the table. "People often know things they don't realize they know. For instance, we were told there was friction between Dirk and Brandon Thorne. Would that be your assessment, too?"

Rye shifted uncomfortably. "Look, I'm not trying to be rude or anything. I just don't feel right talking about my boss. I hope you understand where I'm coming from."

"No problem," Marco said. "I'd like to think my employees would be that loyal. How about the Brandywine residents? Any problems between Dirk and any of them?"

"Just the ones who had things stolen. They're pretty angry about it."

I brought my notebook and a pen to the table. "Would you give me their names?"

After I'd finished writing, Marco asked, "Is it your impression that most people believe Dirk is guilty of those thefts?"

"Yes, sir. Everyone I've talked to believes he's the thief."

"I know Mitzi Kole is one of them," I said.

Rye chortled softly as though laughing at a private joke. "Yep, she's one of them."

His reaction was revealing, but I had a feeling he wouldn't be as forthcoming with his words. So I looked him in the eye and said, "So you're aware they were having an affair?"

CHAPTER SIX

Rye seemed shocked by my question so Marco jumped in. "What my wife means to say is that we've heard rumors about the two of them. We wondered whether they were true."

Rye ran his hands over his thatch of hair, distinctly uncomfortable with the question. "I don't want to answer that, Mr. Salvare, because I don't know for certain."

"Fair enough. Would you verify that Dirk was in Mitzi's house the day before she reported her jewelry missing?"

He ducked his head, using his thumb to scratch between his eyes. "I guess it's okay to tell you since I already told the detective. Yes, Dirk was at her house the day before Mrs. Kole called the police."

"Was he in Mitzi's home alone?" I asked.

Rye just kept scratching his forehead, clearly a signal that he didn't want to answer, so I tried again. "Was Mitzi *there* while Dirk was working?"

After a long hesitation he said, "All I know for sure is that her Jaguar was in the garage while his truck was in the driveway."

I glanced at Marco and raised my eyebrows.

"Thanks for your candor," Marco said.

Rye glanced at his watch. "I should get going. I've got another appointment."

"Just a few more quick questions, if you don't mind," Marco said. "You mentioned something earlier about checking the houses at the end of the day being your responsibility now. Does that mean you've been promoted?"

"I applied for it."

"Is it true that Dirk kept you from being promoted before?" I asked.

"Yes, ma'am. Dirk took a disliking to me for some reason."

"I'm sure you've been through this with the police," Marco said, "but would you mind telling us what you were doing Friday afternoon and evening?"

"I was caulking and painting at the model home on Friday afternoon. I left at four like usual and headed home."

"Did anyone see you at the model?"

"No, sir. I was there alone."

"Was your truck out front or in the driveway?"

"Neither. I walked over from the office."

"Where was Dirk while you were there?"

"I don't have a clue. I spoke briefly with him before he went out for lunch and never saw him again."

"Was it unusual for you not to see him all afternoon?"

"Not at all. We often worked separately. And Dirk kept odd hours. Sometimes he'd get there at ten in the morning instead of at seven like everyone else. Or he'd be gone by three. I never knew what times he'd be there from one day to the next."

"Was that allowed?" I asked.

Rye shrugged. "I don't know if Mr. Thorne was aware of it. Dirk was always on time on the day the boss was due to stop in."

Stealing from residents, slacking on the job, humiliating coworkers—Dirk Singletary sounded like a real piece of work. It made me wonder what kind of husband and father he'd been. "What time did you arrive home on Friday, Rye?"

"It takes me forty-five minutes, so about five o'clock."

"Anyone there who can back you up?" Marco asked.

"No, sir. My wife doesn't get home until ten o'clock—she works evenings part-time—and my boys play sports after school."

I wrote everything down and put an asterisk beside it to indicate an area to explore. Rye had no way to verify his alibi.

He began to twist his baseball cap in his hands. "Look, if this is your way of trying to find out whether I killed Dirk, I can tell you I didn't particularly care for the way the guy treated me, but I wouldn't have killed him. I've got a large family to support, and I can't do that from prison. If you want to know the truth, I've been shopping for another job. I don't want that to get back to Mr. Thorne, though."

"Everything you tell us is confidential," I said.

He let out a breath. "Thank you."

"Other than the robbery victims," Marco said, "can you think of anyone in Brandywine who might have had an intense dislike for Dirk?"

Rye picked up his glass and took a slow drink of tea as he pondered it. "Not *in* Brandywine," he said at last. "Just kind of associated with it."

"I need a name," Marco said.

Without hesitation Rye said, "Maynard Dell."

That name sounded familiar but I couldn't place it. Marco, however, identified him instantly. "The town's building inspector? Why did he dislike Dirk?"

"It was more of a mutual dislike."

"Based on what?"

"I shouldn't really be telling you this, but"—Rye leaned in and dropped his voice, as though afraid of being overheard—"some of the houses here? Dirk said they shouldn't have passed inspection. Their wiring isn't up to code."

"Then why did they pass?" Marco asked.

"You know how the inspector checks wiring? He sticks one of them juice detectors in the electrical outlet to see if it lights up. If it does, it passes inspection. Then there's his fondness for long liquid lunches. Kind of hard to work after one of those."

"He drinks *during* working hours?" I asked as I wrote.

Rye held up his hands, palms out. "I'm only repeating what Dirk told me. It really bugged him that Maynard was earning good money and getting great benefits for slipshod work just because he knew someone on the town council. A patronage job, Dirk called it. Boy, he hated that."

"So do I," I said. "Doesn't that irk you, too?"

Rye shrugged again, but this time I caught glimmers of anger in his brown eyes. "I care about the people here. I hope it isn't true, because I don't want anything bad to happen to anyone 'cause their house isn't safe."

"Does that include our house?" I asked.

"Like I said, this was what Dirk told me. But if I were you, I'd hire an electrician you trust to inspect your wiring."

I glanced around the room, half expecting to see sparks coming from the kitchen's recessed lights. "What happens if the wiring is faulty?"

"It could cause a fire." Rye shrugged, glancing up at the brushed nickel light fixture overhead. "You'd have to rip it all out to fix it."

Rip my walls apart? I was seeing red, and it wasn't from imaginary flames. "What kind of electrician did Brandon Thorne hire?"

"Whoever put in the lowest bid."

I could feel my temper bubbling up fast, but I wasn't sure who to be angriest with, the developer or Maynard Dell. "So if our house catches fire, shouldn't Maynard Dell and the town of New Chapel be responsible?"

Rye nodded, his head bowed as though admitting it embarrassed him. And yet I thought I detected a slight smugness in his expression that made me suspect he was enjoying ratting Maynard out.

Marco said, "Once Dirk knew this was going on, what did he do?"

"He said he was gonna have a talk with Maynard."

"Did he report it to Thorne?"

Rye shrugged.

"Did that talk between Dirk and Maynard happen?" Marco asked.

"Yeah. It happened. I was working at a house over on Thorneapple when Maynard came by, and was he pissed. 'You see I'm doin' my job, don't you?' he asked me. 'If I get fired 'cause of Dirk, I'll kill that sumbitch with my bare hands.'"

Marco looked at me, and I said, "Got it," as I scribbled it down.

*   *   *

After Rye left, I took our glasses to the sink, setting them down with a bang. "When is our appointment with Brandon Thorne? If he's not aware of this deplorable situation with the building inspector, he will be. And he should pay for an electrician to come check our house, too. And while we're at it, we can demand a new floor."

Marco scooped up the sugar and napkins and brought them over. "Hold on a minute, Sunshine. Let's keep our building issues separate from the investigation or we won't get anywhere with the man."

I rinsed the glasses and put them in the dishwasher, trying to calm down. "Sorry. My Irish is showing."

"Good thing we Italians are so even-tempered."

I couldn't help but laugh at that. I slipped my arms around his waist and smiled up at him. "Yes, it is a good thing. I just wish Rye weren't so convinced that Brandon won't give us a new floor."

"To be honest, I'm surprised we didn't notice the floor damage when we did our pre-closing walk."

"I *did* notice, Marco. I told Dirk it looked odd. But it was evening, and Dirk told me it was just the way the lamplight was hitting the surface. It didn't even cross my mind to get down and feel it. And he kept moving, so I moved with him."

"Where was I during this conversation?"

"You took Seedy outside. Where is she, by the way?"

"Out back on her leash. She loves that yard so much I couldn't get her to come inside. We sure picked the right place for her."

With a sigh I said, "I thought it was right for us, too."

"We'll make it right, sweetheart. Don't worry."

I lay my head on his shoulder and let his warmth

and confidence soak in as he rubbed my back. Marco was an expert at making things better.

He kissed the top of my head. "Let's sit down for a few minutes and go over Rye's information while it's still fresh."

I gave him a kiss and then we sat at the table again.

"What's your impression of Rye?" he asked.

"He came across as nice as everyone says he is. He seemed to genuinely not want to say anything bad about anyone here, including his boss. In this day and age, that's unusually magnanimous."

"I agree. He struck me as a salt-of-the-earth kind of guy, reluctant to talk negatively about anyone until he brought up—"

"Maynard Dell. I caught that, too. Rye was more than willing to share everything he knew about Maynard. To tell you the truth, Marco, I almost felt like he enjoyed dishing the dirt on him."

"The question is, did Rye share that knowledge to divert suspicion away from himself or because he's sincerely concerned about the residents here?"

"I didn't get a bad feeling about Rye, but I do see a motive, albeit a weak one."

"To get the promotion he's been denied?"

I gave Marco a high five. "We're on the same page, Salvare. So not only was Dirk humiliating Rye in front of the residents, but he was also keeping Rye from moving up in the company. On Rye's behalf, however, he didn't seem too certain he'd get the promotion even with Dirk gone. We should ask Thorne about that."

"Add it to our list of questions."

I turned to a fresh page and titled it "Brandon Thorne Interview." "I want to be there when you interview

Maynard Dell, Marco. Boy, do I want to be there. I've really got a bone to pick with that man. Actually, let's write to the mayor about him, too. And the town council. They need to know what kind of guy they hired."

"One thing at a time, Abby. Our focus for now is the murder. If what Rye told us checks out, Maynard will go on the suspect list."

"How are you going to check him out?"

"I've got an electrician coming in to do some new lighting around the bar. He's a knowledgeable guy. If there's any scuttlebutt on Maynard Dell, he'll know it."

"Be sure he comes out to inspect our house, too."

"I'm on it. Anything else on Rye?"

"No, let's move on to Brandon Thorne. You're not going to believe this, but he doesn't bond his employees or do background checks on them."

"How did you find out?"

"Mitzi Kole. According to what Detective Wells told her, if Thorne had done a background check on Dirk, he wouldn't have hired him, thus Dirk wouldn't have been around to steal from the residents."

"Did Dirk have a criminal history?"

"All Mitzi said was that at his previous places of employment, complaints were filed but charges were never brought."

Seedy scratched on the sliding glass door so Marco went to let her in. He unhooked her leash and she headed for the kitchen, then paused halfway, sniffed the air, and then began to growl, sinking low to the ground as though she were in danger.

I crouched down beside her and began to stroke her fur. "What is it, Seedy?"

"Maybe she smelled a stranger in the house." Marco

put water in her bowl and called her. Seedy glanced around the room, as though making sure no one else was there, then moved cautiously toward him. "What else did you learn from Mitzi?"

"She claims she was *not* at home when Dirk came in to fix her walls. She said he let himself in and was gone when she got back, which contradicts Rye's story."

Marco leaned against the island, his arms folded over his chest. "Whose story do you believe?"

"At this point, Rye's. Mitzi has a much stronger motive, although she downplays it. You know how people ramble and shift attention onto others when they're feeling guilty? That was Mitzi after I suggested she had a good reason to be angry at Dirk."

"What else did Mitzi have to say?"

"She thinks you're cute."

"Not hot?"

"Did you want her to say you're hot?"

Marco's mouth curved up at the corners. "*You're* hot when you're jealous."

"I'm not jealous over some sad, older woman who dresses like my niece. But I did get a little annoyed when Mitzi told me not to believe everything Theda said."

"Why did that annoy you?"

"She was trying to throw suspicion on Theda."

"Abby, you know we have to look at Theda as a viable suspect."

"I know, and I'll put her on the list because it's protocol, but if Theda were guilty, my inner alarm would be ringing like crazy. You know who makes it ring? Mitzi." I glanced at my watch. "I need to get back. Do we have an appointment with Thorne?"

"Tomorrow at twelve thirty. I wasn't able to reach

Dirk's wife, so I'll try to set up that interview this afternoon."

I brushed my teeth, ran a comb through my hair and hurried back to the kitchen, where Marco was crouched on the floor petting the dog. "Will you keep Seedy with you this afternoon?"

"No problem."

"Thanks, Marco. And I almost forgot. Tonight is the other book club meeting, and tomorrow night Jillian is coming over."

"Damn, that's upsetting. I'll be at Down the Hatch both evenings."

"Yeah, I can see how upset you are." I gave him a quick kiss, grabbed my purse and keys, and raced out the door, only to turn and walk back inside.

Marco was fastening Seedy's leash to her collar. "I was wondering when you'd remember us."

"Sorry. Old habit."

"And by the way, warn me the next time you decide to shop for a vehicle. Now I've got a used car salesman who wants to sell me some silver number you apparently picked out for me."

CHAPTER SEVEN

"I really didn't intend to car-shop for you, Marco. I was waiting for Lisa Wells to get back from lunch, and the used car lot was the perfect place to watch for her. I just happened to be standing by a silver Lexus, and the salesman made the leap from there."

"That doesn't explain how he got the impression *I* was in the market for a car."

"All I said was why the Lexus wouldn't work for you."

"And there was his opening. Now I'll have a pesky salesman calling me with cars he thinks *would* work for me."

Seedy put her paw on the glass and gave a yip, wanting me to roll the window down so she could stick her head out. We were in the passenger seat and Marco was driving. As usual.

"Not today, Seed," Marco said. "It's too chilly."

In a stage whisper I said to the dog, "Although it might cool your daddy off."

"I'm not angry, Abby. I can handle the salesman's calls. And I know you're eager to have your 'Vette back. I just don't think the time is right to take on big monthly payments. You don't mind sharing a ride with me, do you?"

"No." *Sometimes. Yes.*

"When we can afford it, we'll look for a car together. Okay?"

I nodded. He was probably right. I still wanted my car back.

I returned to Bloomers to find Grace wiping down tables in the coffee-and-tea parlor, Lottie ringing up a customer's purchase, and Rosa working on a floral arrangement in the workroom, singing in her off-key voice to a song on the radio. Six completed arrangements sat on the counter, waiting to be delivered.

"Hola," she called as I stepped through the curtain. "Where is our little Seedy?"

"With Marco for the afternoon." I put on my bright yellow bib apron with the Bloomers logo on the front and tied it in back. "You can take your lunch break now."

"I'm okay. I've been nibbling for an hour. I told Grace to go when you got back."

I paused to digest that, then plucked an order from the spindle.

The arrangement was for a young woman's twenty-first birthday party thrown by her parents. Besides giving me a price range, their only other request was to use their daughter's favorite colors, purple and yellow.

Inside the cooler I breathed in the fresh floral scents, feeling all my stress melt away as I looked over my inventory. As I pulled out some greenery I heard Grace say, "I'll be popping out now to make deliveries, and then I'll stop for a quick bite."

I was ready to answer her when I heard Rosa say, "Okay, enjoy your lunch. I will take care of the parlor while you're out."

Hmm. Another moment to digest.

Back at the table, I prepped a six-inch square dark purple glass container and then began inserting bluish-purple anemones. Soon I found myself humming along with the music on the radio, happy to be in my haven, doing what I do best.

With the glass pot nearly full, I added a few yellow daisies and pale yellow Futura lilies and then filled in with tree fern. I wrapped it and placed it in the second walk-in cooler, then started on the next order, a get-well bouquet.

No flowers were specified, so I stood in the cooler, looking at my choices. What would be an uplifting color scheme? Yellow, of course, and I had a fine selection of yellow roses. Maybe red poppies and bright white tulips . . . with lily grass and leatherleaf fern as my greens. But it needed something more, something soft and delicate. My gaze landed on the white larkspur. Perfect.

I chose a six-inch-by-six-inch pale yellow ceramic pot in the shape of a sprinkling can, got out my tools and wet foam, and set to work. I was in the zone, my fingers working in tandem with my brain as the design in my mind's eye took shape. Everything else fell away; it was just me and the flowers, their floral scents, silken textures, and rich hues making all my senses vibrate with energy even as I felt an immense serenity of spirit.

By the time Grace returned from lunch and Rosa rejoined me, I'd finished five more arrangements and was back to my usual sunny nature.

At three thirty, Tara, my fourteen-year-old niece, stopped by on her way home from high school. In bygone days, she'd drop by to watch me work and share the latest schoolyard gossip, but lately it was because Bloomers was handily situated near a popular shop on the square called Jangles. We had, in effect, become her bathroom stop.

Tara Knight was the only child of my brother Jordan and his wife, Kathy. Since Tara and I were only thirteen years apart, she'd always been like a kid sister to me. We even looked alike, with our red hair, freckles, short stature, and feisty tempers. Tara had also adopted Seedy's cute little puppy Seedling when we adopted Seedy.

Until she discovered boys, Tara had loved hanging out with me, admiring my entrepreneurship and love of investigations. Against everyone's better judgment, she had even helped Marco and me solve a murder case because, just like me, Tara was headstrong and curious.

Now, with a quick "Hi," she dropped her backpack on my desk and headed to the restroom. She returned to slide onto a wooden stool and hold out her skinny arm so we could see her stack of colorful bangle bracelets. "Look what I got at Jangles."

"Let me see, let me see," Rosa called excitedly, coming around the big slate-topped table to take Tara's hand. "How pretty they are! And look, they *do* jangle!"

"Everyone's wearing them." Tara began to pick them out individually. "See, this one has a bike insignia on it because I ride a bike, and this one has a dog's face that looks a little like Seedling, and this one has a computer, this one has a book, and this one has a basketball."

"You don't play basketball," I said.

Rosa gave Tara a wink. "But I'll bet her boyfriend does."

They giggled conspiratorially.

"Well, duh, of course," I said, trying to be the cool aunt. "That's Zeth, right?"

"Zeth?" Tara gave me a look of horror. "Aunt Abby, that's so over."

Hmm. I used to be Aunt Amazing. But apparently that was over, too.

"It's Dimitri now, Abby," Rosa said, nudging my niece. "Right, Tara? With his big brown eyes and curly black hair . . ."

They giggled again.

"Want a can of sparkling water?" I asked Tara.

"No, but I do want to *thank* you"—she emphasized the word with a roll of her eyes—"for foisting Aunt Jillian's zoo on me tomorrow evening."

"I didn't foist. I *suggested* she ask you."

Tara looked at Rosa and rolled her eyes again. "Same difference. I'm still babysitting—on a Friday night!"

"So?" I asked. "You'll earn good money. You know Jillian pays well."

"You do it, then," Tara snapped.

"Hey, now," Rosa said, planting her hands on her hips and giving Tara a chiding look. "You do not talk that way to your aunt. You're hurting her feelings, and she was only trying to do you a favor. Now you owe her an apology."

Actually, I was trying to do *myself* a favor, but Rosa had a point.

Tara hung her head. "I'm sorry, Aunt Abby. I didn't mean to hurt you."

I put my arms around her and gave her a hug. "Thank you. And if you don't want to babysit for Jillian, I won't suggest you again."

Tara squeezed me around the waist and smiled. "Thanks. I wouldn't mind if it weren't on Friday. My friends and I always go out for pizza and a movie on Fridays."

Rosa made a waving motion. "Go, Tara. I will babysit for Jillian at my house."

I glanced at Rosa in surprise.

"Thank you," Tara said brightly, hopping off the stool to embrace her. "I mean, *muchas gracias.* You're amazing."

I heard a stifled moan and realized it came from me.

The Books and Bottles club was totally different from that of the Brandywine Babes, aka the Bees. The seven women with me that evening were all about their selection of the week, discussing it at length and in great detail, whereas the Bees seemed more interested in getting through any book talk so they could gossip.

At least I didn't feel underdressed. The code was completely relaxed—jeans and khakis, T-shirts, button-downs, and even a sweatshirt, flats, athletic shoes, and in one case, flip-flops. I fit right in. Reagan's house, too, was comfortably designed, with a cushy but worn brown tweed sofa and matching love seat, a pair of beige armchairs, and a few oak kitchen chairs brought in to seat the overflow.

The novel under discussion was set during World War II, a period I knew little about, so I sat quietly and sipped my glass of wine during their dissection. When they stopped and brought out the appetizers, I was relieved and raring to pick up the latest scuttlebutt on Dirk Singletary's death.

But that didn't happen. Talk turned instead to recipes and garden plans and the latest news about a Whole Foods Market coming to town. I was shocked. A murder had occurred in their neighborhood and they weren't talking about it?

When Reagan realized I hadn't said much, she turned

her attention my way. "You've lived in Brandywine a whole six days now, Abby. How do you like it so far?"

Choice: go into what might turn out to be a lengthy discussion of my floor situation or pump them for information about Dirk?

"So far, so good," I answered chirpily. "Well, except for Dirk's tragic death. There's nothing good about that. I didn't know the man well, but what do you all think?"

"About . . . ?" Reagan asked. They were all gazing at me with blank stares.

"About the tragic circumstances of his death," I said.

"It's definitely tragic," Reagan said, prompting nods all around.

This wasn't going to be easy. "Do any of you feel apprehensive about how he died?"

"I think we all agree it's a matter of concern," said a blond named Carissa. "We're hoping the police will resolve the matter soon."

Spring, the young woman wearing flip-flops and a braid down her back, said, "I feel sorry for his wife." This was addressed to the others, who murmured their agreement.

They weren't getting it. Maybe this club *was* just about books and bottles. I was going to have to be blunt about what I needed.

"It's time for dessert," Reagan announced, rising from the sofa.

"Okay, but before that," I said, standing, "I'm not sure you all know, but my husband and I are investigating Dirk's death. So if you have any information—even a tiny bit—that might add to what we know about Dirk's last day, which was Friday, would you share it with me?"

"Of course," Reagan said, heading toward her kitchen. "I work during the day, so I don't have anything to add. Girls? Anything?"

They looked at each other, then looked at me and shrugged.

"Have any of you had run-ins with Dirk?" I asked.

None of them had.

"And no one had jewelry stolen?" I asked.

Another negative response.

Be blunter, Abby!

"Do you know anything about Mitzi Kole?"

"*She* had jewelry stolen," Spring said.

I felt like a salmon swimming upstream. With hopes of learning anything relevant fading fast, I finally threw in my last gambit. "Has there been any gossip about her and Dirk having an affair?"

I almost fell backward at their burst of laughter.

"Abby, there's always gossip going around about Mitzi," Reagan said, as she and Spring served up the desserts, "some of it from Mitzi herself." She handed me a plate with a brownie topped by a scoop of vanilla bean ice cream, then put her head near mine to say quietly, "We try to keep that kind of talk out of our meetings. Why don't you stay after and I'll give you some information that might be helpful?"

When the meeting was over, Spring stayed to help Reagan clean up, so I joined in. Afterward, Reagan poured us more wine and we sat at her kitchen island to talk.

"I'm sorry I interrupted the meeting," I said. "I expected the gossip to flow as freely as it did at last night's book club."

"We understand," Reagan said, "and I think you'll find we operate differently from the Bees."

"Another thing to keep in mind," Spring said, "is that this is your first time with us. We don't know you very well, so things we might normally discuss, we won't in front of a guest."

"So let us tell you what we know about Mitzi and then you can ask questions," Reagan said.

"Fair enough."

"As I mentioned earlier," Reagan said, "some of what we hear comes directly from Mitzi herself because she takes pride in her conquests."

"When you say *conquests*," I said, "does that mean Mitzi has had affairs within this community before?"

"Yes," Reagan said. "Carissa's husband, for one. Now he's her *ex*-husband. She's the only one in our club who was affected by Mitzi's wandering eye."

Then I was right to mistrust Mitzi. I took out my notebook and pen. There was no way I'd remember everything they said, especially after two glasses of wine. "I don't trust my memory. I hope you don't mind." I looked at them and got smiles, so I proceeded. "Did Mitzi tell you she and Dirk were having an affair?"

"Actually, we didn't hear it from her this time," Spring said. "Mitzi tells about her affairs only after she ends them. She hadn't gotten to that point with Dirk because of the jewelry theft or she would have spread the news."

"Considering everything you know about Mitzi, could she have murdered Dirk?"

"I'd hate to speculate without having all the facts," Spring said.

"What you have to keep in mind is that Mitzi is a

player," Reagan said, refilling my wineglass. "But this time *she* was played."

"And a played Mitzi isn't a woman anyone would want to tangle with," Spring said with a shudder. "We've witnessed how vengeful she can be. If she feels wronged, watch out. She's the reason we split away from the Bees' book club."

I wrote it down and then had a hard time reading it. Time to stop drinking the wine. "Can you think of anyone in Brandywine besides Mitzi who had a major beef with Dirk?"

"I'd have to say Brandon Thorne," Reagan said, and Spring nodded in agreement.

"About what?" I asked.

"Dirk's irresponsibility," Reagan said. "From what I picked up at the monthly meetings, Dirk's careless-ness cost Brandon a lot of money, and Thorne Enter-prises is all about making money."

"I wish you could have witnessed how Dirk behaved toward Brandon during those meetings," Spring said. "Every time Brandon addressed him about a problem in the community, Dirk answered either in a condescending manner or with a smirk, like he knew more than Bran-don. It was apparent to me by the end of the meeting that Brandon could hardly stand to have him in the room."

"Quite apparent," Reagan said.

"I live next door to the clubhouse," Spring said, "and after that last meeting, I could see the two of them argu-ing through the window. I couldn't hear what they were saying, of course, but they were shouting. Brandon even stuffed his fists in his pockets as though he was trying to keep from punching Dirk. Then Connie came in, so Dirk turned around and left the building."

"It might be a good idea to ask Connie what she heard," Reagan said.

I made a note to do just that. "Besides Dirk's contemptuous attitude, was anything discussed at the meeting that would lead to such a heated argument between them?"

"Several hot-button topics came up that Dirk was supposed to be handling," Reagan said. "The biggest one was the moss problem on the pond. When we questioned Brandon as to why nothing had been done after two months, he turned the question over to Dirk, who reported he'd had a pond expert come out to treat it."

"But that never happened," Spring said. "Not only was there no invoice on the monthly financial statement, but also the moss is worse than ever, and the residents who back up to the pond are seething. When we're angry and Dirk isn't responding, we e-mail Brandon, and that makes *him* unhappy. So he took Dirk to task in front of the room, and later, like I said, I saw them arguing. That was probably the reason why."

"Are any of the residents with pond lots furious enough to have confronted Dirk?"

"Theda Coros gets more upset about the moss than anyone," Spring said, "because it's worst behind her house. I think it's even creeping over her lawn. But if you're asking whether she would kill him, I don't know her well enough to say."

That wasn't what I was hoping to hear.

"Another issue Brandon took Dirk to task about was the pond pump," Reagan said. "It's a retention pond, so during a dry spell the water level drops dramatically. A pump was installed to keep water flowing into it from a natural spring north of here, but it broke down last fall. Brandon told Dirk months ago to get it repaired, but as of Friday, nothing had been done."

"What was Dirk's reason?" I asked.

"He claimed he couldn't find a plumber who knew how to repair it," Spring said, "but amazingly, that very day a plumber was going to meet him at the pump after work."

"I'm confused," I said, fearing the wine was muddling my thoughts. "*When* was the Brandywine meeting?"

"Friday morning," Reagan said. "The day Dirk drowned."

"And *did* the plumber meet with Dirk?"

"All I know is that the pump is working again," Spring said.

"Where is the pump?"

"It's on the north end of the pond behind Theda's house," Reagan said. "She should be able to tell you whether the plumber was there."

I wrote it down with an asterisk beside it. "Let's go back to Mitzi's affair with Dirk. If you didn't hear about it from Mitzi this time, who told you?"

"Theda," Reagan said.

I didn't like the way my next-door neighbor's name kept coming up.

CHAPTER EIGHT

I tiptoed across the bedroom in the dark, trying not to wake Marco, but I wasn't as steady as I'd thought and ended up stubbing my toe on the dresser. I muffled a curse and rubbed my throbbing digit only to have Seedy hobble around the bed to see what game I was playing. I whispered to her to go lie down, then carefully slid under the covers and lay still, listening to see if Marco was breathing deeply or if I had disturbed him.

I heard no sound at all so I reached for him and found the other side of the bed empty. What day was it? Thursday? Of course. Marco was at the bar. Silly me.

Sometime much later I heard, "Abby. Roll over. You're snoring."

I was *snoring*? "Sorry," I mumbled sleepily. "I might have had too much wine."

He slid his warm body against my back and put an arm around me, saying in an amused voice, "Enjoy the book club, did you?"

"Mm-hmm." My brain began to chug to life as details of the evening came back. "Those women like wine. Every time I turned around, someone was refilling my glass."

I rolled toward Marco and propped myself up on my

elbow, eyes only half-open. "This group is different from the Bees. They don't gossip; they discuss books. I had to postpone my questions about Dirk's murder until after the meeting. And wait till I tell you what I learned about Mitzi."

Marco yawned. "You sure you don't want to talk about this tomorrow?"

"Too late. I'm awake and thirsty. Anyway, I found out that Mitzi has had numerous affairs, including one with a Books and Bottles book club member's husband. They're divorced now, by the way."

"Two questions. How does that help our case and do I deserve that pointed look?"

I gave him a playful push. "Here's where it gets interesting. Mitzi likes to brag about her flings, but only *after* she's ended them. She hadn't told anyone about her affair with Dirk, which means it was still going on when she discovered her jewelry missing."

"And that makes her the killer?"

"It might, given that Mitzi is known to get even when she's been wronged."

Marco yawned again and turned onto his back. "It sounds to me like Mitzi has been tried and convicted by a court of women."

"Come on, Marco. You have to admit it puts Mitzi in a bad light. And by the way, she's the reason the Books and Bottles club split away from the Bees."

"If she's so bad, why have the rest of the Bees stayed with her?"

"Maybe they're just like Mitzi."

Marco put his arm over his eyes. "Are we done yet?"

"Almost." I sat up and crossed my legs, fully awake now. "The women told me about the issues Brandon

Thorne had with Dirk. I'll tell you tomorrow about the argument one of them witnessed. And here's new information. Dirk was supposed to meet a plumber at the pond behind Theda's house Friday after work. Apparently there's a pump back there to keep the pond filled, but it hasn't been working."

Marco raised his arm to peer at me. "Did they say who the plumber was?"

"No. They don't even know whether a plumber came out, except that the pump is working now. But if someone did meet with Dirk, that person might have been the last one to see Dirk alive, and we may have a new suspect."

Turning away from me, Marco mumbled, "Remind me to call plumbing companies tomorrow."

"Okay. I'll be right back. I need a drink of water."

I returned to the bedroom to find Marco fast asleep. I eased myself under the covers and closed my eyes, but my mind didn't want to turn off. Instead of counting sheep, I was making a mental list of questions to ask Brandon Thorne. I was also preparing my case for a total floor replacement. I finally got so frustrated, I went to the kitchen and wrote everything in the notebook to clear my mind.

Friday

When at last I felt myself drifting off, I could hear birds chirping, which meant dawn was not far off. And when the alarm went off at seven a.m., I waited until Marco left the bedroom then pulled the covers over my head and went back to sleep.

I was deep in a dream when I felt a shake. "Hey,

babe," Marco said, "I let you sleep as long as possible, but you're going to be late if you stay in bed any longer."

"I don't care. I was awake most of the night, so I'm sleeping till nine."

"Sorry, Sunshine. That won't work. I have to be at the bar early to meet the electrician. We're starting the new lighting project today."

"That's nice. You go ahead. I'll come in later."

"On your bike?"

Oh, crap. The car situation. I heaved a frustrated sigh. I had no choice but to get up. I didn't feel safe riding on the hilly country road that led to town.

"Can Lottie or Grace come get you when they go out for a delivery?"

"That might not be until noon, and we're too busy for them to leave midmorning." With a groan, I flung off the covers and stumbled to the bathroom. My eyes were scratchy and my head hurt. Clearly, when it came to alcohol, I was a lightweight.

"I put your coffee in a travel mug," Marco said when I emerged from the bedroom in jeans and white button-down shirt. "You can eat your almond toast on the way. I'll keep Seedy with me."

He tried to make conversation as we rode into town, but I was too crabby and my mouth was full of sticky almond butter anyway. By the time I walked into Bloomers, the coffee had kicked in so I felt halfway human, but as noon approached, I began to drag. I decided to borrow Lottie's car and go home for a nap.

I was putting on my jacket when my cell phone rang and Marco's name appeared on the screen. "Hey, Buttercup. Feeling any better?"

"No. I'm going to skip lunch and head home for a nap."

"It'll have to be a quick one. We have a meeting with Thorne at twelve thirty."

I sighed as visions of curling up on the sofa flew out the window.

"I can meet with him alone if you'd rather nap."

Miss out on an interview? Even in my sleep-deprived state, I couldn't do it. That was my favorite part of an investigation, not to mention the fact that I wanted to address the floor situation. "No, I'll be fine. I'll drink more coffee." Maybe the entire pot. Black.

"Okay. Be out front in twenty minutes."

I glanced at the clock as I ended the call. I had plenty of time to have that java before I went. And then I put my head down on my desk and fell fast asleep.

What felt like seconds later, Rosa shook me awake. "Marco is out front waiting for you."

I jumped up, grabbed my purse, and headed out, stopping to tell Lottie where I was going. "I might be a little late getting back," I called as I headed out the door.

"No problem," Rosa said, coming up to the cash register. "I will make sure everything runs smoothly."

I stopped and turned around.

Lottie and Rosa had their heads bent over an order form.

I ate the sandwich Marco had provided on our way to Brandywine. "Thanks," I said, swallowing a mouthful of turkey. "I was starving. How did your meeting with the electrician go?"

"Joe and I roughed out a design, but Down the Hatch is an old building with old wires, so I have to have some rewiring done before I can start the project. By the way,

I mentioned to Joe what Rye told us about the house possibly not being up to code, and he said he'd be glad to check it out one evening this week."

"Great. Now we just need to get Brandon to agree to pay for Joe's service call. Did you say anything to Joe about Maynard Dell?"

"He's aware of Maynard's shortcomings but was surprised about the code problem because it leaves the city wide-open for lawsuits. But that's what happens when politicians give away patronage jobs."

"And on the subject of plumbers," he continued, "I called every plumbing company in the greater New Chapel area, even into Maraville and up around the Indiana Dunes. Not one of them had scheduled an appointment with Dirk for last Friday or any other day in the past two weeks."

"But someone fixed the pump."

"Put that on our list of questions for Thorne. We also need to ask Theda if she saw anyone working on the pump last Friday."

I took out my notebook and wrote them in. "I've got quite a list for Brandon already. It's what I did last night while you were sleeping."

Marco put his hand on the back of my head. "I'm sorry you had a rough night, sweetheart. Early to bed for you tonight. Shag Jillian out by nine."

Jillian! Another appointment I'd forgotten.

"Also, I arranged for us to meet with Dirk's wife tomorrow morning at eleven."

"Perfect. We can stop for lunch afterward and then hit the furniture store. I'm determined to replace that card table."

We pulled up to the clubhouse and parked beside

Brandon Thorne's black Lexus. "Does Brandon know why we're meeting with him?" I asked, stifling a yawn.

"I didn't give him a reason."

"Then he must think it's about the floor. He wouldn't know we're investigating Dirk's death unless you said something. And I still believe we should discuss the floor today so we can get it resolved. I don't want it to drag on for months."

"I have to disagree, Abby. Today is about the investigation. We'll bring up the floor another time."

Thus speaketh the king. If I weren't so tired, I would've mounted a defense.

I unbuckled my seat belt and put my purse strap over my stiff shoulder. My head felt like a bowling ball propped on a toothpick, and my eyes felt like they were deadlifting a hundred-pound weight. Even my muscles ached from lack of sleep.

Still, I'd spent almost the entire night thinking about what to say to Brandon Thorne to convince him to replace our floor, and as Marco opened the car door for me, I couldn't help but champ at the bit. When would we have this opportunity again? A week from now? Two?

"How about this?" I asked. "We discuss the floor if Brandon brings it up."

"Okay, *if* he brings it up we'll discuss it, but at the end of the interview."

We walked into the clubhouse foyer and turned right into a short hallway that led to the Brandywine sales office. Finding no one there, we checked the small galley kitchen, the fitness room, and a large multipurpose room filled with round tables.

We finally spotted Brandon in the media room sitting at a high-topped table in front of a bank of windows working on his laptop. A pool table occupied the middle of the room and a row of swivel chairs faced a large-screen television on the opposite wall.

"Welcome," Brandon said, getting off the chair to shake our hands. "Have a seat."

He was wearing a crisp blue-and-white checked shirt tucked and belted into blue jeans, and a pair of polished Timberland boots. He was fit, trim, and tanned, and even with silver at the temples, he looked nowhere near sixty years old. He had a firm handshake, an engaging smile, and a pleasant, boyish face that gave him an air of trustworthiness that Theda had warned me not to believe.

"I hope you're enjoying your new home," he said, giving us his winning smile.

"Well," I said as we sat down across from him.

Marco put his hand on my shoulder. "The reason we're here—"

"You're not happy with your home?" Brandon asked.

"We need a new floor," I blurted.

Brandon scratched behind his ear as if this was puzzling information. "Why?"

Marco was pressing his thumb into my shoulder, but I ignored him. I was battling extreme fatigue and annoyance, and that was a bad combination for a feisty redhead. "Didn't Rye explain? He said he'd tell you first thing this morning."

"Rye mentioned something about a little water problem around the patio door," Brandon said smoothly, "but my understanding is that the floor can be sanded and restained."

A *little* water problem? I didn't believe that was what Rye told him. "That's not our understanding, is it, Marco?"

Clearly not pleased with me, Marco folded his arms

across his shirt and gave me a scowl. "No, it isn't. But we can discuss this later."

"Just a minute," Brandon said, his charm slipping. "What is *your* understanding?"

"That the wood is damaged because one of your workers left the sliding door open during a storm," I said. "That the heavy rain may have even seeped down to the subfloor, and that the damage necessitates a new one."

Brandon typed something into his computer. "How big is the damaged area?"

I glanced at Marco for backup, but he was silent. "It doesn't matter," I finally said. "The whole floor needs to come up."

Brandon looked at me over the top of his laptop. "I'm afraid that's not possible."

"Why? Is it bolted to bedrock?"

"What we do in instances like this is sand and refinish the damaged area," Brandon said.

I could feel my temper building up steam. "The wood is so warped it's *rippled*, Brandon. You can't sand away ripples. And Rye said if you tried to replace only that area, the stain would never match."

"Rye isn't a flooring expert." Brandon resumed typing, all traces of friendliness gone. "I'll have someone from the flooring company come take a look."

I was getting more frustrated by the second and still my husband remained silent. "And if the flooring expert says the entire floor needs to be replaced?"

"Then I may need to have someone from the manufacturer come out."

"To do what?" I asked.

"Give an opinion."

"And if he *also* says we need an entire new floor?"

Brandon smiled, but the warmth was gone. "Let's deal with that bridge if and when we cross it."

I glanced at Marco in exasperation, but he was sitting with his arms folded, one hand pinching his lips, his gaze on Brandon.

"In other words," I said, "we have to wait for the floor rep to take a look, and then probably the manufacturing rep as well before we have an answer?"

"That's how it usually works," Brandon said, typing again.

"Will you guarantee that if both experts say we need a new floor, you'll put one in?"

He walked two fingers along the top edge of his laptop. "That bridge, you know?"

I was about to throw my hands in the air and walk out when Marco said, "Let's put that issue aside for the moment. We actually came here to talk to you about Dirk Singletary. As you probably know, I own the Salvare Detective Agency with Abby. We're investigating Dirk's murder, and your name has come up several times."

Brandon stopped typing. "*My* name has come up? In what way?"

"As a person of interest," Marco said.

The developer stared at Marco for a long moment, as though waiting for him to say, *Just kidding.* But Marco merely gazed back impassively. Shutting his laptop, Brandon said, "Then why haven't I been contacted by the police?"

"We're always a step or two ahead of them," Marco said. "We work fast. And if we can clear you, they won't be contacting you."

Brandon thought it over for a few moments, then

took out his cell phone and stood up. "I need to consult with my attorney."

Marco looked at his watch. "Go ahead, but we're on our lunch hour. All we have is twenty minutes. If we miss that window, I can't guarantee that the detectives won't beat us back here to interrogate you."

A flicker of panic went across Brandon's face before Marco corrected his statement. "Sorry. *Interview* you. I know you're not from New Chapel, so just a word of warning: We have a nosy investigative reporter who follows the detectives around, so if they make it here before we do, your name will probably appear in the newspaper. That may not be good for sales."

"Right." Brandon walked away, his phone to his ear. "I'll make it quick."

As soon as he was out of the room, Marco muttered, "So much for Team Salvare."

"Are you mad at me?"

"We're supposed to work as a unit, Abby, and we agreed not to discuss the floor until the end of the interview. What you did puts our investigation in jeopardy. What were you thinking?"

"I'm sorry, Marco. The problem is I'm *not* thinking. I'm sleepy and so frustrated with Brandon's refusal to acknowledge our problem that I had a strong urge to smack him. Then seeing that innocent look on his face while he played dumb about the floor made me want to lean across the table and carry out that urge."

But the thought of leaning over the table made me want to put my head *on* the table, on a soft pillow, with the hum of the air conditioner lulling me into a deep sleep . . .

"Abby."

I jumped. "What?"

"You dozed off in the middle of a sentence."

I rubbed my eyes. "I did? What was I saying?"

"It was my sentence. I was the one talking."

"Then what were you saying?"

"That you should relax. Your mistake might just have worked in our favor."

"How?"

Even though Marco was angry, the corners of his mouth curved up just a little. "Wait and see what happens."

CHAPTER NINE

Brandon returned less than a minute later, his charming demeanor back in place as he sat down at the table. "I couldn't reach him, but I have nothing to hide, so let's proceed."

"Okay," Marco said, looking at the list I'd printed in the notebook. "Let's start with the basics."

Brandon held up his index finger. "First, about your floor."

Marco gave me a quick glance, as if to say, *Wait for it.*

"*You* want a new one. But that's going to cost me money—twelve, fourteen grand possibly. Now, *I*"—he put his hand on his chest—"want to see this person-of-interest label go away. So you make *that* happen and I'll make your new floor happen. We can schedule the installation today."

Cool-headed Marco said, "I'd be happy to make that happen. All you have to do is be completely forthcoming with your answers."

Brandon rubbed his nose, thinking. "Okay, here's the deal. I answer all your questions, you get a new floor *and* you take me off the person-of-interest list."

He'd merely restated his original offer. But that

didn't matter because my clever husband had turned my breach into an opening.

"That will depend on your answers," Marco said evenly. "But then, you did say you have nothing to hide."

"And I meant it." Slick smile. Brandon was a born politician.

"Shall we proceed?" Marco asked.

"Absolutely."

"I mean with scheduling that new floor."

"Rye is at lunch right now. I'll have to talk to him later."

"Tell you what," Marco said, "Abby is going to give you a piece of notebook paper so you can write out your new floor guarantee."

With a disgruntled huff, Brandon took the paper, scribbled a note and signed it, then slid it across the table. Marco and I read it, then, while I tucked it in my purse, he tore out the list I'd made, gave me back the notebook, and began the interview.

"When was the last time you saw Dirk?"

Brandon looked up at the ceiling for a moment. "That would be last Friday. Noonish."

"What did you do after the meeting?"

"Dirk and I had a short business conference, then I left to return to my headquarters in South Haven, Michigan."

Since Brandon had made no mention of the argument, I thought Marco would pursue that line of questioning, but instead he continued on. "Where were you Friday evening?"

"At my office in South Haven."

"On a Friday night?"

"We're starting a new development, and I wasn't

going to be in the office for a few days." He shrugged. "That's the life of a busy developer."

"What kind of relationship did you have with Dirk?" Marco asked.

"The normal boss–employee relationship."

Marco looked puzzled. "Residents we've talked to told us you couldn't stand to be in the same room with Dirk. That he was disdainful and condescending to you during meetings. Is that what you consider normal?"

"We didn't always get along, but I certainly *could* stand to be in the same room with him."

"We heard a report that you and Dirk had a shouting match after your last meeting," I said.

"It was nowhere near a shouting match," Brandon said. "We may have raised our voices, that's all. Who told you that, anyway?"

"What was the argument about?" Marco asked.

"I wanted to know why Dirk hadn't followed through on some issues."

"Are you talking about the moss problem?" I asked.

"Yes, that and other things." He straightened his shirt cuffs.

"You want to elaborate on those other things?" Marco asked.

"Mainly the pump repair. He was supposed to have taken care of both, and as of Friday's meeting, he'd done neither."

"That must have made you angry," Marco said.

"I wouldn't call it angry. More like annoyed."

"Did Dirk say why he hadn't acted on them?"

"He skirted the issues by complaining about Rye. All I could get out of Dirk was that he'd scheduled a plumber to repair the pump Friday evening. From what

I understand, the pump is now working, so at least he kept his word on that. The moss problem, however, is unresolved, and I know several residents are fed up with it, particularly"—he smiled as though a light had come on—"Theda Coros. Of course. She's your next-door neighbor. That's who your source is."

"We've talked to a number of residents," Marco said. "Do you know what plumbing company Dirk used?"

"I have no idea. You have to consider I have many communities like this. I depend on my on-site superintendents to take care of problems when they arise."

"But Dirk *wasn't* taking care of them," I said. "All those issues that weren't being addressed must have been frustrating, especially when you knew how upset many of the residents were."

Brandon didn't comment.

"Is there one plumbing company you use regularly when you build houses in Brandywine?" Marco asked.

"No."

"So whoever puts in the lowest bid?" I asked, blinking hard to keep my eyes from drifting shut.

"That's how it works," Brandon said.

I covered my mouth to hide a yawn as Marco took up the questioning. "Has anything been done about the moss situation?"

"I just instructed Rye today to get on it."

"Let's move on to Rye's relationship with Dirk. We were told several residents witnessed Dirk being purposely humiliating to Rye. Did you know about that?"

"No, I wasn't aware of it."

I woke up at that. "They said they complained directly to you about it, Brandon."

"I have a liaison who handles residents' complaints."

"Doesn't your liaison keep you informed of staff problems?" I asked.

"He should, shouldn't he?" Brandon opened his laptop and began typing. "I'll make a note about that right now."

"Did anyone voice a complaint about Dirk at any of the meetings?" I asked.

"Not that I recall."

I was having a hard time believing him. I was also having a hard time focusing. Two hours of sleep simply wasn't enough for my brain to operate.

Referring to the questions, Marco asked, "Did Dirk ever recommend that Rye be fired?"

"On several occasions," Brandon said.

"For what reasons?"

"Mostly because Rye wasn't capable and wasn't showing up for work on time."

"Yet you didn't fire Rye."

"Rye's been with the company longer than Dirk and has always performed well, so I didn't see any reason to let him go."

"Doesn't that make you wonder what Dirk's motive was?" I asked. It sure made *me* wonder why Dirk wanted Rye out of the picture.

"I didn't really stop to think about it," Brandon replied smoothly.

"What is Rye's future with the company?" Marco asked.

Brandon shrugged. "He *has* a future, if that's what you mean."

"Will he take over Dirk's position?"

"Yes. I'll be making that announcement at our next meeting."

"Have you told Rye?" I asked.

"I told him on Tuesday. He was very happy."

That didn't match with Rye's story. In fact, it was the second time someone else's account hadn't matched Rye's.

"When you heard that some of the residents had accused Dirk of theft," Marco said, "what action did you take?"

"I cooperated fully with the detective investigating it."

"What have you done to insure a situation like that won't happen again?" I asked.

Brandon gave me a smile. "What does that have to do with Dirk's death?"

"Did you do a background check on him before you hired him?"

"No, and I still don't see what that—"

"Are you doing background checks now?" I was on a roll.

"I will be, going forward."

"With all the uncertainty surrounding Dirk, why wasn't he fired?"

"It wasn't proven that he took any jewelry."

"The residents here believe it. Isn't that enough?" I began listing reasons on my fingers. "Dirk was accused of theft and questioned by the police three times. He didn't take care of critical issues. He was rude to you and condescending to the residents, and he was outwardly cruel to Rye. And yet you kept him on."

Brandon just stared at me.

"Did he have something on you?"

"Okay, that's it," Brandon said, rising, his face turning an angry red. "We're done."

That was called avoiding the question. My radar was beeping *Liar*.

"Would you rather talk to the detectives?" Marco asked.

Brandon walked away and then came back, pointing a finger at me. "I don't want you to make me feel like I had a reason to kill Dirk. Understand?"

"No one can make you feel that way but you," I said.

I heard the front door open and close and then Connie stuck her head in to see what was going on. "Sorry. Didn't mean to bother you."

"We're almost finished," Marco said.

Brandon jerked his chair out and sat down.

"Is there someone who can verify that you were in your office in Michigan Friday evening?" Marco asked.

"I don't know," Brandon snapped. "I think I was there alone."

"You think?" Marco asked.

"I was there alone."

"Did anyone see you arrive or leave?"

"I don't know."

"Are there any houses nearby?"

Brandon shook his head.

"Did you use your cell phone?"

"Why?"

"We can locate the pings that registered at the nearest cell tower."

"I may have used it."

I could tell by the pinched look on the developer's face that it was dawning on him he was in trouble. But as Marco continued to question him, I realized I was in trouble, too. My exhaustion was catching up with me, and it was affecting my ability to take notes. They were starting to look like scribbles.

"Do you keep tools in the back of your SUV?" Marco asked.

"Just a tire jack."

"Where are the tools that Rye uses?"

"In a closet just beyond the men's restroom."

"Is it locked?"

"No."

"Mind if we take a look inside after we finish here?"

"Be my guest."

Marco looked over the questions. "Okay, that should do it. Thanks for your cooperation."

Wait, what? That wasn't the end of the list. There was one question left.

Brandon shut his laptop and rose, tucking his computer under his arm. "I'll have Rye set up an appointment with the flooring rep this afternoon to get your new floor installation scheduled."

"Thank you," Marco said.

"Am I off your person-of-interest list, then?"

"We'll have to digest this information and see how well it matches up with what we already know."

"Then I hope you'll have good news for me tomorrow."

"You didn't ask the last question," I whispered to Marco, then called to Brandon as he reached the door, "One more thing. Are you aware that some of the homes here aren't up to code?"

"Abby," Marco whispered.

Brandon paused in the doorway. "That's not true. They all passed inspection."

"So no one told you that the town's building inspector may have passed them fraudulently?"

"Abby," Marco said, sharper.

"I don't believe that," Brandon said.

And I didn't believe *him*. "You'd better talk to Rye. He tells a different story."

Marco shot me a look that I couldn't decipher. Brandon stared at me for a moment and then strode out without replying.

"I'll bet he knows exactly what I'm talking about," I said to Marco. "And what was that look for?"

"Are you trying to get Rye fired?"

"What?"

"We don't know if Rye was telling the truth. What if he made that up about Maynard Dell to throw us off his trail? And if Brandon is truly in the dark on this, why *didn't* Rye tell him? How do you think that made Brandon feel to hear it from us instead of from his employee? If Rye is as concerned about the residents here as he professes to be, shouldn't he be complaining to his employer and not to a new resident?"

I didn't know what to say.

"You forgot a major rule, Abby. Everything discussed in our interviews is confidential. You even told Rye so yourself."

Marco was absolutely right and I felt awful. "What can we do?"

"It's out there now. We'll have to let Rye know so he's not blindsided when Brandon asks him about it."

"Marco, please believe that I am deeply sorry."

"I don't doubt that, Abby, but it was a mistake for you to come. When you're dealing with people's lives and livelihoods, you have to be on your toes."

I couldn't have felt any lower if I'd tried. "Honestly, I thought I was fine. My lack of sleep is affecting me more than I realized."

"I was going to suggest we stop to talk to Connie, but you're clearly not up to it."

"No, we're here and so is she, so we might as well take advantage of it. I'll stay quiet and let you handle it."

He gave me a skeptical glance. "Then we'll have to make it quick. I really do have to get back to the bar."

We found Connie in her office, making a pot of coffee. Before we went in, Marco pulled me aside. "Are you sure you can stay awake? I don't want any mistakes this time."

"I understand. Let's do this."

A big-boned woman with short brown hair, twinkling eyes, and a dimpled face, Connie had on her standard uniform of brown slacks and a print top with brown loafers. We'd gotten to know Connie when she helped us choose the fixtures, flooring, cabinets, and paint for our house prior to construction. She had struck me then as a fair and competent saleswoman.

"Hello, you two," she said, pouring herself a cup of coffee. "What are you up to today?"

"Do you have time for a few quick questions?" Marco asked. "We're investigating Dirk Singletary's case."

"I wondered if you would be," she said. "Some of the residents were taking bets. Would you like some coffee?"

Like. Need. Crave. I knew Marco wanted to make it a fast stop, but if he wanted me to stay awake, he had to give me this. "I'll take a cup—black, please."

"I saw the article about Dirk in today's paper," Connie said, handing me a cardboard cup filled with strong-smelling brew. "I see they've officially declared it a murder. It's so hard to believe something like that could happen here."

I nodded in agreement but didn't comment. I took

a drink of coffee instead and nearly spit it out. It was so strong my tongue curled, but I forced myself to drink more, hoping it would kick-start my energy.

"What appointments did Dirk have scheduled for Friday after the meeting?" Marco asked.

As I set the cup on the filing cabinet beside me and opened the notebook to a clean page, Connie swiveled her chair toward her desk and flipped through an appointment book. "He was scheduled to meet with the Rosenbaums at two o'clock, with Mrs. Nabhan at three o'clock, and then nothing until seven thirty, when he was supposed to meet with Theda."

"Did Dirk always work that late?"

"Just on Fridays. It had something to do with picking up one of his children after a sporting event. I heard him talking on the phone with Jane about it."

"Jane is his wife?" Marco asked for verification reasons.

"I'm sorry. Yes, Jane Singletary."

"Did Dirk keep his Friday appointments?"

"Two of them. Theda said he didn't make it to hers."

"Is there any way to verify her claim?"

"Not without asking Dirk, unless Theda's neighbors saw him there. Oh, that would be you, wouldn't it?" She laughed.

"We hadn't moved in yet, but Mitzi Kole might know," Marco said.

I paused as a big yawn overtook me, then made a note to ask Mitzi, only it looked like *Arf Mitsu Hobe.*

Marco continued. "How long did Rye Bishop work on the day of the murder?"

"I leave at five, so I couldn't say how long he stayed beyond that time."

"Doesn't Rye usually leave at four?" I asked, then remembered my promise. I gave Marco an apologetic look.

"Rye stayed later on Fridays because Dirk did."

Another contradiction to Rye's story.

"What appointments did Rye have last Friday afternoon?" Marco asked.

Connie checked the appointment book again. "He doesn't have anything written down, but that's not unusual. He's our troubleshooter, so he goes where he's needed. It's often a spur-of-the-moment thing."

I leaned my elbow on the filing cabinet, overcome by a desire to lie down.

"Did you hear Dirk and Brandon argue after the meeting?" Marco asked.

"I came in at the tail end of it. I had been out showing a model home."

"Do you know what their argument was about?"

Connie shook her head. I gave mine a shake, too, trying to wake myself up.

"Did you hear anything that was said?" Marco asked.

"Of course," I answered, then realized Marco had directed that to Connie. I coughed into my hand, trying to make it sound like *Of course*.

"Well," Connie said, "I hate to speak ill of the dead, but—"

I closed my eyes as the conversation swirled around me, the words blurring into meaningless sounds. My elbow slipped off the cabinet and jerked me awake. Fortunately, the coffee didn't spill.

But I did come to just in time to hear Connie say, "As Dirk passed me he said, 'Tell Brandon to go jump in the pond.'"

That struck me as so ironic I had to choke back a chuckle. Marco shot me a quizzical look and I bowed my head, which was not the smartest move, because I began to fall asleep again.

"That's not something people normally say to their boss," Marco said.

"That was how Dirk talked to Brandon."

"Shouldn't that have gotten him fired?"

Connie smiled. "I wish I could comment on that. And I'm sorry, but I do need to leave. I have a meeting with prospective buyers at the model home in ten minutes."

"No problem, Connie," Marco said. "You've answered our questions for now. Thanks for your help."

As soon as Connie was out of earshot, I said, "Sorry that I laughed at Dirk's comment, but the irony of him telling Brandon to jump in the pond struck me as funny."

"That's okay. It made me wonder how Brandon felt. Maybe it angered him so much he decided Dirk should be the one in the pond."

We left the office and walked up the hallway to the large storage closet beyond the men's restroom. Inside were an industrial vacuum cleaner, a squeeze mop, two blue plastic buckets, brooms, several pairs of thick yellow work gloves, a shovel, and a large rusty red tool chest. Marco crouched in front of it and snapped the fasteners on the front, then opened the lid, revealing an assortment of small wrenches, screwdrivers, scrapers, and loose nuts and bolts. He lifted the top tray and found more of the same beneath it.

"No large wrenches or hammers, and I would've expected to find some." Marco closed the chest, shoved it back inside, and shut the door. "We'll have to ask Rye if there's another location where tools are kept."

Back in the car, now toasty warm from the sun, I buckled myself in, lay my head against the head rest, and shut my eyes. They hurt so much they felt like sandpaper.

As Marco backed out of the parking space he said, "I got the impression Connie didn't care for Dirk. Did you catch that, too?"

"Mm-hmm." Didn't catch it at all. Had I slept through it?

"First thoughts about Brandon's interview?"

"Born politician," I muttered. "Born . . . to be . . . a politician." I spun off into a dream that I was lying on my bed listening to music on the radio. Then the newscaster broke in to say, "You need a nap, Abby."

"Abby?" Marco shook my arm. "I'll handle the situation with Rye. You take the afternoon off."

"Can't," I mumbled. "There'll be a coup in my absence."

"You're not making sense, sweetheart. Just stay awake until I get you home. You're too tired to be using sharp tools today. I'll call Lottie and explain."

I turned to the side and rested my face on my hands. "It won't matter," I said on a sleepy sigh. "Rosa will override you."

"You're really not making sense now."

He carried me into the house, put me on the bed, pulled off my shoes, and tucked the comforter around me. "I'll call you in ninety minutes. If you sleep longer than that, you'll be awake again tonight."

"Okay," I said on a sigh, as sleep carried me off. "Good night, my liege."

CHAPTER TEN

By the time Jillian arrived at seven o'clock that evening, I was rested, refreshed, and realizing what a horrible mistake I'd made. I prayed that Marco was able to mitigate it somehow with both Rye and Brandon. I also came to the conclusion that while some people were able to function on a few hours' sleep, I wasn't one of them. I'd have to apologize to Marco again. I didn't want to lose his trust. At least I was awake enough now to deal with my fussy cousin.

Jillian Ophelia Knight Osborne was a year younger, a head taller, twenty pounds lighter, and way prettier than me. She had a waterfall of glorious copper-colored hair, large golden brown eyes, creamy skin, and just a sprinkling of freckles across her pert little nose. Mine was more like a rain shower.

Jillian was the pampered wife of Claymore Osborne, the wealthy son of one of the scions of New Chapel. He was also the younger brother of the man I would have been calling my husband, had that man not dumped me after I'd flunked out of law school.

It was history now, a tragedy back then, which had turned out to be a blessing. As with most things, I didn't see it that way for a long time. Now I could look back and breathe a sigh of relief. If all that hadn't happened, I wouldn't own Bloomers and be married to my hero.

I didn't sigh in relief that evening, however—only in irritation because of the first words out of Jillian's mouth.

"That Rosa is amazing."

She dropped her Kate Spade tote—white with a black trim—on the sofa and shrugged off her white leather jacket with black trim and silver buckles. Underneath she wore a black top, black-and-white checkered leggings, and knee-high black boots. Jillian always made a statement, even for a casual evening at her cousin's.

"I almost cried when Tara told me she wasn't able to babysit," Jillian said, removing a white leather notebook from her tote bag. It, too, had black leather trim. Did she have one to match every outfit?

"But Harper took to Rosa just like that." Jillian snapped her fingers. Her nail polish, I noticed, was black with white polka dots. "I was shocked. You know how attached that baby is to me."

"Yes, well, be careful. You might find your position as mother usurped."

"What are you talking about?"

I plunked down on Marco's old tan sofa beside my cousin, who was sketching the room on her iPad. "I don't know if I'm imagining it or not, but sometimes it feels like Rosa is taking over my shop."

Jillian laughed. "No one is going to push you out of your own business."

I had to agree it sounded ridiculous. "You're right. Okay, what do we need to do to get this house decorated? My party is coming up soon."

"Do you have a floor plan to scale?"

"Somewhere. I'll have to dig it out."

"I'll need that. Next is a questionnaire that will help me determine your decorating style."

"I don't have a decorating style. That's why you're here."

Jillian stopped drawing to look at me. "Seriously? You want me to decorate your house in *my* style?"

I did a quick once-over of her outfit. "Probably not."

"Back to the questionnaire. Here you go. Fill it out while I make a list of furniture pieces that we can use."

I looked over the questions on her tablet and found one I could answer. Favorite colors: yellow, orange, purple, green.

Jillian did a full sweep of the living room and came back. "Well, that was easy."

"Really?"

"Yes. Everything in this room must go."

"I don't think Marco will want to give up his recliner."

Jillian heaved a sigh, one hand at her waist. "Do you want a beautiful house or not? If you do, then that beat-up recliner goes. Let me see your questionnaire."

I handed it over and she did a quick scan. "You answered one question."

"It's the only one I could answer."

"So what you're saying is that you want your house to look like a children's playroom."

"Do you understand now why I asked for your help?"

Jillian put down the tablet then formed a square with her fingers as though looking through a window. "Envision this room stripped down to nothing."

I mimicked her hand position. "No problem. That's what it was six days ago."

"Now in your mind's eye, put one piece of furniture in the room. Let's make it a sofa. What color is it?"

"Tan."

Jillian glared at me. "Not the one that's already here."

"I can't do it, Jillian. I can't envision something that's not here. You do it."

"No! This is a team effort, Abby. Stop being difficult and focus. If you were designing a floral arrangement, what color would you start with?"

"That would depend on the type of arrangement."

"Then pretend you're designing a chic but comfortable arrangement for a living room."

"A comfortable floral arrangement?"

Jillian heaved a frustrated sigh. "Go for dressy casual, then."

"That sounds like an outfit."

"I'm a fashion consultant, Abby. Would you bear with me here?"

"Bright yellow."

"Okay. That's a start. But you might not want such a bold color for a large piece of furniture. How about we use yellow for your accent color?"

"That'll work."

"*Now* what color is your sofa?"

I squinted my eyes and tried to imagine the room. "Tan."

Jillian heaved a sigh then checked her watch. "Could I have a glass of chardonnay, please? This is going to be a long evening."

Saturday

At breakfast the next morning the first thing I did was apologize to Marco for the terrible mistakes I'd made during Brandon's interview. I couldn't help but thank God that it had worked out to our advantage. And then as I refilled our coffee cups, I filled him in on my planning session with Jillian.

"Here's my problem. I can picture a floral arrangement before I pull the flowers for it, but when it comes to imagining a room, I draw a big fat blank. Last night was like banging my head against the wall. I actually felt sorry for my cousin."

"So basically it took two hours to decide on yellow pillows."

"She gave me homework to do when we're out shopping today. I have to take photos of every piece of furniture I like. We're going to meet again Monday evening to go over them."

"Taking photos is pure genius. I'm impressed, Abby. It sounds like Jillian knows her stuff."

"But what if I like everything?"

"You won't like everything. Do you like our dining room table?"

"It's nice—for a card table."

"Now you're being difficult. Push your anxiety aside and see what we come up with today. I think you'll be pleasantly surprised."

"It will definitely be a surprise. I'm not sure about the *pleasant* part."

"Would you have a little faith in Jillian? You're the one who said she's an expert."

I took a drink of coffee and sighed. "I wish I had your optimism."

"You know your cousin isn't going to steer you wrong. She wouldn't want her name associated with anything tacky. Trust her on this, Abby."

I took my plate to the sink. "She could do it if she wanted to. She understands my tastes as well as I do."

Marco finished his oatmeal and joined me at the sink to rinse out his bowl. "I know you too well to let you get away with this, Sunshine. You're afraid your choices won't be designer enough, so you're trying to force Jillian into making your decisions."

"Would you like to make them instead?" I asked as he headed toward the bathroom to brush his teeth.

"With some team effort, I'll bet we could do it. You're always saying how in sync our tastes are."

"We don't have the decorating knowledge, Marco. For instance, look at your recliner."

He stopped and turned to stare at me. "What's wrong with my recliner?"

"Jillian said it's worn-out and has to go."

"Not going to happen," he said, and shut the door behind him.

"What about *Have faith in your cousin* and *She's the expert*?" I called.

"Not going to happen."

Jane Singletary sat across from us in the expensively furnished living room of her spacious two-story colonial, watching us with tired but wary eyes. She had welcomed us with some reluctance and had ordered her boys to go up to their bedrooms immediately.

An attractive, physically fit woman, Jane had shoulder-length light brown hair held back with a bright blue headband, accenting her vivid blue eyes and light complexion. She wore a wedding ring with an enormous diamond setting, and if she had on makeup, I couldn't detect it. The deep purple circles beneath her eyes stood out clearly. Wearing a light blue T-shirt that said *Pump Up the Heat*, a pair of black workout pants, and black sneakers, she had a light sheen of perspiration on her forehead as though she'd just been exercising.

"We'd like to express our condolences on the loss of your husband," I said.

I had expected a tearful reply but instead got a terse "Thank you."

"When is his funeral?" I asked.

"Tomorrow. They just released his body yesterday. Would you like coffee or anything?" This was asked perfunctorily.

"No, thanks," I said. "We won't take up any more time than is necessary."

"As I explained on the phone," Marco began, "we're conducting a private investigation on the matter of your husband's death at the behest of a resident in Brandywine who fears she will become a target for police detectives."

"And as I said on the phone, I've already been over everything with detectives. Can't you get information from them? This is difficult for me."

"I wish they would permit that," I said. "Also, we try to look at a case from all angles, which they don't always do, so our questions may be completely different."

Jane didn't reply, but her expression said plenty. She wanted to get it over with.

"Let's start with some basic information," Marco said, reading from the list of questions we'd written that morning. "How long were you and Dirk married?"

"Twelve years." Anticipating the rest of our questions, she began to rattle off information. "Our boys are Chad, ten, and Chase, eight. They attend private school.

We moved here from Fort Collins, Colorado, and before that we lived in Wilmington, Delaware. I don't work outside of the home, and I was out last Friday evening from six p.m. until sometime after nine.

"I dropped my oldest son at baseball practice at six then went to the grocery store, the drugstore, and Target. My youngest son stayed with my mom at her home across town. Dirk normally picks Chad up from practice at seven thirty, but he said he had a late appointment, so I arranged for my mom to get Chad that night."

Jane got up from her aqua blue armchair, placed a piece of paper on my notebook, and sat down again, while I wrote furiously to keep up with her. "Here's her telephone number and address if you'd care to check the facts."

Jane was one prepared woman.

"Do you have receipts from the three stores?" Marco asked.

She shook her head. "I can print out my credit card statement, though."

"Why did Dirk pick your son up from practice every Friday?" Marco asked.

"I take a jiujitsu class on Friday evenings."

"Why didn't you go last week?"

"I had too many errands."

"Did Dirk say who his late appointment was with?"

"One of the residents, but her name escapes me. I know it concerned moss. Dirk said this woman was driving him crazy about it." She added bitterly, "Believe me—for him that was a short drive."

"Do you think Dirk would have harmed this woman?" Marco asked.

"I'm sure he would have been nasty to her, but nothing more than that."

"Was the resident Mitzi Kole?" I asked.

"No. It was a foreign-sounding name. Athena? Thena?"

"Theda?" I supplied.

"That sounds right."

"Did Dirk say anything about meeting a plumber?"

"No."

"Do you know whether he kept that meeting with Theda?" Marco asked.

She shook her head.

"Did Dirk keep a large wrench in his truck?"

"He kept a lot of things in his truck. Why?"

"The police believe the murder weapon may be a wrench or similar tool. Where is the truck now?"

"Parked behind the garage. The police brought it back yesterday, but they didn't say anything about a wrench."

Marco studied her for a moment. "I don't mean to get too personal, but how would you describe your marriage?"

Jane crossed her arms. "Fine until a detective showed up at my door two months ago to tell me my husband was a jewel thief."

"Does that mean you believe the accusation was false?" Marco asked.

"I hoped it was, but when the detective came a second time, she brought proof. How could I deny it?"

"What kind of proof?"

Jane began to list it on her fingers. "Witnesses' statements. The fact that he had access to the victims' homes and knowledge of when they were away. And a pawnshop owner who identified Dirk from a photo."

"Why wasn't he charged with theft?" Marco asked.

"I was told the detectives were still building their case against him when he died."

"Before that first visit by the detective, did you have any inkling that Dirk had stolen anything?" Marco asked.

She averted her gaze. "No."

Marco and I exchanged glances; he didn't believe her, either. "Did Dirk ever bring you an expensive piece of jewelry or make an extravagant purchase with money you knew you didn't have?" he asked.

She kept her gaze lowered, nibbling her lower lip as though she couldn't bring herself to say it. After some thought, she finally nodded.

"Did you ask him how he got the money for those purchases?"

She shook her head.

"Didn't you wonder?"

She curled her hands into fists and said angrily, "Of course I wondered, but I wasn't allowed to question him. When we had to pack up suddenly and move from our home in Wilmington, I couldn't ask why, nor could I ask when we moved from Fort Collins to New Chapel. *Just do it* was the motto I lived by. It made life easier."

"Was Dirk abusive?" I asked.

"Verbally," she said, "but only when I crossed him, so I didn't. He was away most of the time anyway, so we didn't see him much. I raised my sons myself and thank God for it."

"Looking back," Marco said, "do you think you had to pack and move because Dirk was stealing in those other cities as well?"

"I'm sure it was something he didn't want to go to jail for."

"Why did you stay with him?" I asked. It wasn't on the list, but I had to know.

"I can give you a whole slew of excuses. The boys were young. The money was good. And look at this house. I knew deep down we couldn't afford a place like this on his salary, and yet here we are." She shrugged. "It took a visit from the detective to force me to face reality. That was when I consulted a lawyer about a divorce."

"What was the outcome?" Marco asked.

"The outcome was that Dirk died, so I told my attorney not to file the papers."

"What lawyer did you see?"

"Gary Gillen."

I wrote it down. I'd met Gary several times while clerking for Dave Hammond. Since Jane hadn't proceeded with the divorce, I was hoping he'd be able to verify what Jane had said.

"Was there a will?" I asked.

"Why would Superman need a will?"

"Excuse me?"

"That was how my husband thought of himself. So now we have to go through the long probate process. Luckily Dirk put away a lot of money in CDs—which I didn't know about until my attorney did some research. They're in my name, thank God, so I can withdraw money to live on."

"They're solely in your name?" Marco asked.

"Yes. And if you want to know how it's possible that I was unaware of them, the answer is that Dirk taught himself how to forge my signature. He was probably trying to protect the money in case someone came after him."

"Did Dirk know you were going to divorce him?" I asked.

"No way. I'd planned to take my boys and go stay with family on the day he was served his papers."

"You were that fearful of what he'd do?" I asked.

"I didn't know how he'd react. That was the thing about Dirk. His moods were so mercurial, you just didn't know from one moment to the next."

"Was Dirk ever unfaithful to you?" Marco asked.

"I don't have any names, but I've long suspected that he was cheating on me." Jane glanced at her watch. "I need to feed my sons lunch."

"Sure." Marco rose, so I put away my notebook and stood up beside him.

"Your boys are well behaved," I said. "I haven't heard a peep out of them."

"Thanks. They're my life." She walked ahead of us and opened the door. "I'd do anything for them."

CHAPTER ELEVEN

"Jane was certainly prepared for that interview," Marco said as we headed home. "She ran through her answers as though she'd memorized them. And I didn't get the feeling she's grieving much."

"Can you blame her? He cheated on her, stole, forged her signature, dragged her around the country, and verbally abused her. I'm guessing he wasn't Mr. Nice Guy with the boys, either."

"All of which gives her a very strong motive. I also find the timing of Dirk's death interesting. If Jane had divorced him, she'd get just a portion of his estate. Now she'll get all of it."

Marco was building a case against her. "She signed the papers, Marco. She was ready to go through with it. That takes a lot of courage."

"What's rule number one, Abby?"

"I know. Verify. I'll make a call to Gary Gillen on Monday. I think he'll remember me, but whether he'll tell me anything, I don't know."

"What are your thoughts about Jane's alibi?"

"It sounded like a typical busy evening for the mother of two kids."

"I saw it as the perfect way to set up a crime. Jane left

her house at six o'clock in the evening and returned after nine. That three-hour window gave her enough time to buy something quickly from each store to establish an alibi then be at Brandywine to wait for Dirk to show up for his late meeting with Theda. How convenient that she didn't keep her receipts, because the time stamps would show what times she made her purchases."

"But she did offer to show us her credit card statement."

"All the statement would show was that someone had made purchases with her card on that date. Here's another point to consider. Jane usually attends a jiu-jitsu class on Friday evenings, but last Friday she opted to go shopping instead. If she had shown up for class and then left early, someone would have noticed."

"She said she had errands to run."

"They couldn't have been done on Saturday or Sunday?"

"Maybe they couldn't, Marco. We didn't ask her that. And besides, Theda was waiting for Dirk to show up. Don't you think she would've said something to us if she'd seen him and Jane behind her house, especially if there was a struggle?"

"Why would Theda be watching her backyard? Wouldn't she be waiting for Dirk to come to her front door?"

"Okay, so how would Jane know where Theda lives?"

"For a smart woman, I don't think that would be a problem. I would even bet that Dirk kept a Brandy-wine directory on his computer. As far as I'm concerned, Jane had the means, motive, and opportunity, and right now she's at the top of my suspect list."

"I'll give her motive and opportunity, but she'd have

to be pretty strong to knock Dirk out and drag him into the water."

"Desperation gives people incredible strength." Marco pulled into our driveway and pushed the button on the garage door opener. "And think about her last comment. She would do anything for her sons. Maybe that includes murdering her husband."

After lunch and a walk with Seedy, Marco and I headed to a large furniture store in Maraville where there were more choices than at the smaller store in New Chapel. But once inside the warehouselike showroom, I began to think I would've been better off with a limited selection.

"Now, *that's* what I'd like," Marco said, and began to weave through living room suites. I started to follow then saw a spring green sofa and love seat and detoured toward that instead. I pulled out my phone and snapped a photo of them and then saw two upholstered chairs in a pastel orange that looked pretty.

"Abby, come take a look," Marco called.

"Just a minute." A sofa and love seat in a purple-and-green abstract print were calling to me, so I took a photo before going to see Marco's pick.

He was seated on one end of a massive sectional sofa, running his hands over the leather cushions. "Isn't this awesome?"

I was appalled. "That's a lot of black, Marco."

"But look at this." He pressed a button and a footrest sprang up. He folded his arms behind his head and smiled. "Isn't it great? There's one on the other end. Try it."

So much for our tastes being in sync. I sat down on

other end and had to scoot myself back, which caused my legs to dangle like a child's. "It's really big."

A saleswoman came scurrying up, a spiral binder in her hands. "I see you've found *the* most popular item on the floor. Isn't she a beauty? Such fine leather, too, but tough. Really tough. I promise this sectional will make quite a statement in your house."

The Black Hole of Calcutta?

She turned to Marco. "Did you see that the armrest folds back to reveal cup holders?"

Marco folded it back, smiling like a child opening a Christmas present. "Nice."

"If you press that button, your chair will become a recliner, too," she said to me.

"Doesn't matter. My feet won't reach the footrest."

"Nonsense." She fluttered over to demonstrate then stood back, a frown on her face, as she contemplated my situation.

"I told you," I said.

"Just stretch out on it," Marco said. "That's what you usually do anyway."

I turned over the price tag hanging off the armrest then showed it to Marco. He put his footrest down and rose. "Okay, then."

"We have a smaller sectional over here, also in leather," the saleswoman said, motioning for us to come with her as she headed off in another direction.

Marco was about to follow until I said, "Hey. Leather Man. I don't want a dark living room or all-leather seating or something that's too big for me. I need color, soft fabrics, and a seat that fits *my* seat."

"Then show me something you *would* like."

Which I did. But he didn't go for the purple-and-green print. Or the spring green set. Or the orange armchairs. Or the pesky saleswoman who kept trying to show us more leather. "We'll let you know if we find something," he finally told her. She handed him her business card and faded away.

"How about this?" he asked, sitting on an over-stuffed dark brown tweed love seat.

"The fabric is rough and almost as dark as the black leather. How about that set back there?"

"The navy set? I'd go for navy."

"Behind it."

"I'm not sure which set you mean."

"That one."

"The yellow?" Marco gave me a look. "Really? A yellow room?"

We wandered around the floor for another hour, and although I took a lot of photos, we couldn't decide on anything. I finally said, "What do you say we look at kitchen tables?"

Fortunately, within half an hour we found a table and chairs in a medium brown stain just like Jillian had suggested. What made it even more stylish was that the chair backs and legs were in a darker shade of brown than the table and the seats. The set also came with a self-storing leaf and two extra chairs. It was to be delivered on Tuesday around noon, and Marco would be home to accept delivery.

"What are we going to do about the living room?" I asked as we drove home.

"We'll have to come back when we have more time."

"Marco, we were there for three hours. Do you really

think more time will help? Do you see why Jillian needs
to do this? All I have to do is tell her what we don't want
and let her do the rest."

"Are you absolutely sure that's the route you want
to take?"

"I'm positive."

At home we took Seedy for a walk, changed clothes,
and headed for Café Venezia, a rustic Italian restaurant in town, to meet Marco's mom for dinner. I
couldn't wait to find out what the surprise was. With
Francesca, I never knew what to expect.

She was already seated at a table for four covered
with a red checkered cloth. She waved when she saw
us, but I'd spotted her even before she lifted her hand.
A woman as strikingly beautiful as Francesca Salvare,
with her large dark eyes, voluptuous mouth, and prominent cheekbones—a Sophia Loren lookalike—was hard
to miss.

Her thick dark hair framed her classically Italian face
and fell in loose waves onto her shoulders. As usual, she
wore black—tonight a black silk blouse and black slacks
with red heels and a red patent leather purse that she'd
hung on the back of her chair. I suspected her color pref-
erence had influenced Marco's tastes, too.

"Buonasera," she said, giving us kisses on each cheek.
"How are you, my precious son? And Abby, you look
bellissima this evening."

I glanced at Marco for a translation and he whispered,
"Pretty." Francesca liked sprinkling Italian words into
her conversation.

"I hope you brought your appetites with you," she
said as Marco pulled out a chair for me. He took the
seat to my left, directly opposite his mom.

"I'm starving," I said, to no one's amazement.

Marco took a long, thirsty drink from his water glass. "We shopped for furniture this afternoon."

"I ordered a bottle of a nice Italian Chianti," Francesca told us. "It should be here momentarily."

That was odd. She hadn't questioned us about the results of our shopping expedition. I picked up the menu just as a waiter in a white shirt, black tie, and black pants stopped at the table to take our orders.

Francesca waived him away. "We're not ready. Just bring the wine."

"So what's your big surprise?" Marco asked.

"Not yet, Marco," she said, her dark eyes dancing mischievously. "Be patient."

As I perused the menu, many ideas crossed my mind as to what that surprise might be. Perhaps Marco's younger sister, Gina, was having another baby. She'd always said she wanted three children. Or Francesca was taking us on a cruise to Italy. She'd been longing to do so for years.

On the other hand, maybe Marco's mom had decided to move back to Ohio. She often mentioned missing her friends there. Or perhaps she had decided to build a house in our new subdivision. She'd talked about it at Christmas, but I'd assumed she was joking.

I took a sip of water and then nearly spit it out. Dear God, that was it. She was going to build a house across the street from us so she'd have a perch from which to direct our lives. She would make our bed, rearrange my kitchen cabinets, and organize my closets while I was at work. And I didn't even want to think about what she'd do with my messy underwear drawer.

She'd already tried reorganizing my things at Bloomers while we were on our honeymoon. I'd arrived after a blissful week to find all my florist's tools and supplies, every single item that I'd placed so carefully, put in alphabetical order. It had been a disaster. Marco and I had spent a day putting everything back the way I liked it.

I gripped Marco's arm to warn him just as the sommelier delivered the Chianti. As the man wielded his bottle opener and chatted with Francesca about the vintage, I leaned close to Marco's ear to whisper my terrible suspicion. He pulled back to search my gaze and I could see that my worry had now become his.

After the sommelier had poured our wine, Francesca raised her glass and invited us to do the same. "To my new adventure," she said, and we clinked rims.

"Are you going on a vacation?" Marco asked, a note of desperation in his voice.

"I might," she replied, then took a drink of wine. "But that's not it."

Marco and I exchanged glances.

Another waiter stopped behind Francesca's chair, so I said, "We need a few more minutes." But instead of leaving, he leaned down and wrapped his arms around Marco's mother's neck.

Marco was on his feet before Francesca tilted her head back and said with a laugh, "Here you are at last!" As my startled husband sat back down, his mom pulled the waiter around beside her. "Marco, Abby, I'd like you to meet Alfie."

If someone had taken our photo at that moment, they would have captured us with our mouths open. This pudgy, balding server was her new adventure?

As it turned out, Alfie wasn't a waiter at all. His choice of attire was just unfortunate. He was a pleasant-looking middle-aged man, although a bit on the short side and slightly overweight, with a spare tire around his waist, a double chin, and thinning brown hair combed over to one side. Because of his girth, his pants sat low on his hips and his shirt bagged over his belt. He was not the type I'd ever imagine the classy Francesca to be interested in.

The new adventure extended a hand toward Marco. "Alfred Donnerson. It's a great pleasure to meet you, Marco. Your mom talks about you all the time. Yep, she sure does. So I know all about Down the Hatch and your Army Ranger years and your private investigation business and your stint on the police force and, well, every amazing thing you've done. Wow. That's all I can say. Wow."

He sat down beside Francesca then reached across the table to shake my hand. "Abby, also a pleasure to meet you. I've heard all about your charming flower shop and your fondness for investigations and how you pulled yourself up by your bootstraps after flunking out of law school. Franny has told me what a remarkable young woman you are, but she didn't warn me about how pretty you are."

"That's so kind of you to say," I said, while my brain was whispering, *Franny?*

Francesca poked him in his soft belly. "Don't tease, Alfie. I did too tell you how pretty my daughter-in-law is." She looked at us, smiling radiantly. "Alfie loves to tease me."

Amazing. Francesca's infamous Italian temper usually made teasing a no-no.

"This is our favorite restaurant," Alfie said, draping an arm around Francesca's shoulders. "We actually met here, one of those *Our eyes met across the room* moments. I keep saying fate brought us together, don't I, Franny?"

Seriously, *Franny?*

He squeezed her shoulder and she laughed like a little squeak toy and dipped her head, fluttering her eyelashes at him. I'd never seen her look so girlish. I had to smile with them as they whispered together and laughed, sharing a private moment.

The real waiter appeared and before anyone could wave him away, Marco said, "I think we're ready to order. Abby, ready?"

I glanced at him. Marco didn't look or sound happy. "I'm ready."

Francesca leaned close to Alfie and said, "Abby is hungry," as though excusing Marco's terseness.

"Oh," Alfie said, looking startled as he picked up his menu. "Well, then I'll just have the lasagna." He handed the menu to the waiter then said to Francesca, "But no one makes lasagna like you do, Honey Bun."

As Francesca gave her order, I whispered to Marco, "Are you okay?"

"Let's just get this over with."

Once our server had gone, Marco gave Alfie a penetrating stare. "What do you do, Alfred?"

Alfie shrugged and said with a smile, "Not much, to tell you the truth. I retired a few years back and my goal now is to enjoy life." Gazing at Francesca with puppy dog eyes, he said, "Your mom is helping me accomplish that goal."

"Really." Marco crossed his arms over his shirt. "And how does that work exactly?"

CHAPTER TWELVE

Marco's question was followed by a strained silence. A server came by to freshen our water and I caught him giving us puzzled glances. Then Francesca calmly unrolled Alfie's napkin and shook it out before placing it on his lap. "Alfie and I share a passion for art and musical theater."

"Sounds exciting." Marco turned toward Alfie again. "Have the two of you gone to any art galleries or seen any musicals?"

"No," Francesca answered, narrowing her eyes at her son, "but we're going up to Chicago next Sunday to see *Joseph and the Amazing Technicolor Dreamcoat*."

"Now, that is one heck of a play," Alfie said. "I saw it years ago when Donny Osmond starred in it. I loved it so much, in fact, I went back two more times. I can't wait to share that experience with your mom."

"Have you ever been married?" Marco asked.

"Yes, I have."

"Any children?"

"Nope." Alfie paused as two servers delivered our salads. "But I sure am enjoying getting to know Franny's grandbabies. What a delight they are. That little Christopher is as smart as a whip and, boy, can he put on a show.

I keep telling him he ought to be on the stage—and there's one leaving in an hour." Alfie laughed at his own joke and Francesca laughed with him. It was so corny, even I chuckled.

"I just remembered another musical we've got to see, Franny," Alfie said. "*Paint Your Wagon.* What a great musical that is. Funny lines, clever lyrics . . . and then there's *Phantom of the Opera.* A true classic."

He continued his discourse about his favorite musicals while we ate our salads. He finally ran out of stories about the time our entrees arrived.

"Everybody's food looks *dee-lish*," Alfie said, scanning the table.

"What did you do before you retired?" Marco asked, cutting into his chicken.

"Oh, boy," Alfie said, loosening his tie. "That's a story for another day. I don't want to bore everyone on such a nice evening. I'll bet that's not how you feel, Marco. It must be exciting to track down suspects and pinpoint the guilty parties."

"There's nothing exciting about sitting in a car or at a computer for hours at a time," Marco said stiffly.

Francesca gave Marco a warning glare.

"We do a lot of surveillance," I said, feeling sorry for Alfie. "That can be really boring. But you're right. When we finally catch our man—or woman—there's nothing like that feeling of justice being done. My favorite part is interviewing suspects. It's like playing a game of chess, and Marco is a genius at it."

"Is that right?" Alfie turned an admiring gaze on my stone-faced hubby. "You mentioned you spend a lot of time at the computer. Do you use search engines to find your perps? Do you have certain Web sites that are your go-to places for information?"

"I have my methods," Marco replied.

"I'll bet you can find just about anything on anybody on the Internet these days, can't you?" Alfie waited a moment for him to reply, and when he didn't, turned to me. "I hear you're awesome at making flower arrangements. Franny said you won a trophy."

"Right," I answered. "The woman I bought the shop from won the trophy two years ago and then I won it last year."

"She'll win it again," Francesca said to Alfie. "She's very talented."

"Thank you, Francesca." I didn't have the heart to tell her I wouldn't be entering this year.

"So tell me," Marco said, swirling his wine, "where do you live?"

"Gosh." Alfie glanced around the room. "What direction are we facing? Where's north?"

"That way," Marco said, pointing toward the front.

"Then about an hour that way," Alfie said with a smile.

"Alfie has a retirement cottage on a lake," Francesca said, smiling at him, "and one of these days he's going to take me up there to see it." Then she turned to Marco and asked in an accusing tone, "Why?"

"It's okay, Franny," Alfie said gently, patting her hand. "He's just being a good son. He's concerned about his mom."

She smiled at Alfie and then turned toward Marco again, and though her voice stayed sweet, her eyes were flashing fire. "You don't need to be concerned about me, Marco. I'm not senile yet."

"I care for your mom a lot, Marco," Alfie added. "I'm sure I'd react the same way if my mom sprang her boyfriend on me."

He was calling himself her boyfriend. I knew that wouldn't sit well with Marco, so I said quickly, "Anyone having dessert this evening?"

"Nothing for me, *bella*," Francesca said. "Actually I think it's time for us to go, Alfie. I feel a headache coming on." She gave Marco a pointed look as she lifted her hand to signal the waiter. "But you stay and enjoy the rest of your dinners."

"Two boxes and the check, please," she told our server.

"Now, Franny," Alfie said, reaching for his wallet, "let me get this one."

"Put your money away," she ordered. "I invited my children here to celebrate my happiness. And now I'm paying for it."

He slid his hand out of his pant pocket.

As soon as Francesca signed the bill, they said good night and left, no handshakes or cheek kissing involved. I drained my wineglass while Marco just sat there tapping his fork on the table, deep in thought.

"Marco, I know you can't help worrying about your mom, but I think she's in good hands. Alfie seems likable—a little goofy, but he obviously adores her."

"He called her Franny. No one calls her Franny."

"He said 'perp,' too. Are you going to shoot him for it?"

"A headache? My mom doesn't get headaches."

"I believe she was referring to you, sweetie."

"Something's not right, Abby. I can feel it." He put down his fork. "Are you ready to go?"

"Not before you tell me what your problem is."

"You already know what my problem is. I don't trust *Alfie* or whatever his real name is. You know how you get bad vibes about people? Well, he gave me bad vibes."

"He didn't give me any. Alfie seemed like an ordinary, kind of nerdy guy who adores your mom. I think you're being overprotective because this is the first time in our experience that she's dated. I know how much you admired your dad, but he's been deceased a very long time. Maybe it's time your mom spread her wings."

"That man wouldn't answer my questions, Abby, about what he did for a living or where he lives."

"That man has a name, and your mom told us where he lives."

"*On a lake* is not an answer. *An hour that way* is not an answer. Tugging on his tie *is* an answer. He evaded my questions. And why was he so interested in how I search for people? That really raised my suspicions."

"You need to trust your mom a little more, Marco. She got along fine with your dad without your help."

"That man is nothing like my dad, Ab. Nothing. My dad was a strong, proud man who wasn't ashamed to admit where he worked or lived. Did you see how Alfie caved in when Mom gave orders? My dad wouldn't have done that."

"So he would have argued with her?"

"That's how they operated, Abby. They argued. They were two passionate people who voiced their feelings. This guy is a wimp. She doesn't like wimpy men."

"Maybe you should let your mom decide what kind of man she likes."

"Maybe she *is* getting senile."

"Stop it. You know she's not."

"She's not making wise decisions, either. How do we

know he's not a stalker or a gigolo who marries women for their money? Or a bigamist or drug dealer?" He finished his wine in one gulp. "Let's go. I have to take care of a few things at the bar."

"You have to go back tonight? I thought you took the evening off."

For the first time that evening, the tiniest flicker of a grin played at the corner of his mouth. And then it dawned on me. "Marco, tell me you're not going to investigate Alfie. Your mom will kill you."

He put his napkin on the table and stood up. "Let's get out of here."

As I motioned for the waiter, Marco said, "Mom already paid."

"I know, but there's half a bottle of Chianti left. I'm not leaving that behind."

Marco sat and put his elbows on the table, resting his chin in his hands, thinking.

No doubt about it, Alfred Donnerson was about to be the subject of Marco's personal investigation.

Sunday

After a chilly, rainy morning, the afternoon turned sunny and warm, so we took Seedy to the park for exercise. As we strolled along the path that circled the park, I said, "Did you notice how my mom avoided answering me after church today when I asked her what she's working on?"

"She answered you. She's working on the next book in her children's mystery series."

"She wouldn't look me in the eye, Marco. We both

know what that means. And she didn't come into the shop at all last week. Rosa said they're working on a project together, but she wouldn't say what it was, so once again I'm the outsider."

Marco merely said, "Hmm," and then tossed a stick for Seedy.

It wasn't his normal reaction. Something was on his mind, but I knew not to press him. He would talk about it when he was ready.

In the meantime, the sun was shining, the air was fresh, Seedy was happy, and I was determined to put all of my worries and frustrations aside so I could enjoy a nice afternoon with my husband. As we ambled along, I inhaled deeply and let out my breath with a *whoosh*, completely in the moment.

In my blissful state of oneness with the Universe, I sat down beside Marco on a cedar bench to watch Seedy romp with a friendly pup. Marco rested his arms along the back of the bench and said out of nowhere, "Donnerson has been divorced four times."

It took me a moment to remember who Donnerson was.

"Four times, Abby. Four women couldn't stand him."

"It seems more surprising that Alfie's been *married* four times. And honestly, Marco, it could've been the other way around. Maybe he couldn't stand them."

"Does that make it better?"

"Isn't it possible he just never found his soul mate?"

Seedy loped up with a tennis ball in her mouth that she'd found somewhere, so I tossed it for her. "Go get it, Seedy!"

"He has five stepchildren from the last three marriages."

"Okay. And?"

"He lied. He said he had no children. I'll bet my mom doesn't know that."

"If she doesn't, it's because Alfie doesn't think the time is right to tell her. There's no reason to hide step-children from her. I still think your mom is savvy enough to know if Alfie isn't the one. Let that relationship develop or fall apart on its own."

Seedy returned with the ball, so Marco got up to toss it for her. "Let's walk down to the pond. I want to see the pump."

He'd changed the subject because he wasn't inclined to change his mind. I had a feeling it would come to a showdown between Marco and Francesca, and I didn't want to be there when that happened.

We couldn't find the pump until Marco went back to the house and got a pair of rubber boots so he could wade into the water to cut through the moss and the thick cattails that rimmed the north end of the pond. I stood on the mossy shoreline with Seedy, who kept tugging at her leash, wanting to go with him.

The pump was a cast-iron device that looked like a large spigot on the head of a thick pipe. "It's working," Marco said. As he turned toward me his boot struck something and he nearly tripped. Reaching into the water, he pulled out a two-foot shovel. Seedy barked and wagged her tail, thinking he'd found a toy.

"Hello, you two!"

I turned to see Theda walking toward us, a hooded white cardigan draped over her shoulders. "Enjoying the beautiful afternoon, I see. What did you find there, Marco?"

As he waded out of the water, he held up the dripping two-foot-long wooden tool with a black handle and a shiny metal shovel.

"That looks like my garden spade," Theda said. "How did it end up in the pond?"

I knew by Marco's expression he was wondering the same thing. "When did you lose it?"

"Oh, dear. Sometime this month. I used it to dig out the moss that was growing in the mulch around my lilac bushes. When I went to look for it in the garage last week it wasn't there." She took the shovel from Marco and turned it around. "It's in remarkably good shape, isn't it?"

"I was thinking the same thing," Marco said.

Theda studied it a moment longer, her eyebrows drawing together. "I'm assuming it's mine, anyway. Where else would it have come from?"

"I'd like to give it to the police," Marco said. "Maybe they can find out."

Theda gave Marco a quizzical look as she handed it back. "Do you think it's connected to Dirk's death?"

"It's a possibility" was all he would say.

As the three of us started toward our houses, with Seedy close behind, I said, "Speaking of that, while you were waiting for Dirk last Friday evening, did you notice anyone working on the pump or see anyone near the pond?"

"I'm afraid not," Theda answered. "I was in the living room watching TV and waiting for my doorbell to ring. I don't recall even looking out my back window."

"The pump's running," I said. "So someone was out to fix it."

"The last time the pump needed to be repaired, I saw a plumber's van parked in front of my house," Theda said. "I can say for sure there wasn't any such vehicle there on Friday. There *was* an older-model black Ford sedan parked across the street, but I assumed Betsy had company. Have you met Betsy yet? Very nice woman."

"Not unless she's in one of the book clubs," I said.

"She's not. I'll introduce you next time I see her outside," Theda said.

"Have you ever met Dirk's wife?" Marco asked.

Theda shook her head. "He wouldn't have brought her to any functions."

"Why?" Marco asked.

"He wouldn't have been able to flirt with Mitzi with his wife present. That's not to say Jane hasn't been to Brandywine. I believe someone told me she was dropping him off in the mornings and picking him up at night when his truck was in for repairs."

"Has she ever been to your house?" I asked.

"Not that I know of." As we stopped by her front door, she said, "Would you like to come over for dinner tomorrow evening? I thought I'd make a juicy pork roast."

"Unfortunately, I'll be at the bar," Marco said.

"I'd love to come," I said. "I even have some Chianti. Oh, wait. Scratch that. My cousin Jillian is coming over tomorrow evening."

"Bring her with you," Theda said. "We'll have a party."

I exchanged glances with Marco. "I don't think that's a good idea."

"Why? Does she have two heads?" Theda laughed at her own joke. "Bring your cousin, Abby. It'll be fine."

I loved the way people were so optimistic—until they met Jillian.

"That shovel looked too new to have been submerged for weeks," Marco said as he opened the garage door.

"Then maybe it isn't Theda's shovel. She didn't seem sure. Maybe it belongs to the plumber who fixed the pump." I took an old towel off a shelf. "Sit, Seedy. I need to clean your paws."

Marco pulled newspaper out of the recycling bin and rolled the shovel in it. "Why would a plumber need a shovel to fix a pump?"

"Let's find the plumber and ask him."

"At the moment I'm more interested in who owns the black Ford. Let's go introduce ourselves to Betsy and see what she says."

Betsy Hendricks was a sweet-natured senior citizen who shared a home with her invalid sister Sally. Neither of them knew who the sedan belonged to, but Betsy thought she recalled seeing it in the neighborhood before. We asked the neighbors living on both sides of Betsy, but no one had answers.

"We need to find the owner of that car," Marco said as we returned home. "I wonder if Rye owns a vehicle besides his pickup." He unlocked the door then paused. "Did you notice a car in Jane's driveway?"

"No, and I didn't even think to ask what she drove."

"We'll need to pay her another visit."

CHAPTER THIRTEEN

Monday

I arrived at Bloomers the next morning with a dog eager for one of Grace's homemade pet treats and a stomach ready for Lottie's egg skillet breakfast—only to find Rosa once again in charge of the kitchen. Fortunately, I was hungry enough to eat whatever was put in front of me. But afterward, as Lottie and I counted our stock in the cooler, I said in a whisper because the door was open, "So are we going to be having huevos Marisol from now on?"

Lottie was typing information into the iPad but paused. "Don't you like them?"

How could I put it tactfully? "I'm not a fan of chili peppers first thing in the morning. I like your eggs better."

"I'm sorry, sweetie. I was just trying to include Rosa in the team. We don't want her to feel like an outsider."

"Honestly, I don't think that's a problem."

Lottie stopped typing again. "Is something the matter?"

She seemed so innocently puzzled that I began to think the problem was all in my head. "I'm burping peppers."

Lottie put her arm around my shoulders. "How about I make my eggs next week? And then Rosa and I can rotate Mondays. Will that help?"

"Lottie?" Rosa squeezed in behind us. "Did you find those flowers you told me about?"

"I will when I finish this, sweetie."

I squeezed myself out. There wasn't enough room in the cooler for two sweeties.

As I sat down at the computer to put in an order with one of my suppliers, I heard Rosa say, "These will be perfect, Lottie. Thank you so much. Our arrangement is going to be *estupendo*."

"It's all your doing, Rosa. Your idea and your design. I'm just here to give you a few pointers."

I turned around as they walked out. "What arrangement is that?"

Rosa pressed her hands together, her face glowing with excitement. "I'm going to enter the live floral design competition at the flower show." She turned toward the woman who had steered me through many rough shoals. "And Lottie is going to guide me."

Who feels like the outsider now?

I turned toward the computer, blinking back a sudden mist in my eyes as they conferred in quiet tones at the table. What was wrong with me? I didn't have the time to devote to the contest. So why was I feeling so blue?

My cell phone rang and Marco's photo appeared on the screen. I excused myself and went to the bathroom to talk.

"Hey, Sunshine, how was breakfast?"

"Rosa cooked again," I whispered, shutting the door. "And she's entering her own design in the flower show."

"I can barely hear you. Who's entering what?"

"Rosa," I whispered. "In the flower show. I don't know why it's bothering me."

"How about we meet for lunch and you can tell me more then?"

My phone dinged and Jillian's name popped up. "Okay. I've got another call. See you at noon." I clicked over to the other line. "Jillian, I was going to phone you. My neighbor Theda invited you and me over for dinner at six o'clock tonight. Want to go?"

"Claymore is going to babysit this evening, so I'll have to make sure he doesn't stay at the office late. What is Theda serving?"

"Roast pork. But you're under no obligation to come. I'm just passing along—"

"Perfect. See you at six."

"Wait, Jill. What did you call for?"

"Oh, right. I almost forgot. Tell Rosa I won't need her tonight after all, but thanks for the amazing job last week."

When I returned to the workroom, Lottie and Rosa were still discussing the flower contest, with Lottie sketching ideas on paper for her, so I looked up the number of the attorney Jane Singletary had seen and called his office. I explained about our investigation to his secretary and asked to speak to Gary Gillen.

"I used to clerk for Dave Hammond," I told her. "I'll bet Gary will remember me."

She put me on hold and came back moments later to tell me I'd have to make an appointment. "His next available is a week from Friday."

"That's too far out. It's important I speak with him right away. Could you ask him if he'd just give me five minutes of his time?"

She put me on hold again, then came back on the line. "He's got a court case across the street in twenty minutes. Can you come right now?"

Gillen Law Office occupied the second floor of a bank on the other side of the square. The building had been constructed in the 1960s, so it was a lot more modern than the one that housed Bloomers. I took the stairs to the second floor, opened a glass door, and stepped into a waiting room. Within minutes, the receptionist was whisking me up a carpeted hallway, past a room where secretaries were working, to an office at the end.

"Abby Knight to see you," she said, knocking. She opened the door and stood back to let me enter.

"Abby, how are you?" Gary Gillen said, coming over to shake my hand.

"I'm great, but I wouldn't have recognized you. When did you grow the goatee?"

Gary smiled, stroking his neatly trimmed red beard. "A month ago. My wife hates it. What do you think?"

"I think you look distinguished in a Scottish Highlands sort of way."

"Can I quote you on that?"

In his early fifties, Gary was a man who stayed fit and appreciated fine clothing. Today he wore a slim gray pin-striped suit, a white shirt, a gray, purple, and white tie, and expensive-looking black loafers.

"I appreciate you squeezing me in," I said, "and I'll keep it brief. I know you have to get to court."

"My secretary told me about your investigation," he said as he put files into his briefcase. "I'd love to hear more about it sometime, but what can I help you with today?"

"You were representing Jane Singletary, right?"

"Actually, no. I never entered my appearance."

"She told me the divorce papers were ready to be filed when her husband died."

"Then she made a mistake. We met twice, the first time for a consultation and the second time so I could analyze their finances and her antenuptial contract. After I explained everything to her, she decided not to proceed."

"So they had a prenup?"

"Correct. Dirk had her sign it before they married, and whoever prepared it knew how to close loopholes. All the assets collected before and during their marriage would go to him if she divorced him in the first twelve years of marriage. So Jane would've been stuck for another three years."

"Why would anyone agree to that?"

"She said Dirk tricked her into signing it and she regretted not having her own attorney look it over. Apparently Dirk was quite a con man."

"Wouldn't there have been a way she could break the contract?"

"Possibly, but the attorney fees would be costly, and then there'd be no guarantee a judge would grant her petition. Judges hesitate to break contracts. On top of that, Dirk had racked up significant debts, so even if she was able to get half of the marital assets, she would've lost most of them paying off their debts. I really felt sorry for her."

"But you don't anymore?"

"She should be fine now. Dirk had a multimillion-dollar life insurance policy."

"Did Jane know about the policy before Dirk died?"

"After I found the policy mixed in with the financial papers, she sure did. Dirk had never told her about it."

I was stunned. Everything Gary was telling me gave Jane a strong motive for murder. And yet my internal radar hadn't buzzed around her at all. "When was your last meeting with Jane?"

"My secretary can answer that better than I can." He snapped his briefcase shut. "I've got to head over to court. Do you want to walk and talk?"

"I think you've answered all my questions. Thanks for the help, Gary."

He left me with his secretary, who brought up the appointment calendar on her computer monitor. "Here we go," she said, swiveling the screen so I could see.

I wrote down the date, thanked her, and headed back to Bloomers. I felt sick inside, and it wasn't from Rosa's *huevos.* Jane had told her attorney to cancel the divorce action one week before her husband was killed. The implications of that gave her the strongest motive of any of our suspects.

But I wasn't giving up on my gut feeling about Mitzi yet, so I made one more phone call before I started on my work for the day.

Down the Hatch was only partially full when I arrived at noon, so we were able to sit at our booth. We put in our orders then I briefed Marco on my conversation with Gary Gillen ending with the date the divorce action had been canceled.

"I know what you're going to say about Jane, Marco, but maybe she lied to us because she feared she'd look guilty if we knew the truth."

"And lying *wouldn't* make her look guilty? Come on, Sunshine, you don't really believe that, do you?"

With a sigh, I said, "I guess not."

"Timing is everything, Abby. What really tips the scales for me is that Jane learned about that life insurance policy one week before her husband was killed. Do you understand why she's my top suspect?"

Unfortunately I did, especially after the call I'd made to Mitzi Kole's hair salon.

"I did some other fact-checking this morning," I said. "I spoke with the salon owner, who verified with Mitzi's stylist that Mitzi was there last Friday from six thirty until nine p.m. for her spa evening."

"So Mitzi told the truth. Don't look so glum about it."

"I can't believe my radar is that far off about both women."

"Guts can be wrong, Abby, but facts never lie."

"My gut has always steered me right before. And now I have a pedicure appointment tomorrow evening that I don't even need. That was going to be my excuse to get Mitzi's stylist to talk to me."

"What torture."

"Why don't you come with me? We can have our toenails done together."

Marco looked at me through lowered brows. "Me?"

We paused as our sandwiches were delivered, then Marco said, "I met Joe at the house this morning. He said our electrical wiring meets code and our electrical box is correctly labeled, but we'll probably have to start replacing light switches in a year or so because the quality is so poor."

"I've never heard of having to replace light switches."

"It wasn't a problem when switches were manufactured in the USA. At least we don't have to worry about our house catching fire."

"That's good news."

"I also did some research on Mitzi's husband and was able to verify that he was indeed out of town on business. His employer even offered to sign a sworn statement, so I'm taking him off the list." Marco dipped a fry in ketchup. "Now tell me what you were whispering about on the phone this morning."

I squeezed Dijon mustard onto my turkey and spread it with my knife as I described the morning's events, ending with, "And there I sat feeling like an outsider."

"You're not on the outside, Abby. You're the boss."

Why did he make it sound so simple? I tore the paper off my straw and stuck it in my iced tea. "You're not getting it, Marco. With Rosa and Lottie planning Rosa's contest entry right behind me, I felt so—"

"Then enter the competition yourself."

I sipped my tea, turning his idea over. "Planning an award-winning design takes a lot of thought and creativity. You have to have an image in your head first and then—"

"So what if it takes time? You have free evenings."

I put down my glass. "Are you in a rush?"

"No, why?"

"You keep cutting me off."

"Sorry. Go ahead."

If Marco wasn't in a rush, why did he keep glancing up at the clock over the bar?

"Anyway, I've already told Rosa and Lottie that I don't have enough time. Besides, if I entered my own design, how would that make Rosa feel?"

"Enter both arrangements."

"I can't compete against my own employee."

Marco took a drink of beer and glanced at the clock again. "I'm out of ideas."

And apparently out of patience for that particular subject. "Were you able to talk to Rye about my gaffe?"

"Yes. He was very gracious about it. He said Brandon had not contacted him. He also said the pickup truck is his only vehicle. His wife has an old white Chevy Cavalier."

I breathed a sigh of relief on both counts. "What's next on our agenda?"

"Verify Rye's wife's car and interview the building inspector. If you want to go with me tomorrow, I'll find out what time Maynard Dell normally takes his lunch and we can plan your lunch break around it."

From the corner of my eye I caught a flash of bright blue and looked up to see Francesca step inside the bar. She spotted me and waved.

"Marco," I said, trying not to move my mouth, "your mom's here and she's coming this way."

He breathed a sigh of relief. "It's about time."

I gaped at him. "You invited her and you didn't tell me?"

He reached over to take my hands. "I wanted you here with me when I discuss her boyfriend."

Marco had set up an ambush and made me his accomplice. Now she'd be angry at both of us. "I'm not saying a word," I told him, taking my hands away.

"Abby, *bella*," Francesca said, leaning in to kiss my cheek and give me a hug. She scowled at her son and said, "Marco." She didn't kiss or hug him, just scooted in beside me and sat facing him.

Francesca was wearing a peacock blue silk jacket

over a white blouse with black slacks and flats, carrying a black shoulder bag. She brushed her glorious dark hair away from her face and folded her hands on the table as Gert came to take her drink order.

"A cup of coffee, thank you." Then, as Gert hurried away, Francesca leveled her gaze at her son. "What did you want to talk to me about?"

He leaned back and put one arm along the tufted orange bench. "Alfred." Francesca slapped both hands on the table and sat back with a disgusted look. "That's what I thought."

"*Mama*, that man is deceiving you," Marco said.

Francesca didn't say a word, just kept her unsmiling gaze on him.

"Alfred Donnerson has been divorced four times. His fourth marriage lasted a year and ended a short two months ago. He lied about having children. He has five, in fact. Five stepchildren, all grown, some with children of their own."

In a low voice she said, "You didn't ask about *step*-children. Only *children*."

Marco went on. "I found two addresses associated with his name. The first I traced to an abandoned food factory, the other to a multimillion-dollar mansion on a gated property, both a far cry from that cozy lake cottage he told you about. You know what else I found on Alfred Donnerson? Nothing. It's as though someone has gone to great lengths to erase his past. Know what that tells me?"

"That he's smarter than you are." Francesca slid off the bench, put her purse over her shoulder, and left.

I sipped my tea through the straw, watching my husband's expression change from surprise to anger to frustration and then to determination.

"Donnerson might *think* he's smarter than me . . ." Marco said, picking up his beer bottle. He didn't finish his thought, just tipped the bottle back and took a long drink.

"Marco, drop it. Your mom doesn't want you interfering."

"Not going to happen. I care about her too much."

Too much was exactly the right term.

"You're always asking me to trust your instincts, Abby. How about this time you trust mine?"

CHAPTER FOURTEEN

When my mom stopped in at Bloomers after school, I was actually relieved to see her and gave her a warm hug. A slender woman with the peaches-and-cream complexion she'd inherited with her English genes and a honey blond bob that never had a strand out of place, Mom wore her standard teacher's outfit of neutral slacks, a coordinating print blouse with a cardigan sweater over her shoulders, and sensible flats.

Rosa and I had been busy putting together arrangements for a bridal shower, but everything stopped when Mom arrived. Even Lottie and Grace joined us to see what Mom had made, no doubt because of her unusual absence the week before. However, she hadn't brought the new art project Rosa had said she'd been working on, just bookmarks she'd had printed for her children's books.

"I love them, Mom," I said, and handed one to Lottie to see. "Good job."

"It's cute, Maureen," Lottie said. "Bright and colorful." She handed it to Rosa, who said, "I've seen it already," and passed it to Grace.

"When did you see it?" I asked Rosa with a smile.

Rosa and Mom exchanged smiles as Mom said, "I showed her when she came over to help me with my project."

After an awkward silence, Lottie said, "So when do we get to see this project?"

"When it's ready," Mom said, and again she and Rosa smiled at each other.

I smiled, too, and before I made my escape into the cooler, forced myself to say, "I can't wait to see it."

Mom didn't mean to exclude you, I told myself. *She's just busy with her books and excited about this new art project.*

Inner child to Abby: *She wasn't too busy to share her project with Rosa.*

"Abigail?" Mom called.

I gave a start, grabbed a handful of daisies, and stepped out. "Yes?"

"I'm taking off now, honey." She gave me a kiss on the cheek, did the same to Rosa, then headed toward the curtain. "Remember, dinner at our house this Sunday."

"Are you talking to me or Rosa?" I asked.

"You," she said. "But, Rosa, we'd love to have you and Petey come, too."

"*Gracias*, Maureen, but we go to my *mamá*'s house on Sundays."

I turned away so they wouldn't see my relief.

As I took Seedy for a walk around the neighborhood after work that evening, I saw Rye Bishop coming out of the model home wearing a thick black belt loaded with tools. My first inclination upon seeing him was to do an about-face and hurry the other way. But common sense intervened; the investigation was more important than my embarrassment, and the opportunity was just too perfect to pass up.

"Let's go talk to Rye, Seedy. He won't hurt you."

She began to growl and got low to the ground, just as she'd done after Rye had been to our house. Her reaction was odd—Seedy usually hid when she saw a strange man—so I had to pick her up and carry her. As we approached him, she tucked her head under my elbow, still growling.

"Evening," Rye said with a shy smile. He had on his usual hooded sweatshirt, baggy work pants, with his baseball cap on backward. "Hi, Seedy." He tried to pet her, but she merely increased her growls and stuck her head farther beneath my arm.

"I'm surprised you're still here," I said. "I thought your day ended at four."

"A toilet problem in the model needed a fix."

"You do plumbing work?"

"If it's an emergency situation and not too complicated. Brandon can't sell homes if people see problems in the model."

"So, listen, Rye, I know Marco talked to you, but I wanted to tell you myself how sorry I am that I brought up your name in our meeting with Brandon. I know it's not an excuse, but I was operating on two hours of sleep."

"I know you didn't mean nothing by it. Besides, maybe it's time Brandon got a wake-up call so he's aware that people are finding out what's been going on."

"I'm not sure about that wake-up call. He stated firmly that all the homes here passed inspection."

"They passed, all right. My point was that some of them shouldn't have."

I walked with him as he headed back toward the clubhouse. "If you were aware of the fraudulent home inspections, why didn't you tell Brandon?"

"Because Dirk said I shouldn't try to usurp his

authority by reporting it myself. He gave me his word he would report it."

"And yet Brandon seemed shocked by the news. Do you think Dirk lied about telling him?"

Rye shrugged. "Either that or Brandon knows and is lying to you. Guess it comes down to who you want to believe."

We paused to wave at a neighbor driving by, then I said, "Did you ever see Jane Singletary here in Brandywine?"

"Yep, on a couple of occasions when she had to bring Dirk to work."

"Do you remember what kind of car she drove?"

"It was an SUV—a Honda CR-V, if I remember correctly."

"What color?"

"Black."

The color worked but not the model. "Do you know anyone who drives a black sedan?"

Rye scratched his neck. "Seems like Dirk had a black sedan of some sort—or maybe it was navy. He mentioned it once, but I never saw him drive it. He liked his big blue Toyota Tundra too much. And then there's Mr. Thorne's black Lexus."

"The residents would recognize Brandon's car, wouldn't they?"

"I'd expect so."

"And I hate to ask you again, but what time did you say you left last Friday?"

"Four o'clock. Is there a question about the time?"

I couldn't mention what Connie had told us, so I said, "I forgot to write it in my notes and couldn't remember what you'd said. But you're sure it was four?"

He took off his hat and scratched his head, then put his hat back on. "Now that I think back, it might've been later. Seems like I remember getting stuck at the Nabhans' house fixing more things than I'd planned to. So maybe it was later than four."

"Duly noted. By the way, congratulations. I hear you got that promotion you wanted."

Rye's face turned red. "Yeah, I was surprised."

"Why didn't you tell us about it when we talked Thursday?"

"Well"—he took off his cap again and put it back on, a nervous habit, perhaps—"I wasn't sure I was going to be staying here. I was hoping to get another job, but that fell through."

That seemed a plausible reason. "I don't want to embarrass you, Rye, but would you be honest with me about why Dirk wanted you fired?"

He glanced at me in surprise. "Who said he wanted me fired?"

The name was on my lips when I remembered the rule. "I can't divulge that."

He studied me a moment. "So Mr. Thorne told you. I have to say it's the first I've heard of it, but I'm not too surprised."

We stopped behind Rye's pickup parked in front of the clubhouse's small lot. "Why is that?"

"Dirk didn't like me because I knew how often he was getting to work late and how many times he left early."

"Did you ever tell Brandon about Dirk's work ethic?"

He shook his head. "I don't do that to people. I'm just grateful Mr. Thorne didn't listen to Dirk."

"Quite the opposite. Brandon said you've always

done a fine job . . ." I stopped abruptly, realizing I'd just broken the rule again. Fortunately, Rye didn't notice.

"That's good to hear, especially since it looks like I'll be staying." He climbed into the bed of his truck and unlocked a built-in chest to put away his tool belt.

"Here's another question for you," I said. "Is there another location besides the supply closet in the clubhouse where tools and equipment are stored?"

"Nope. That's it. Why?"

"Marco noticed that there weren't any hammers or large wrenches in it."

"Things go missing a lot around here," he said, closing the chest. "Subcontractors take things and never return them. That's why I keep my stuff locked up. If there's anything in particular Marco needs, he can borrow it from me."

"He'll appreciate that. In fact, you don't happen to have a large wrench, do you?"

Rye opened the chest again and pushed his tools around. "That's strange. It's not here."

CHAPTER FIFTEEN

Once in a great while, Jillian surprised me by being normal. And for a short while she did so at Theda's house, as we dined on scrumptious food and laughed at stories of Theda's crazy Greek family. It helped that Theda did most of the talking, and when she paused, I jumped in with questions so Jillian couldn't get the proverbial word in edgewise. No sense tempting fate.

But the normalcy ended at the conclusion of a story in which Theda mentioned her late husband.

"Poor Theda," Jillian said, before I could start a new topic of conversation. "I can't imagine losing my husband. Can you, Abs? Who would take care of me?"

"You'd learn to take care of yourself," said Theda, a reflective look in her eyes.

Jillian leaned forward on her elbows. "How did your husband die?"

"He drowned in our swimming pool."

Jillian turned to me with wide eyes. "Can you imagine?"

"Will you look at the time?" I tapped my watch. "We'd better get started on my living room project, Jillian."

She was not to be deterred. "Who found him, Theda?"

"Jillian," I said, poking her under the table, "it's a painful subject."

Theda put down her wineglass. "That's okay, Abby. I was the one who found him."

My cousin put her hand over her mouth, her eyes welling with fat tears. "I'm so sorry," she whispered. "How horrible."

"I try not to dwell on it."

"We're both very sorry for your loss," I said, scooting back my chair. "I apologize if we upset you. Jillian, we really should be going. Thanks for a lovely dinner, Theda."

Jillian didn't move. "Was it like in the TV shows, where the police try to get you to say you pushed him in?"

"Jillian, stop," I hissed.

Theda wiped her mouth with her napkin, placed it on the table, and said calmly, "Exactly like that."

Jillian looked at me again, her eyebrows making tiny tents above her shocked gaze. Then to Theda she said, "But you didn't, right?"

"Time to go," I said as I tugged my cousin to her feet. "I'm sorry, Theda. Jillian has a bad habit of blurting the first thing that comes into her head."

"I didn't mean to offend you, Theda," Jillian said.

"I understand. And to answer your question, Jillian," Theda said, trying to keep a straight face, "I didn't push him in. That's not to say I hadn't thought about it."

We laughed, but there was something about the gleam in Theda's eye that said she was quite serious.

Jillian sat on the sofa with me and scrolled through my photos. "You're sticking with the playroom theme, I see."

"I can't help it. I like color. But Marco likes black and navy, so what do we do? I refuse to live with this old beater sofa another month."

Jillian tapped her chin then typed something on her

tablet and began to scroll through more photos. "How about something like this?"

She showed me a white leather sectional. "Nope. No leather and not white. I want something colorful, comfortable, and cushiony."

She went back to scrolling. "Do you believe Theda's story?"

"Which one?"

"That she didn't push her husband into the pool."

"Of course I believe her. What I don't believe is that you asked her about it."

"You have to admit it's freakishly coincidental that another man drowned behind her house, and, yes, I know it's not the same house, but it *is* the same woman. And that last comment she made? How telling is that?"

"Oh, come on, Jillian. She was joking."

Jillian studied me a moment, then with a grin, pushed my arm. "You don't believe that's a joke any more than I do. She may have been smiling, but she was dead serious."

"She's not a killer, Jill. She's my friend and next-door neighbor."

"Okay." She gave me a skeptical lift of her eyebrows. "You know what they say, though. There are no coincidences. So how do you feel about this sofa?"

Tuesday

I didn't get a chance to talk to Marco until breakfast the next morning, where I relayed my conversation with Rye and the information I'd gleaned from it.

"So he can fix plumbing when necessary, and one of his heavy tools is missing even though he keeps the chest locked," Marco said over his second cup of coffee. "We may have found our mystery plumber."

"I'm not so sure. I asked Rye how it was possible for someone to take his wrench, and he said he might have left it behind when he was working at one of the models."

"For someone who keeps his tools locked up, his cavalier attitude about leaving one behind raises a red flag with me. We'll need to follow up on that to see if he located the wrench. I'd love to get my hands on it first and have it tested for blood residue.

"By the way, the garden shovel was sent for DNA testing, but the police won't get results for weeks, so we have to assume any heavy tool could be the weapon. And as for the black sedan, we'll need to ask the neighbors whether they would recognize Thorne's car. I have a strong feeling that if we find the owner of that Ford, we'll find our killer."

I finished my coffee and got up to rinse my cup. "The Ford could have belonged to Dirk. Rye said Jane drives a Honda CR-V, but Dirk owned a third car that he didn't use for work. Maybe he brought it that day."

Marco brought his bowl to the sink. "Doesn't work, sweetheart. If it was Dirk's car, it would've been there when the police came." He paused, thinking. "Still, we should find out what his third car is. I'm off tomorrow evening, so let's pay Jane a call either at noon or after dinner. I'll phone her to see when she's available.

"And I did talk to someone in Maynard Dell's office, but she said his lunch hour varied. She suggested we drop by at eleven forty-five. Can you get away that early today?"

"I'll make it a point. I'm sure Rosa will *love* taking over for me." I followed that with an eye roll.

"What's going on, babe? I thought we had that sorted out."

I waved it away. "Never mind. I was trying to be funny."

Marco studied me a moment. "I know you too well, Sunshine. You're going to dwell on this thing with Rosa until you get it resolved. How about sitting her down for a talk? She might not have a clue how she's coming across to you."

That was true; she probably didn't. And if I told her, she'd be hurt and upset and go overboard trying to convince me otherwise, making the situation even more uncomfortable. But I didn't feel up to a debate on the subject, so I brushed it off with a simple "Good idea."

"About Maynard Dell," Marco said, "my strategy is going to be to first get him to admit to his deficiencies and then tell him we know Dirk was blackmailing him. His reaction will show us whether we hit the nail on the head. And Abby, I know how eager you are to tear into the man's work ethic, but you have to keep in mind that all we have are Rye's allegations. That doesn't mean we can't ask hard questions, but we have to maintain a professional attitude while interviewing him. So if you don't mind, I'll do the questioning. I think you're a little too touchy about the subject."

That stung. "If you're basing this on what I did at our interview with Brandon, you know I was asleep on my feet. It won't happen again."

He leaned over to kiss my cheek then got up to rinse out his cup. "What did you and Jillian decide about the living room?"

"She isn't happy about it, but I convinced her to work around your recliner."

"That was nice of you," he said. "Any sofa decisions?"

"No, but now she has an idea of what we like, so she's going to put together a plan, and we'll meet again Friday evening."

"Did she behave at dinner?"

I rinsed my plate and put it in the dishwasher. "You know Jillian. She always manages to stick her foot in her mouth." I didn't mention her questioning Theda about her husband's drowning because I knew it would only raise Marco's suspicions further. "So are we meeting at your bar or at Bloomers before we go see Maynard?"

"I'll walk down to get you."

I backed toward the hallway. "Great. I just have to brush my teeth and then I'm ready to go. Want to put Seedy's leash on?"

As I opened Bloomers' yellow frame door I could hear all three women chattering happily in the coffee-and-tea parlor. But at the tinkling of the overhead bell, all talk ceased. I shut the door and bent down to unhook Seedy's leash.

"Abby?" Lottie called.

"I'm here."

I heard whispers and then Grace called, "We're in the parlor, love. Come join us for coffee."

Seedy jumped up into the big bay window at the front of the shop, taking her usual spot on a dog cushion Lottie had bought for her, so I tucked her leash under the counter and walked into the parlor. There I found my assistants sitting at a table near the beverage counter in back. A place had been set for me.

As I sat down, Grace poured my coffee and returned to her seat. I noticed them casting glances at each other over the rims of their cups, so I peered into the creamy liquid. "Did you put poison in my cup, or what?"

"No!" Rosa exclaimed, looking offended. "Why would you say such a thing?"

"Because you all have guilty looks on your faces."

"Sweetie," Lottie said, "you're working that murder case too hard. Take a look around. Notice anything different?"

I did a quick surveillance and was about to say no when it hit me. We had new centerpieces, small white ceramic baskets, about four inches in diameter, each basket holding an arrangement of crepe paper flowers in lime green, light pink, and white. I wasn't sure what the purpose was of having fake flowers when we had a shop full of live blossoms, so I merely made a comment to the effect that they certainly were bright.

And then I asked what they were.

"The Marisol. My namesake flower," said Rosa. "Usually they are very big, like dinner plates, and made from paper. I made these small to fit the room better."

Giving her a pat on the back, Lottie said, "Great centerpieces, sweetie."

"Charming," said Grace. "A lovely addition to our parlor, Rosa."

"I thought it was time to shake things up a bit," Rosa said. "People like what's new. New flavor of scone, new brew of coffee . . ."

New boss?

Our morning meeting over, the day proceeded normally, with Grace handling the parlor, Lottie ringing up customers, and Rosa and me taking care of orders. At one point I found myself alone with Lottie in the shop, so I said, "Do you really like Rosa's centerpieces?"

"You don't?"

"I asked you first."

Lottie put her arm around me and said quietly, "I know what your objection is, and I agree with you: Live flowers are better. But she was so pleased to be helping that I couldn't find it in my heart to say no to them. Why don't we leave them a week or two and maybe they'll fade or get dusty?"

And that was the last word on the subject.

As I made deliveries later that morning, instead of focusing on questions to ask Maynard Dell, I found myself thinking of a new floral design, or, to be specific, an *award-winning* floral design. I tried to block those thoughts, yet I couldn't deny the tingles of excitement they gave me.

My phone beeped, so as soon as I parked our delivery van, I read the text message from Marco: *Jane refused meeting request. Suggest you attend Mitzi's book club tomorrow night.*

Oh, boy. There was something to look forward to.

As I walked back to Bloomers, I kept seeing a white floral arrangement in my mind's eye and once again felt those tiny pulses of excitement at the thought of creating something new and unique, an Abby Knight original.

Brain to Abby: *You don't need the extra pressure. You've got enough to do as it is.*

Abby to brain: *Killjoy.*

When I got back to the workroom, Rosa was at my desk filling out a form online with Lottie at her shoulder, guiding her through the process.

"Are you teaching her how to place an order?" I asked, pulling the next slip of paper from the spindle.

"Nope," Lottie said. "We're entering her into the floral competition."

"There!" Rosa exclaimed. "I did it." They gave each other high fives and turned to me with hopeful smiles.

"Congrats," I said, returning the smile, then went into the cooler to pull flowers. But instead of looking for the blossoms I needed for a sixteenth birthday party arrangement, I found myself scanning my supplies for what I had in mind for the contest.

Curly willow—check. White Casablanca lilies—check. Dendrobium—

"Sorry to interrupt your concentration," Lottie said from behind.

I jumped and said guiltily, "I wasn't concentrating on anything important."

Lottie looked at me oddly. "Okay. Would you hand me some fern?"

I handed her the greenery, gathered my birthday flowers, and pushed all thoughts of the contest out of my mind so I could get back to work.

The order specified orange and yellow, so I used mini cosmos, gerbera daisies, ranunculus, and white roses, a bright combination of yellow, orange, and white, and then filled in with baby's breath and statice, all in a glass ball base filled with clear marbles.

"You're humming," Lottie said, patting my back. "I haven't heard you hum in ages. You must be happy."

She caught me by surprise. I'd been thinking about that contest entry again.

We arrived at the Building Commission office in the administration center at eleven forty-five a.m. only to learn that the building inspector had already checked out for lunch.

"What time will he be back?" Marco asked.

One of the two women behind the counter, a young woman whose name tag lay partially hidden beneath her long blond hair, glanced at the other woman, who seemed old enough to be her grandmother. The other woman, wearing a name tag that read *Diane*, waggled her hand. "It varies."

"Would you give us an approximation?" Marco asked.

Another exchange of glances. Then the young woman flipped back her long hair, giving me a view of her name—Hevyn—and opened her mouth to speak, but Diane cut her off. "Leave your name and phone number and we'll have him contact you."

We were being given the runaround. Marco focused his penetrating gaze on Diane, causing her to blush hotly. "Do you expect him back at all today?"

"I really can't say what his schedule is like," said Diane, pushing a piece of paper and a pen across the counter. "As I said, it varies."

Marco laid his business card on the counter, ignoring the memo paper. "Just give him this and tell him it's important."

Diane didn't even glance at the card, but her young associate did, her blue eyes widening. I made eye contact with her and smiled. "If Mr. Dell does show up this afternoon, would you be sure to call us? Any help would be appreciated." I slipped one of my cards into her hand. "If you can't reach my husband, you can find me at Bloomers Flower Shop. I'm the owner."

*   *   *

"I wonder why they were being so secretive," I said, as we made our way down a back staircase. We'd opted to skip the crowded elevator and get a little exercise instead.

"I don't know, but something's up." Marco opened the glass door at the bottom and we stepped outside into bright sun.

"What if he doesn't call?"

"Then we'll either stake out his office, find his home address, or—"

"Mr. and Mrs. Salvare?"

We turned to see Hevyn leaning out the door, glancing around as though she was afraid of being seen. She held out a scrap of paper. "You can find what you need here."

I opened it up. *Washtub Tap* had been hastily scrawled on it. "Thank you," I said, handing it to Marco.

"What he's doing?" she said. "It's not right." And then she was gone.

Hevyn had answered our prayers.

The Washtub Tap, located northwest of New Chapel, was an old wooden building with peeling blue paint and a flat roof. It was so named because of the ancient, rusty, claw-footed bathtub that sat by the door. The tub was planted with geraniums just starting to bud. I stopped to break off some yellow leaves while Marco surveyed the exterior.

"No sign of a black sedan in the parking lot," he said, opening the door for me.

The inside of the bar looked as decrepit as the outside, with scarred, creaking wooden floorboards and old plaster walls whose white paint had bronzed with age and was flaking off in potato chip–sized pieces. More light came from windows on either side of the door than from the low-wattage coach lights that rimmed the room.

The wide L-shaped bar was made of a dark wood and kept well polished. The mirror behind it was tarnished and missing much of its silver backing. The wooden stools had red seats, the padding cracked from years of use. Age-darkened ladder-back chairs nestled around square oak tables, filling the rest of the space.

Marco's bar looked stunningly modern by contrast.

Having never met Maynard Dell, we asked an amicable bartender to point him out. He indicated a table in the back corner where one man was holding court. His round pate gleamed like a billiard ball and his double chin held a tangle of thick, wiry gray hair that ran from one ear to the other, giving him the appearance of having his head on upside down. He wore a button-down blue denim shirt tucked loosely into black pants held up by red-striped suspenders that curved around his generous belly.

Maynard and his cronies, men of different ages but all dressed in similar clothing, were laughing uproariously and clinking beer bottles, swigging for a long moment and then sighing in unison. When we approached, they regarded us curiously.

"Mr. Dell?" Marco handed him his business card. "Marco and Abby Salvare. We'd like to have a word with you."

Maynard glanced at the card then flicked it away, sending it skittering across the table. Another man picked it up and read it, then passed it to someone else. "I'm at lunch," Maynard said in a bored voice. "If you need an inspection, call my office."

"This isn't about an inspection," Marco said. "It's about a murder investigation."

Maynard looked at him with a baleful eye. "And just why is it you came to me?"

"We believe you have information that may help us."

Maynard snorted, causing his cronies to snort, too. "Do I, now?"

"Yes, sir. So we can either talk here in front of your friends or go somewhere private. It's your choice."

"Son," Maynard said, "you're misinformed. I know you're talking about that fellow from Brandywine and I'll tell you straight out I don't know anything about him except what I read in the papers." He folded his hands across his belly and grinned at his buddies as though proud of his tough stance.

"Then you're ready to swear to the police that you've never had any dealings with Dirk Singletary?" Marco asked. "Because that's the fellow I'm referring to, and also the one you've been dealing with at Brandywine for several months—unless the building commissioner was also misinformed."

Maynard eyed Marco but didn't comment.

"If you don't talk to us now," Marco said, "you will be talking to detectives later. I can guarantee that."

"Really?" said Maynard with a smirk. "And just why is that?"

"Because I'm prepared to tell them about that little arrangement you and Dirk had regarding the homes you were supposed to inspect in Brandywine."

Maynard sat forward, his heavy neck growing red as he stabbed a thick finger at Marco. "Now don't you go making aspersions like that in front of my friends."

"Then I suggest we find somewhere else to talk,"

Marco said, "because I have more aspersions, and you'll like them even less."

At the hushed murmuring among his cohorts, Maynard got up and adjusted his pants over his belly. "There's a private room up the hallway."

CHAPTER SIXTEEN

We sat at a long pine table in a room at the back of the building. Marco placed me at the head of the table then took a seat opposite the annoyed building inspector. In the light from an overhead fluorescent tube, Maynard looked old, with wrinkled bags beneath squinting eyes, deep marionette lines that ran from his bulbous nose to his Brillo pad beard, and yellow fingernails on his cigar-stub digits.

As I started a new page in the notebook, Marco began the interview. "Who inspects new construction in New Chapel?"

"I do."

"Did you inspect the homes in Brandywine?"

With a glare Maynard said, "I just said I was the guy, didn't I?"

"What makes you the expert on building construction?"

"Forty years of experience, that's what makes me an expert. Tell me, son. How many years would you say you've been an expert in your field?"

Marco ignored the dig. "What kind of electrical education have you had?"

Maynard rubbed a hand over his beard, muffling his words.

"Did you say a two-week course?" I asked.

"Two days," he mumbled, looking out over the room.

"So roughly fourteen hours," Marco said, "whereas a journeyman electrician needs a five-year apprenticeship before he can call himself an expert. Are you certified?"

"Hold on a second," Maynard said hotly. "You told me this was about Dirk Singletary. You keep your questions on that subject or I'm gonna walk right out of here."

"All right," Marco said evenly. "Let's get right to the investigation. We've learned that some of the homes in Brandywine were not properly inspected and are not up to code but passed anyway."

"Says who?" Maynard demanded, his fat fingers gripping the table edges.

"Says someone who knows wiring."

Maynard sat back, crossing his arms. "Give me proof."

"I can do that. I know a journeyman electrician who's willing to come out to inspect one of the homes later today. He's promised to give me an honest assessment from top to bottom. Would you like us to come back with that proof and bring the police investigators with us or would you rather continue now?"

Maynard slammed his fist on the table. "I tested every one of those houses. The wiring was fine."

"What method do you use?"

"Method? I don't have a method. I have a specialized tool."

"What does this *specialized tool* do?"

"It tells me whether electricity is flowing through the wires."

"Do you go outlet by outlet to check?"

"What are you getting at?"

"Do you go outlet by outlet?"

Maynard ran his fingers through his beard, tugging at the snarls. "A random sampling is all that's necessary."

"Would I be able to buy this *specialized tool* at the hardware store?"

Maynard shrugged.

"Isn't it, in fact, a twenty-four-dollar GFIC tester that anyone can buy to see if their outlets work?"

Maynard glared at Marco but didn't reply.

"Do you inspect the electrical boxes?"

"Yes."

"Do you check to see if the switches connect to what they say they do?"

Again Maynard only glared.

"How can you say a house meets code if you don't inspect those things?"

Maynard shoved his chair back, hitting the plank wall. "I don't have to sit here for this—this—witch hunt."

Marco sat forward, his expression intense, his forearms on the table. "It's a murderer hunt, Mr. Dell, and you, unfortunately, are a suspect."

Maynard was so flustered he couldn't speak. Now Marco had him where he wanted him and was about to turn up the heat. "Dirk Singletary knew you were passing Brandywine homes fraudulently, didn't he?"

"That's a lie! I did my job—*do* my job—to the best of my ability."

"But your ability is the problem, isn't it? You don't have the certification to do a proper job, so you pass homes that might not be up to code. They might, in fact, be dangerous to live in. Dirk Singletary knew it, and yet he didn't report you because he knew he could make money from that knowledge. So what was his price?"

The building inspector was on his feet, bristling with outrage. "You're talking nonsense!"

Marco stood, too, and placed his palms on the table, leaning forward to shorten the distance between them. When he spoke his voice was absolutely calm and utterly, deadly serious. "Sit down, Mr. Dell, and pay close attention to what I'm about to say."

As Maynard took his measure, I held my breath, worried that we'd lose our chance to question him. But it must have finally sunk in that Marco meant business because, with what was left of his pride, he sat down once again and adjusted his chair.

And then Marco began again. "We are fully aware of Dirk's money-making schemes. Rest assured, Mr. Dell, you aren't the only one affected, but you *are* the only one being uncooperative, and there is *nothing* that makes a detective more suspicious than an uncooperative suspect.

"Now here's the important part," Marco continued. "We have a credible witness who will testify that you threatened to kill Dirk Singletary."

"What?" he choked out, on his feet again.

"You heard me. So it would behoove you to cooperate because detectives generally go easier on cooperative witnesses. Got that? Because, believe me, my wife and I have no vested interest in protecting you from police interrogation. So I'll ask you again. How much did Dirk ask you to pay him?"

It was a calculated move on Marco's part. If he'd guessed wrong about the demand for money, Maynard could tell us to go take a hike and walk out the door. But he merely studied Marco with calculating eyes before resuming his seat.

"And just so you know," Marco said, "where the detectives go, so goes Connor MacKay. You're familiar with Connor, right? The crime scene reporter for the *New Chapel News*? Imagine what a scoop he'd have."

Maynard continue to regard Marco, and I could almost hear the wheels turning in his brain. After another minute, Marco glanced at his watch and said to me, "Let's go. We still have time to catch Detective Wells before she leaves."

"All right!" Maynard cried. He collapsed against the back of his chair, all his bluster gone. "All right."

I went to the bartender and ordered coffees for us—Maynard seemed to need something more sobering than alcohol—and as we waited for them to be delivered, he asked, "Just what are you proposing to do with the information I give you?"

"Turn it over to the detectives and impress upon them how cooperative you're being," Marco said.

Maynard rubbed his heavy hand across his mouth, his crafty gaze on my husband. Finally, he put his hands on the table, folded together pleadingly, as he took on a new persona, that of a beleaguered old man. "You have to understand where I'm coming from, son. I'm a year away from retirement. My health isn't good. My wife is sickly. I've got a roof that needs replacing, an old furnace . . . I'm in no position to hand out money.

"So when Dirk approached me out of the blue, insinuating that he could get me fired because of a few things he claimed to have seen, well, you can imagine my shock. Something like that could cause an old man to collapse right there on the spot. I told him if he thought I had any money he was barking up the wrong tree, but he didn't care one whit about me or my problems. No, sir. He was desperate. He had to have that money now or else. I explained that the only money I had was in my life insurance policy, and that scumbag was okay with me cashing it in. And then he gave me a deadline."

Marco waited while the bartender came in with a tray, placing steaming mugs, a bowl of coffee creamers, and packets of sweeteners in front of us. Then he asked, "What was the deadline?"

"I don't remember the exact date, but I think it was sometime next week."

Marco and I exchanged glances, then I wrote in the notebook: *Doesn't remember blackmail deadline?*

Marco said, "So you agreed to pay the money."

"Yes, sir. I had no choice."

"What was Dirk going to do if you didn't meet your deadline?"

"He told me he had proof that I wasn't doing my job that he could show to the mayor and commissioners."

"What kind of proof?"

Maynard picked up his mug with both hands as though he was having trouble keeping it steady. "Photos is what he said."

"Did he ever show you the photos?"

Maynard shook his head then used his trembling hands to bring the mug to his lips. I guessed it was an attempt to make us feel sorry for him.

"Do you have any idea what the photos show?"

"No, sir. When I was on the premises at Brandywine, I was inspecting. I don't know what he could've seen."

"Wouldn't a reasonable person ask to see the photos before handing over money?" Marco asked.

Maynard stared into his cup as though embarrassed. "I didn't think of it."

I had to pinch my lips to keep from scoffing. I didn't believe him for a second.

"Mr. Dell, what kind of car do you own?" asked Marco.

"It's parked right out front, a white van with the town logo on it. A company car."

"What about your wife?"

"She drives a red Buick LeSabre."

"Where were you from seven to ten o'clock on the Friday evening Dirk was found murdered?"

"Home with my wife."

"What time did you leave work that Friday?"

Maynard stroked his beard for a moment. "Five o'clock."

"Is that the time you usually quit?"

He nodded.

"Did you stop at Brandywine before heading home?"

"No, sir."

"What time did you arrive at your residence?"

"About seven o'clock."

"Why so late?"

After a noisy sip of coffee, he said, "I usually have a few beers with my buddies after work on Fridays."

"Here?"

"Yes. It's on the way home."

"Do you live in New Chapel?"

"Not New Chapel proper, no."

"Why are you here now?"

"I'm on my lunch break."

"I didn't see any food."

Eyeing Marco over the mug, Maynard said slyly, "I was warming up to it."

"How long is your lunch break?"

"An hour."

"So if I ask the bartender how long you usually stay, he'll say an hour?"

"Maybe a little longer."

"Maybe all afternoon?"

"No, sir," Maynard said. "I might stretch my lunch hour on occasion, but I'm a hardworking man who puts in an honest day's work."

I had to stop myself from snickering.

Marco studied him for a moment, then said to me, "Anything I missed?"

I shook my head.

"Okay, Mr. Dell, that will do it for now."

Maynard downed the rest of his coffee then rose with an exaggerated groan and lumbered out of the room.

Marco looked at me. "Let's see what the bartender has to say about that Friday night."

Our habit was to go over all the information we'd gleaned after every interview, so once we were in the car heading back to town, I opened the notebook. "Ready."

"First question," Marco said, "why were you so quiet?"

"You were on a roll, Marco. My function today was totally supportive."

He put his hand on my arm. "I just wanted to be sure it wasn't because of anything I said about our last interview. We're a team, Sunshine. Never forget that."

I smiled at him. Actually, it *was* a little about what he'd said to me. My goal now was to redeem myself in his eyes.

"What did you think of Maynard's answer to the deadline question?" Marco asked. "If someone were blackmailing me and gave me a deadline, you'd better believe I'd know it down to the minute. Also I question why he didn't ask to see those photos. No one in their right mind would pay up without seeing proof. And for that reason I think he knew what the photos would show. It's also why he just moved to number one on my suspect list."

Mitzi was still my number one. "Wasn't it pathetic how Maynard suddenly tried to make himself out to be a helpless old man?"

"Quite an act. So our next step is to verify that the white van is Maynard's only vehicle and that he can take it home. I doubt there's any use in talking to his wife about what time he got home that Friday—I'm sure Maynard will coach her—but I'll give her a call anyway."

"The bartender wasn't much help about that Friday night, but at least we found out ourselves that Maynard could've easily made it to Brandywine before seven thirty."

Marco pulled into a public parking lot. "I'm going to ask Jane if she found any photos among Dirk's things. If she thought it would take the heat off her, she might share them with us. And that might be a way to get in the door again." He shut off the engine and reached over to tweak my nose. "Now on to a more pleasant subject. How about dinner at the bar tonight?"

"As long as you haven't invited your mother."

The corners of Marco's mouth turned up impishly. "No more ambushes, I promise."

CHAPTER SEVENTEEN

Marco stayed true to his word and we had an enjoyable dinner together, setting aside all talk of business for an hour to just enjoy each other's company before he had to return to his bar duties. Back home, I took advantage of the mild weather to go for a walk with Seedy, where we encountered Reagan and several women from her book club sitting on her porch with glasses of wine.

I stopped to ask if they knew what kind of car Brandon Thorne drove, and all of them did. But when I asked if they knew anyone who owned a black Ford sedan or if they had ever seen one parked in the neighborhood, I got the opposite response. No one had.

"We'll keep our eyes peeled," Reagan promised. "If we see that car, we'll call."

As I came back around to my house, Mitzi was standing outside her garage, waiting for her fluffy dog to do her business. When Mitzi spotted us, she scooped up her dog and headed inside her garage, as though she wanted to avoid talking to me.

"Mitzi, wait," I called, stopping at the bottom of her driveway.

She came toward me with her dog tucked beneath

her arm and a wary look on her face. Judging by her red dangle earrings and stack of red bangle bracelets, off-the-shoulder navy knit top, tight white jeans, and navy heels, I was betting she was on her way somewhere.

"Hello, Seedy," she said, patting the top of my dog's head as though she were contaminated.

"I won't keep you," I said. "I just wanted to ask if you've ever seen a black Ford sedan parked in the neighborhood or know anyone who drives one."

"Sorry. I don't know anyone who owns a car like that, but I feel like I've seen it around. Why? Do you think that's the car the killer drove?"

She'd jumped to that conclusion pretty rapidly. "Theda saw it parked across the street the evening Dirk was killed."

"Oh, *Theda* saw it." Mitzi rolled her eyes.

"I don't know if there's a connection, but we're checking into it. Do you recall seeing Dirk behind Theda's house anytime that Friday?"

She thought for a moment, tapping her chin. "Did I see him? I *might* have. He was there one day last week, but was it *that* Friday . . . ?"

I had a feeling Mitzi wanted to say yes so she could throw more blame on Theda, but apparently her conscience wouldn't let her. "The only person I saw was Theda."

"What was she doing?"

"Attacking the moss with her shovel."

"What time was this?"

"After dinner. I'm not sure exactly what time but it could've been around dusk." She put her hand over her dog's ears and whispered, "Is Theda still a suspect?"

"Unfortunately, I can't discuss an ongoing investigation. Were you out with your dog when you saw her?"

Mitzi stroked her pet's head. "Yes, for the umpteenth time. My poor little Peanut has a weak bladder. Don't you, Peanut?" She rubbed noses with her dog, then glanced at me coyly. "You know Theda hated Dirk, right?"

"*Hate* is a strong word."

"Theda has strong opinions. Actually, she's a strong woman. Have you ever seen her carry a big bag of mulch from her garage to the back of her house? I have."

"Your opinion of Dirk is pretty strong, too, Mitzi. At least, that was the impression I got the last time we talked."

She put one hand on her hip. "How would you feel if someone you trusted took your most valuable jewelry? I have every right to feel strongly about him."

"I'm not arguing that at all. In fact, I agree with you. You opened your heart to him and he betrayed you."

She gaped at me in disgust. "Opened my heart? What are you talking about? My relationship with Dirk was completely professional."

"It's been established that you were having an affair with him."

"That's a lie." She put her dog down and said angrily, "I would never, *ever* let that creep in my bed."

I gave her the long, steady look for which Marco was famous. "Come on, Mitzi. It's all your book club could talk about last week."

"I told you we were joking."

"We also have a witness who saw Dirk entering and leaving your residence several times over the last few weeks, as well as seeing your car in the garage while Dirk's was in the drive—"

"Theda! She told you, didn't she? That old busy-body, always at her window, spying on my comings and goings. How dare she!" Mitzi burst into noisy sobs, her hands covering her face. "I made a mistake . . . never should have . . . a momentary lapse of judgment . . . regret it for the rest of my life . . . so humiliated . . ." She grabbed my hands. "Abby, you have to believe me! I didn't kill Dirk. I hated him, but I would never hurt another human being. It was Theda. Theda killed him, and now she's trying to make me look guilty. She was furious about the moss problem, and Dirk wouldn't do anything about it."

Before I could respond, she blurted, "Or Rye. He wanted Dirk's job. Everyone knows that, and even Dirk told me so. He said he always had to look over his shoulder when Rye was around. Have you investigated Brandon? You know Dirk was trying to blackmail him, don't you?"

"Whoa. Slow down. Dirk was blackmailing Brandon Thorne?"

"*Trying* to blackmail him." Like turning off a spigot, the waterworks stopped and she wiped her eyes with her thumbs, careful not to smudge her eyeliner. "He told me a few days before he was killed. 'Mitzi, sweetheart,' he said, 'Brandon is going to have to pay big bucks to keep me quiet, and when he does, we're going to the Bahamas and never coming back.'" Mitzi started crying again, but this time it was obviously forced. "And two days later he stole my jewelry. Lying rat bastard! I'm glad he's dead."

As soon as the words were out of her mouth, she gasped and grabbed my hands again. "I didn't mean that, Abby. I'm not glad he's dead. I just meant that he deserved to die. No, that's not what I meant, either. He should be alive so he could go to jail for stealing my jewelry." She searched my face pleadingly. "You understand, don't you? I'm not the murderer, Abby. I'm a victim."

If Mitzi wanted sympathy, she wasn't getting it from me. "Did Dirk tell you how he was going to blackmail Brandon?"

"No, just that it was going to be a lot of money."

"So you don't know whether he actually contacted Brandon?"

She scooped up Peanut and began backing toward her garage. "Oh, I think he contacted Brandon. Dirk was brash like that. He didn't fear anyone." She hit the button to close her garage door, then called, "Will we see you tomorrow night at book club?"

"I'll be there."

"Great," she said with forced enthusiasm.

How about that? I wasn't dreading her book club meeting. In fact, I couldn't wait to hear what the Bees would be talking about this week.

Marco made it home by eleven o'clock that night. He'd texted me earlier that he wouldn't be late, so I waited up, eager to share my new information.

"How's my favorite female?" he asked, kissing me on the cheek.

"Feeling idiotic. I took Seedy for a walk and forgot all about my pedicure appointment this evening." I was propped up in bed reading, with Seedy stretched out beside me. At his entrance she rose and wagged her tail, waiting for her turn.

"Yes, I'm happy to see you, too," he said, giving her a good rub behind the ears. "Can you reschedule your appointment?"

"I did. It's Thursday evening."

He pulled his T-shirt off over his head and stuffed it in the hamper in our closet. "Guess who came to see me this evening."

"Your mom?"

"No. Your friendly car salesman. He found the perfect vehicle for a busy private investigator." Marco unzipped his jeans and stepped out of them.

"Are you serious?"

"Those were my exact words to him. I almost kicked him out of the bar."

"I'm sorry, Marco. I'll go see him tomorrow and tell him to leave you alone."

"No, Sunshine. *I* will go see him tomorrow and tell him to leave me alone." He pulled on his pajama bottoms and flopped down beside me. "You've done enough."

"Okay, then."

He tweaked my chin. "I just mean I need to take care of my own problems."

"Duly noted. Want to hear how my evening went?"

"Other than forgetting to get your toes painted?" He propped up his pillow and relaxed beside me. "Go for it."

I told him about my discussion with the neighbors concerning the black Ford. I also told him about my chat with Mitzi but I left out the part about her seeing Theda because I didn't believe her. "The more Mitzi tells me, Marco, the more strongly I feel she's our killer. She was throwing everyone under the bus tonight, including Brandon."

"Sounds like we need to have another talk with Brandon Thorne."

"That's your takeaway from my conversation?"

"Blackmailing someone, or even attempting to, isn't something to take lightly."

"No one is taking it lightly, Marco, but Mitzi admitted to being behind her house the night Dirk was killed, not at her salon for a spa treatment like she claimed. She was right here when the murder happened."

"As was Theda."

"But Mitzi got her stylist to lie for her and back up her alibi. Don't you think that's a tad more damning? And what about her assertion that Dirk tried to blackmail Brandon? For all we know, she might have lied about that, too."

Marco rolled off the bed. "I get it, Abby. Question her stylist again when you go for your pedicure. It's possible Mitzi went for a late appointment."

He paused at the door. "Want some ice cream? I've got a taste for that chocolate coconut milk you bought last week."

"My gut doesn't lie, Marco."

"Okay, suit yourself."

As he walked out, I called, "I mean about the case, not the ice cream."

Wednesday

White delphinium, perhaps? Or would the Casablanca lilies be better?

"Abby?"

I glanced over at Marco as he pulled into the parking lot. "Yes?"

"I asked if you were coming back to the house with me at noon for delivery of our new dining table, but I guess you were somewhere else."

I *had* been somewhere else—inside my head designing

that flower entry for the contest I was not going to enter. "I can't. We've got to finish the bridal shower arrangements and get them to the banquet center before noon, then do two funerals before four o'clock. Text me photos of the table. I can't wait to see it in our dining room."

When we reached Bloomers, Seedy and I walked into the shop only to find both the parlor and the salesroom empty. Hearing voices coming from the back, I parted the purple curtain and saw Grace, Lottie, and Rosa around the big slate table working on the bridal shower centerpieces.

"Look! We're almost finished," Rosa called buoyantly when she saw me.

I spotted a row of completed arrangements sitting on the back counter. "You must have come in pretty early to get so many done."

"Petey had to be at school early, so I thought, why not get a head start? We have so much to do today."

"And I was totally on board with it," Lottie said. "I'm up early anyway to get my four eating machines off to school."

"Rosa had everything efficiently organized assembly line style when I got here," Grace said, "so I was able to help, too."

"All of you came in early?"

"We thought it would give you more time to work on the investigation, sweetie," Lottie said, as she placed another finished centerpiece on the back counter.

"And now that you're here, I'll go set up the parlor." Grace washed her hands at the sink, got one of her special biscuits out of her pocket for Seedy, who was waiting patiently at her feet, and headed toward the curtain.

"I'll start loading the van," Lottie said to Rosa.

"I just have this last one to finish," Rosa replied.

I glanced at her arrangement from the corner of my eye as I went to sit at the computer. It looked perfect, an exact replica of the design I'd made yesterday. "Thanks for getting them finished, Rosa."

"Abby," she said, putting her arms around my neck, "you don't have to thank me. I was just doing what needed to be done. Now we don't have to worry about having time for the funeral arrangements."

It was true. The rush—and the stress—were gone. Now I could enjoy creating new arrangements all morning and afternoon and still have time to go back to the house with Marco. Yet I felt deficient, like I had fallen asleep at the wheel. Why hadn't I thought of coming in early?

Maybe Rosa *would* make a better boss.

As I walked up the sidewalk heading toward Down the Hatch just before noon, I spotted Gert rushing out of the bar motioning for me to hurry.

"Come on, Abby," she called, practically hopping up and down.

"What's going on?"

"Nothing if you hurry." She linked her thin arm through mine and led me through the noisy, crowded bar, calling over her shoulder, "Didn't you get Marco's text?"

I patted my pocket. "I must have left my phone at Bloomers. Why?"

Gert stopped in front of Marco's closed office door, her small pruned face a mask of fury, and whispered, "Because your neighbor showed up here unannounced a little while ago, and we've got to do something about it."

"Which neighbor?"

"Mitzi something or other. She burst in on Marco

and began setting up a cozy little picnic for two right on top of his desk. Marco made up an excuse to get the heck out of there and told me to bring you down fast 'cause you weren't answering his text."

I pushed past Gert, opened the door, and saw Ms. *Something or Other* leaning across Marco's desk, giving me a perfect view of her red leather miniskirt–clad derriere, bare legs, and red stilettos.

"I hope you found that bottle of bubbly you promised me," Mitzi said, setting out another carton of food. "But I have to warn you, champagne makes me very, *very*"— she turned around, full cleavage in sight and a seductive pout on her face that instantly turned to openmouthed shock.

"Very what?" I asked.

CHAPTER EIGHTEEN

Mitzi looked exceedingly guilty as she smoothed her red miniskirt down her thighs and straightened her skintight white V-neck top. Not a trace remained of the teary-eyed victim who'd attempted to play on my sympathies the day before.

"Abby!" she said with phony enthusiasm. "You made it after all. I was afraid my invitation got lost in cyberspace."

"Gert?" I said to the woman behind me. "The door, please."

Gert shut it quietly, leaving me alone with Mitzi. I walked around Marco's desk and stood facing her, my arms folded over my blouse. "I didn't receive an invitation."

"Oh, well," Mitzi said lightly. "That's the Internet for you."

I stacked the plates she had put out and handed them to her. "I'm afraid we're going to have to decline your lunch, Mitzi."

"But I went to all this trouble."

I collected the plastic utensils and put them in the picnic basket. "An important development has come up in our investigation that we need to take care of right away."

She stared at me with her big doe eyes as though

having difficulty processing the news, so I continued with the packing.

"Does this mean you're close to finding the murderer?" she asked, placing the plates back into the basket.

"Yep." I handed her a container of potato salad, pleased to see her blanch.

"So someone is going to be arrested soon?" she asked, trying to appear casually interested.

"Absolutely," I said.

She closed the hamper, put the handles over her arm, and said with a pasted-on smile, "Well, maybe we can do this some other time."

As she made for the door, I called, "I'll see you tonight. Seven o'clock, right?"

She paused, looked back as if she wanted to say something, then with a tight smile gave me a nod. She opened the door and nearly collided with Marco. With an uneasy smile, she sidestepped him and hurried away.

I followed her up the hallway and into the bar area. At the exact moment she entered it, Gert, standing behind the bar, shut off the music. As Mitzi passed her, Gert said to Rafe in a loud voice, "She may have snuck in on us, but she sure as heck ain't sneakin' out."

Rafe and the two other bartenders, their arms folded, gave Mitzi steely glances. That caused all the customers to follow the direction of their gazes and part to let Mitzi through. No one spoke. The only sound was the clicking of her stiletto heels on the linoleum as she made her walk of shame, wobbling twice and nearly stumbling but keeping her head high and her eyes straight ahead. When she exited the building, the music went on, a cheer went up, people resumed their conversations, and Marco and I retreated to his office.

"I know what you're thinking," Marco said, "but the bottle of champagne was my excuse to get out of there. And in my defense, she said you were on your way."

I put my fingers over his lips. "It's okay, Marco."

He took my hand and kissed my fingertips. "You know I wouldn't have let anything happen."

"Of course I know that, and I'm proud of the way the three of us—you, me, and Gert—handled it. But don't you see now why Mitzi should be our number one suspect? She just showed the kind of underhanded deed she's capable of."

"Seduction isn't the same as murder, Sunshine."

"Are you kidding? If she had succeeded in seducing you, there'd be two more murders in New Chapel."

We kissed, hugged, and then headed out the back door, where Marco had the car waiting in the alley. "I hope the delivery van doesn't beat us to the house," I said.

"They'll wait. How did you get away from Bloomers? I thought you were too busy for lunch."

"Rosa asked Lottie and Grace to come in early so they could finish the bridal shower arrangements before noon, which they didn't bother to let me know. And before you say anything, I know Rosa was being helpful. But I would've come in early, too, if she'd just informed me."

"Then we all would've had to go in early."

The car thing again. I sighed morosely as I buckled my seat belt.

"I still say you need to talk to Rosa. Tell her how things like that make you feel. You have to get these things off your chest, sweetheart."

I folded my arms. "Really?"

"Absolutely. You don't do that enough."

"Would you like me to start with you?"

Marco glanced at me for a moment. "Why don't I call Gert and put in an order for some food for you when we get back? I'll bet you're hungry."

On our way to the house, Marco told me he'd contacted Jane Singletary about Dirk's photos. "She wasn't cooperative initially, but once she understood I was only interested in Dirk's photos, she warmed up. She said Dirk would've used his phone, which the detectives confiscated, to take them. However, all their photos back up to the cloud, so she could still access them through her iPad. She said if she finds any pictures from Brandywine, she'll let me know. I'm hoping that conversation opened the door for further dialogue because we still need to question her about other issues.

"I also called Maynard Dell's wife, who claimed she couldn't remember Maynard ever coming home late. When I inquired about her car, she said they'd sold her Buick because she can't drive anymore due to her cataracts."

"That contradicts Maynard's statement."

"Yep. She confirmed that Maynard uses the town's vehicle, which she appreciates because that allows them to park wherever they like, and since she has bad knees, that's a blessing. She was very talkative but in a nervous way. I want to set up a surveillance to see what Maynard's work habits are like, maybe take some photos. If they're what I suspect, my pictures might get him to cooperate even more."

We drove into our garage and got out of the car just as the furniture van pulled up. The deliverymen unloaded the dining set and brought it in, but I barely had time to admire it because Mitzi's unexpected visit had shortened my lunch hour.

"I wish we had time to have lunch here," I told Marco, "but I have a lot of funeral arrangements to do this afternoon."

Yet who knew? Maybe when I got back, *those* arrangements would be finished, too.

My fears were unfounded; there were still tickets waiting on the spindle. Rosa and I worked steadily all afternoon until, by four o'clock, all the arrangements had been delivered and all the other orders that had come in during the day were done. That left me with time to check our stock and place overnight orders to replenish the basics. And once again, as I stood in the walk-in cooler making my list, I found myself working on my imaginary contest entry.

Curly willow, white Casablanca lilies—or had I decided on white dendrobium orchids? How about both? Most certainly centurion white delphinium and maybe some antherium, too.

Pleased with the image in my head, I decided to write my selections down on the off chance I would want to use them at some later date. I flipped my notebook to a new page and drew a sketch of my design, listing all the flowers and accent stems I'd need. When I finished, I stood in the workroom in front of the shelves containing a large assortment of containers and vases, trying to decide on a pot to compliment my design.

"What are you looking for?" Rosa asked, startling me.

"Um, just checking to see if I need to order anything."

"Is that your list?" She pointed to my open notebook.

I hugged it to me and smiled. "Yep." And then I walked away.

As soon as Rosa left the room, I tore out my design to tuck in my purse, away from any prying eyes. But that was silly; I wasn't going to enter the competition. I stuffed it inside the top desk drawer instead and shut it with a bang. There. Now it was off my mind. Subject closed.

Marco came home for supper at six o'clock, and as we enjoyed a garden salad, grilled chicken, and wild rice at our new table, he reported that his buddy Sergeant Reilly had been able to access information showing that the cell pings associated with Brandon Thorne's phone number had indeed come from a tower in South Haven, Michigan, close to Thorne's headquarters, on the Friday Dirk drowned.

"The odds are high that Thorne was in South Haven that Friday," Marco said. "In addition to the fact that no one saw his car here that evening, there were no pings anywhere close to here, either. In fact, later that night, they came from a tower near his home address in Michigan."

"What about Mitzi's allegations that Dirk tried to blackmail Brandon?"

"If the proof shows Thorne wasn't in the area, then her allegations are just that. She may have made them up anyway."

"Are we crossing Brandon off the suspect list?"

"I'm still waiting to confirm that the e-mails he sent out that evening came from a server in that area, but I don't see any reason to keep him on."

"Couldn't he have hired someone to kill Dirk?"

"He could have, but would that be likely? I think we need to focus on our remaining suspects for the time being and leave that as a secondary theory."

"Then that leaves Mitzi Kole, Jane Singletary, Rye Bishop, and Maynard Dell."

"With Rye, there's no evidence to tie him to the murder unless we can locate his large wrench for testing or if the DNA results on the shovel show his involvement. If we could find an alibi witness to say he was at home during the time period of Dirk's death, we could cross him off."

"Are you actively looking for one?"

"I'll need to canvass his neighbors during a time they're most likely to be around, so it's on my schedule for Saturday. Tomorrow I'm going to run surveillance on Maynard. If you want to go, you'll need to take a late lunch hour."

"Done. What about a meeting with Jane?"

"I'm waiting for her to phone me about the photos. If I don't hear anything, I'll give her a call."

I put my chin on my palm. "And then there's Miss Spread the Blame Mitzi. I can't wait to see what happens at book club tonight. And tomorrow is my pedicure. I'm determined to get the truth from Mitzi's stylist."

"You'll miss Reagan's book club."

"Priorities, Marco."

We clinked glasses at that and then I noticed the time. "I need to get ready. Book club starts in twenty minutes."

As we carried our dishes to the sink, the doorbell rang, so I went to answer it.

"Hi, Abby," said a woman I recognized as one of Mitzi's Bees. "I just wanted to let you know that club is canceled tonight."

"That's too bad. I was looking forward to it. I hope Mitzi's all right."

She gave me a polite smile. "Well, anyway, have a nice evening."

"Thanks. I'll see you next week, then."

"Um, sure."

I watched her as she hurried up the sidewalk, and then I shut the door and leaned against it, waiting a moment before looking out the peephole. Just as I suspected, the woman glanced my way then darted up Mitzi's sidewalk and into her house.

"That was interesting," I said to Marco, returning to the kitchen. "I think I just got expelled from the Bee hive."

With my evening wide-open, I made a call to Mitzi's beauty salon and managed to reschedule my pedicure with her stylist for the last appointment of the day. When I went next door to ask Theda to watch Seedy for me later, she invited me in for a cup of tea. I could tell something was on her mind, so I got Seedy and brought her back with me.

We'd barely stepped into her front hall when Kitty jumped out at Seedy then ran off, his tail curved into a question mark. Seedy yipped and then hobbled off after him for a game of hide-and-seek.

"I love the way those two get along," I said, sitting down at Theda's kitchen table. "You'd think they were raised together."

Theda filled our cups with lemon mint tea, then sat down across from me. "Kitty is a special cat. I wish I could keep him. Sadly I go away for several months in the winter and have no way to take him with me. It's why I foster cats instead of owning them.

"But that's not why I invited you here, Abby. When

they pulled Dirk's body out of the pond, Kitty's collar was clutched in his hand. Now I have to go back to the police station with my attorney tomorrow, and I'm concerned."

I was so stunned I sat there for a minute before reason kicked in. "Wait a minute. How would they know it was Kitty's collar?"

"My name and contact information are on the ID tag."

That would do it. "Did you know his collar was missing?"

Seedy chose that moment to stop by my chair and whine to be picked up. "Go play," I said, but she ignored me and continued to paw my leg.

"Seedy, down," Theda said with a snap of her fingers. Amazingly, Seedy trotted off. "Yes, Kitty lost it weeks ago. I used to let him sit in the backyard with a nylon rope attached to his collar, similar to what you do with Seedy's leash, so he could do a bit of roaming. He loves to sit down by the pond and watch the carp swim.

"But one day Kitty tugged the rope free. He was gone for hours and when he finally showed up at the door, his collar was missing. That's why I use a harness on him now. I just can't figure out how that collar ended up in Dirk's hand."

"What did Dave Hammond say?"

"He told me to answer their questions truthfully but not to offer any additional information. Keep it short and sweet, he said. They've asked me to take a polygraph test, but I told Dave I wouldn't do it."

"But, Theda, think about it. A polygraph could clear your name."

Theda held out her hands, concern etched in her strong features. "Do you see how I'm shaking? I'm afraid I wouldn't pass because of my nerves."

A quick thought flashed in my mind: Was that her real reason for not wanting to take the test? Then I felt guilty and erased it. "Don't worry, Theda. We're getting closer to finding the killer. Just do what Dave tells you and trust that the real murderer will give herself—or himself—away soon."

La De Da Salon and Spa was in a strip mall on the east side of New Chapel, sandwiched between a Chipotle and a frozen yogurt shop. It hadn't been open long, and as empty as it was that evening, I wondered if it would last another month. There was only one other client, an older woman getting a cut and style.

A young woman was at the hot pink reception counter playing a game on her cell phone when I walked in. She wore a shiny black smock and had short purple hair. Her dark eyes were rimmed with heavy black liner. Her fingernails sported black polish.

With an expressionless face and a decidedly Russian accent she said, "Here for pedicure?"

"Yes, I'm Abby."

"I am Sonja. Come *wis* me."

I followed her through the ultramodern shop decorated in hot pink, glossy black, and lots of shiny chrome, to one of three pedicure chairs along the back wall. She instructed me to place my bare feet in a tub of frothing water then said, "Use remote on chair arm to control massage." Then she returned to the reception counter.

I played with the controls until I found a relaxing setting then leaned back to enjoy a massage while my feet soaked. When Sonja reappeared, I had to shake myself from the massage-induced coma so I could remember what questions to ask her.

Sonja sat on a low stool in front of my lounge chair and lifted my left foot out of the water to set it on the footrest and pat it dry with a towel. She didn't seem inclined to talk, so I jumped right in. "I may have told you on the phone, but my neighbor Mitzi Kole recommended you. She had high praise for your work."

Sanding the dry skin off my heel, Sonja said in a flat voice, "How nice."

"How long has Mitzi been your client?"

"We have been open four months. She comes here also four months."

"Only four months. Did she tell you about the tragic accident that happened in our neighborhood almost two weeks ago?"

"You mean man who drowned? Terrible."

"Yes, it was. It really shook Mitzi up. She couldn't even remember what time her appointment was that day,"

Sonja said nothing. The woman getting her hair done, as well as her stylist, had gone quiet, obviously listening in.

"Anyway, I thought I'd check for her."

Sonja had me switch feet then began to scrub my other heel. "What for Mitzi needs to know? She was here last week already."

"I guess the detectives investigating the case need to know. Do you have it written down in your appointment book?"

With a frown, she began to scrub my heel so hard I was afraid it would start to bleed. "I don't keep book. Owner keeps book."

I finally said, "Ouch," and pulled my foot away. "Is your owner nearby?"

Sonja shook her head. "She is already gone."

If the appointment book went home with the owner, how would Sonja know when her next appointment was? "When you think back to the Friday evening that Mitzi came in for a full spa treatment, was it after supper?"

The sullen stylist put my foot into the water, took out the other foot, dried it, and began to paint a coat of clear polish on my toenails, not looking at me at all. "Could be."

"Was it dark outside?"

"I don't remember."

"You're talking about Mitzi Kole, right?" said the other stylist, a young woman with a friendly smile.

"Yes."

"You have to remember that night, Sonja. Mitzi got here late and you were majorly annoyed because you wanted to leave early that evening for a date."

Sonja frowned harder and merely gave a shrug.

"What time did Mitzi finally get here?" I asked.

The young woman stopped using a curling iron on her client's hair. "Oh, gee, let me think. Maybe eight o'clock? It wasn't before eight. I'm sure of that. I was getting ready to leave when Mitzi showed up all apologetic and flustered."

"When you say *flustered*, what do you mean?"

The young woman thought for a moment. "Her clothes were kind of—I don't know—like she'd just thrown something on. That wasn't Mitzi."

"Were her clothes wet, or did they appear damp?"

The stylist looked puzzled. "I don't remember that—do you, Sonja?"

Sonja turned to glare at her coworker. "Her clothes were not wet, and we do not talk about clients behind their backs."

I ignored her to ask the other stylist, "Did Mitzi say why she was late?"

The other stylist looked uncomfortable and said in a subdued tone, "Not to me."

I didn't even bother with Sonja. She was clearly prepared to defend Mitzi no matter what. "Thanks," I said to the other stylist. "You've been very helpful."

"No problem," she said, and turned her attention back to her own customer.

Sonja finished my toenails in record time, mainly due to her not wasting a moment on conversation or doing a particularly neat job. Perhaps it was intentional so I wouldn't come back. I paid at the counter and left with the worst pedicure ever.

"Your toes don't look *that* bad," Marco said when I showed him the purple mess later that night. I was in bed reading, and he'd come over to check out my feet then went back to removing his work clothes.

"Yes, they look that bad, but it's not really about my toenails. It's about Sonja refusing to answer questions and Mitzi showing up late that Friday evening, flustered, and nervous. Eight o'clock, Marco, plenty of time for Mitzi to do her dirty work after the sun set and still keep her appointment at the salon. This is why she's my prime suspect. The puzzle pieces just keep fitting around her."

"I'm not saying you're wrong, Sunshine. I just don't think Mitzi has the courage to pull off a murder. I see her as all show, no go."

I didn't want to argue, but I did have to trust my instincts.

Marco sat on his side of the bed to remove his socks. "I'm more interested in this cat collar the police found.

The way I look at it, and undoubtedly the detectives do, too, Dirk was trying to show who his killer was."

"And that would be Kitty?"

"You know what I mean."

"No, I don't. If Dirk was knocked in the head hard enough for someone to get him into the water, how would he have the presence of mind to search for a way to identify his killer?"

"Maybe he came to."

"That's weak, Salvare, and you know it."

"Then how would you explain it?"

"The wind could've blown the collar into the water. Theda said Kitty liked to sit near the pond. Maybe Dirk was trying to grab onto something and snagged it from the bottom."

Marco got up to put his socks in the hamper. "It's a reasonable explanation, but you know as well as I do that the detectives and the prosecutor aren't going to look at it that way. They need to pin this murder on someone soon to keep the voting public happy. And I'm telling you, babe, that the cat collar combined with means, motive, and opportunity, and no way to verify her alibi makes Theda the perfect suspect.

"On top of that, her reaction to the polygraph test is unreasonable. An innocent person will always opt to take it. They cops will see that as another sign of her guilt."

He came back to sit on the bed. "I know you don't want to hear this, but maybe the detectives *are* looking at the right suspect."

"No, Marco. It's Mitzi. Every time I'm around her I can feel in my gut that she's guilty. And somehow I'm going to prove it."

CHAPTER NINETEEN

Thursday

Before Marco and I went our separate ways that morning, we made plans to do surveillance work on Maynard Dell after lunch. To make that happen, Marco was going to have to get Maynard's schedule from Hevyn so we'd know where to find him. To make *that* happen, he was going to wait outside the building inspector's office until Hevyn's coworker took her break, then swoop in and work the Salvare magic on our little helper angel.

Since a lot had to fall into place to make everything work, we came up with plan B: Stake out the Washtub Tap while Maynard was having lunch and follow him from there. The hitch in that plan was that it would eat up a lot of time, and I couldn't spare more than an hour away from Bloomers. So if we had to default to plan B, it would be Marco's alone. I wasn't overly concerned about it because I didn't believe Maynard was the killer. But we had to rule him out before we could move on.

When Seedy and I entered Bloomers just before eight o'clock, Grace, Lottie, and Rosa were buzzing excitedly about the upcoming flower show. Rosa had just learned her entry form had been accepted, just one day before the deadline on Friday. The show was one week away.

I celebrated with them over a blend of coffee Grace used only for special occasions. And all the while my brain was sending me messages: *Do it. Enter the contest. One day left. What are you waiting for? You have a great design.*

I did have a great design. What *was* I waiting for?

How about permission from my conscience?

They continued chatting, so I slipped off to the workroom to study my sketch. The more I envisioned it coming to life, the more my excitement grew, and the more my excitement grew, the more I wanted to make it. All it needed was the perfect container.

I swiveled my chair for a look at the shelves on the opposite wall and spied a tall glass cylinder etched with crosshatch marks just begging to be used for something unique. With river rocks at the bottom, curly willow branches spiraling out the top, and all-white blossoms of staggered heights, it would be an eye-catcher.

With excitement rippling through my body, I pulled up the form online and filled it out. And yet when it came time to hit *Enter*, I couldn't get myself to do it. How could I undermine Rosa's chance to win?

What would Lottie want for you? the little voice in my head whispered. *Wouldn't she tell you to go for it? Aren't two entries better than one?*

I heard the confab in the parlor break up and knew Rosa would appear shortly.

Now or never, Abby. Do it!

I held my breath and hit *Enter*. Now I'd have to let the others know and hope Rosa wouldn't be upset. I cleared the screen just as Rosa and Lottie came through the curtain still talking about the flower show.

"We can go together," Lottie said. "I'll pick you up on my way."

"How long will we be gone?" Rosa asked. "I need to let my mother know because she will be watching Petey."

"All day," Lottie said. "We can buy lunch at one of the food booths. That's what Abby and I did last year. You'll be home in time for dinner." She put her arm around Rosa. "We'll have so much fun. And I have a very strong feeling that you're gonna win."

"Do you really think so?" Rosa asked.

"I do, sweetie. I really do."

Rosa pressed her hands together. "How exciting! I've never won anything in my life. *Mi familia* will be so proud. But tell me what the contest is like. I'm nervous already."

I couldn't hear the rest of their conversation because of Rosa's words echoing in my mind: *I've never won anything in my life.* I plucked a ticket from the spindle and said nothing about what I'd done. As soon as I had some privacy, I'd contact the contest committee and quietly withdraw my entry.

I lived with my unhappy secret until Marco picked me up at two o'clock for our surveillance work. Thanks to Hevyn, we now had the address of a new subdivision not far down the road from Brandywine where Maynard Dell was supposed to be inspecting homes under construction. On our way there, I dug into the sandwich Marco brought me and was about to tell him about my contest gaffe when he surprised me with news about his mother's new boyfriend.

"Get this, Abby. Alfred's fourth wife filed a restraining order against him prior to their divorce."

It was the first bit of information that actually made me doubt my instincts about Francesca's beau. "What was the reason listed on the order?"

"A credible threat to her safety."

I swallowed a bite and wiped my mouth with a napkin. "Okay, before we jump to any conclusions, let's keep in mind that a restraining order is not uncommon in divorce actions. I remember from my days clerking for Dave Hammond that some lawyers file them automatically with their petitions for divorce."

"Automatic or not, Abby, this judge granted the woman's petition, so something Alfred did convinced him that a restraining order was necessary."

"What did the order state?"

"He was not to harass, annoy, telephone, contact, or communicate with his wife in any way and was to stay away from her residence and place of employment."

"That's standard language. I still wouldn't jump to any conclusions until I investigated it further."

"The order was filed out of state, which will make it more difficult to investigate. And on top of that, my mother was talking about taking a trip with Alfred to his cottage soon. Timing is everything, Abby."

"Then I guess you'll have to tell her what you found and let her decide what to do."

"Right. Like that plan worked the last time I tried to talk to her."

"I hope you're not going to ask me to tell her."

He patted my knee. "Don't worry. I have something else in mind."

"Are you going to share it with me?"

Marco made a left turn into a subdivision named Winding Creek Woods and pulled up in front of a house under construction. "I'm going to have a man-to-man talk with Alfred."

"Is that Army Ranger code for something I don't want to know?"

"It's exactly what I said, a man-to-man talk."

"Alfie will probably tell you to mind your own business. And I don't think your mom is going to be pleased when she finds out about this little chat, either."

"I'm not doing it to please my mom, Sunshine. I'm doing it to save her."

As its name suggested, the forested lots of Winding Creek Woods bordered a wide, curving creek with streets on each side connected by bridges at opposite ends, creating a long oval community. Only seven of the prospective forty houses had been completed, so we parked in front of the first in a line of houses still under construction and talked to a painter priming the front door. He informed us that the building inspector had been there early that morning to do a final walk-through.

"Did you see him perform the inspection?" Marco asked.

"No, sorry. I was outside the whole time."

"Do you know Maynard Dell personally?"

"I know who he is. I've been painting homes in New Chapel for twenty-five years. I knew the last two inspectors, too."

"Does Maynard do a good job of inspecting?" I asked.

The painter gave a shrug. "You'd have to ask the electrician or one of the plumbers or heating guys."

"Are any of them around?" Marco asked.

"Nope. Long gone."

"How long was Maynard here?"

"Ten, fifteen minutes. Usual amount of time."

"Fifteen minutes doesn't seem adequate to even check out the electrical wiring, let alone everything else," Marco said.

The man shrugged. "What can I say? Complain to the town council."

At the next house, we were told the same thing by a pair of trim carpenters. Maynard had been in early to inspect and had left his official tag verifying that the heating/cooling system, electrical, and plumbing were up to code. We went to five more houses in various stages of construction with similar results. Maynard had been there, performed his job in less than fifteen minutes, and left.

"If Maynard was telling the truth," I said, as we crossed the bridge to start up the other side of the subdivision, "then who's the liar, Dirk or Rye?"

"Either is possible, but keep in mind that we've only seen the houses inspected before noon. Do you see that white van up ahead with the New Chapel logo on it? I'm betting that it belongs to Maynard."

The van was parked in front of an excavated lot that had recently had its foundation poured, but when we pulled up behind it, we saw no sign of the building inspector. "Could he have climbed down inside?" I asked.

"Abby, look, the motor's running."

"Maybe he's in a hurry to finish and get out of here."

"I don't have a good feeling about this." Marco shut off the engine and opened the car door. "Stay here."

CHAPTER TWENTY

As Marco cautiously circled the vehicle, I got out my cell phone and prepared to dial 911 at his signal. He approached the driver's side, bent down to look inside the window, then reached inside. Then he pulled out his cell phone and snapped a photo before returning to the 'Vette.

"Is Maynard in the van?" I asked.

"Yes, and he's either napping or passed out. He had a steady pulse, but I couldn't rouse him." Marco showed me the photo. "See that silver object on the passenger seat? That's a hip flask with its cap off, and there's a strong odor of alcohol inside the van even with the window open."

"What should we do?"

"I'm going to take more photos. Then I'm going to wake him up."

Marco returned to the van, took more pictures, one with his watch to show the time, then stuck his phone in his pocket and rapped on the doorframe. "Maynard! Are you all right?"

It took several attempts before he got a response. Marco spoke to him briefly then returned to our car and started the engine.

"Are we done?" I asked.

"No, but I want Maynard to think so."

"Did he recognize you?"

"It took him a minute, but he did remember. He wasn't pleased to see me."

"Did you tell him why we're here?"

"Nope, but I have a feeling he figured it out. Keep your eye on him as I pull away."

I swiveled to watch out the back window as Marco turned the car around and drove off the way we came in.

"He's getting out of the van," I reported. "He's leaning against the side so he doesn't fall. It looks like he's watching us leave."

The street curved at the bridge so I lost sight of Maynard. Marco pulled off the road, got his phone out, and made a call to the Washtub Tap.

"As I thought," Marco said when he ended the call, "Maynard just finished a two-hour liquid lunch. And we have photos of the results of that lunch. If we need to interview Maynard again, the photos will make him much more inclined to be honest."

"We need to report him to the town council, Marco. That's unconscionable behavior."

"In good time. Let's catch a killer first and deal with Maynard later."

While heading back to town, my cell phone rang and Jillian's image popped up on the screen. "What's up?" I asked her.

"Have I got fantastic samples for you, Abs. Get excited, because your dream room is about to happen. I'll be there at seven o'clock tonight. Have the wine poured."

When I ended the call, I said, "Jillian's bringing living room samples over tonight. She says they're fantastic."

"And once again, damn! I'll be working."

"Don't look so pleased about it. I really appreciate all the time she's spending on us. I can't wait to see what she chose."

"You're letting her decide everything?"

"Why not? She knows our tastes."

"Did you tell her I like navy?"

"Yes, I did. And before you drop me off, have you heard from Jane Singletary?"

"Not a word. We're going to have to catch her at home this weekend so we can find out what her third vehicle is. We also need to investigate Rye's missing tools. Let's take a walk around the neighborhood during our lunch hour tomorrow and talk to some of the construction crew. I want to find out if tool theft is a common problem."

As he pulled up in front of Bloomers to let me off, I spotted Seedy in the bay window, wagging her tail eagerly. "Look, Marco. She knows the car."

"She's one smart pooch."

"You wouldn't believe how Seedy gets along with Theda's cat. They're best buddies now." I leaned over to give him a kiss. "Dinner at the bar tonight?"

"That depends."

"On what?"

"On how long it takes me to have that talk with Alfred. I'll text when I'm on my way back to Down the Hatch."

I opened the car door. "Good luck with that."

Marco only smiled.

Bloomers was so busy all afternoon, I never found time to call the director of the regional flower show to have my entry pulled. It wasn't until we closed for the day and my assistants had gone home that I finally had an opportunity. Unfortunately, my call went to voice mail, so I had to leave a message. To be doubly sure, I went online and got an e-mail address to send yet another message canceling my entry.

I felt much better afterward. Now no one would ever need to know.

Marco and I met at five thirty for dinner, with Seedy happily retiring to Marco's office for a nap. With all the traffic in and out of Bloomers that day, she'd had her fill of people. We ordered our entrees then sat in the booth with our drinks to talk.

"Tell me how it went with Alfred," I said.

"It went nowhere. First of all, he wouldn't agree to meet face-to-face, and when I told him over the phone what I'd learned about the restraining order, he basically said to mind my own business."

Exactly what I'd predicted.

"After that conversation I phoned my mom to tell *her* what I'd found out."

"Let me guess. She told you to mind your own business, too."

"Yep."

"At least she knows, Marco. You did what you could to warn her."

Marco merely took a drink of beer. The wheels in his brain were still turning. He wasn't finished with Alfred Donnerson yet.

Jillian arrived thirty minutes late that evening muttering about Claymore coming home an hour after he was supposed to, Harper being cranky, and Princess tearing up one of her sofa pillows. She was carrying a box loaded with fabric samples, sported a large burgundy patent leather tote bag over one shoulder, and, despite the turmoil at home, had excitement sparkling in her big golden eyes. Jillian was in *the decorating zone*.

"Wait till you see what I brought," she sang, dropping the box in the middle of my living room. She took off her plaid Burberry raincoat and tossed it over the back of the sofa then glanced around the room. "Where's the wine?"

"Coming up."

When I returned from the kitchen, Jillian had laid out three piles of samples on the floor and was sitting cross-legged in the middle of them, her iPad on her lap. She took the wine, drank a sip, then set it on the old black trunk we were using for a coffee table. She directed me to sit beside her, then began.

"In the first pile we have this ultramodern, very hip look that Marco will just adore. Here's the sofa fabric, and here's the armchair fabric, the throw pillow fabric, a piece of the area rug, and the wall paint sample."

It took less time to study it than to explain it. "It's all gray, Jillian. The area rug is gray, the sofa is gray, the side chairs are gray—"

"I beg your pardon. The *outsides* of the chairs may be gray, but the seat and back cushion fabric is a lively pattern of gray, yellow and white dots. And the area rug isn't solid gray. It's a gray-and-white wave. Gray is the new neutral, Abs."

"So what you're saying is that the bold yellow accent color I asked for is a few polka dots on the insides of the chairs—which don't look at all comfortable, by the way."

"They don't look comfortable because they have modern lines. That doesn't mean they *aren't* comfortable. And I beg to differ about your accent color. There's yellow in the throw pillows, too. See right here?"

I squinted at the pillow fabric. "You mean that thin squiggly line between the heavy gray squiggly line and the thick black squiggly line?"

"Don't wrinkle your nose until you see it put together." She scrolled through photos and showed me the finished product. In one word: bland.

I pointed to a tall object behind the dull gray sofa. "What's that?"

"Your orange lamp."

"That's a lamp?"

"It's a torchiere."

"Doesn't look like any torchieres I've ever seen."

"You wanted a modern look, Abby. This is a modern look."

"Not *that* modern." I reached for my glass. "What else do you have?"

Jillian set that pile aside and turned to another. "You've got to love this one. Here's your sofa fabric, your toss pillow fabric, and this is your chair fabric, which we'll also use for the roll-down window shades."

"Is this drab gold satin supposed to be my bright yellow accent color?"

"You can't use bright yellow on this kind of blue, Abs. But isn't this bold gray-and-white peacock pattern amazing for the armchairs? Look at the completed room." She showed me another photo on her tablet.

"Again, Jillian, they're gray. And now you've got gray covering my windows, too. And didn't I tell you I was opposed to a leather sofa?"

Jillian frowned at me. "You're being difficult."

"I know what I don't like, and I don't like a gray room or a leather sofa. Color and comfort, Jill. Remember?"

With a frustrated huff, she began to put the piles of fabric into the box.

"Don't you want to show me the third group?"

"No. You won't like it."

"Now you're pouting."

"You hurt my feelings."

"I'm not trying to hurt your feelings."

"Well, you did a good job of it."

"I'm sorry. I'll try to be more open-minded next time you come."

"Next time?" She sat back on her haunches. "No way am I doing this again. Either we work on it together *tonight* or I'm done. *Together*, Abby. I can't do it without you. No, make that I *won't* do it without you. So you decide. We work as a team or you live with"—she gestured toward the old furniture—"this."

"Fine."

"Fine."

We sat on the sofa with our wine, sipping silently, not looking at each other. Then I said, "I don't want to live with this old stuff. And my party is nine days away."

She set her glass down, turned her tablet back on, and began to scroll through a collection of living room sets on a design Web site.

"What are you doing?"

"I have an idea." She put the iPad in my hands. "Tell me what you like about this room."

I studied it for a moment. "The coffee table and end tables are nice. Modern but not too modern."

"Let's call them contemporary." She marked them and moved on. "This room?"

"The area rug is colorful, and I like the free-form design."

"Also contemporary." She marked it and moved on. We worked in this way for over an hour. Then she packed up her tablet and put on her raincoat. "See how easy it is when we work together? Now we'll schedule a day to go up to the Chicago Merchandise Mart and pick out your new living room suite."

Remembering how much trouble I'd had at the furniture store, I balked. "I don't have a whole day to spend in Chicago. Won't you do it for me, please?"

"What happened to our team spirit?"

"We're still a team. You just have to operate for both of us."

She scowled at me for a long moment then carried her box to the front door. "Fine. I'll do it on one condition. You have to accept whatever I choose."

My gaze landed on the ugly fabrics in her box. What if I hated her selection?

Reading my expression, Jillian shook her head in disgust. "You still don't have faith in my decisions. Thanks a lot, Abby."

"No, wait, Jillian. That's not true. I'll accept whatever you choose."

"Seriously?"

"Seriously."

She smiled. "It's a deal."

She kissed me on the cheek and stepped outside just as the rain started. As she hurried toward her car I thought of something and called, "Jillian! No gray, please."

She got inside and rolled down the window just long enough to say, "None that you'll notice."

A severe thunderstorm hit half an hour later, sending Seedy scampering for cover and me dashing to close the bedroom windows. As I locked the last one, I caught movement in Theda's backyard and saw what appeared to be a human shape moving toward the water's edge.

Afraid the person was up to no good, I ran for my cell phone to alert Theda. I knew she was home because I could see the flickering light from her television in her side window. But her phone rang four times and then went to voice mail, so I turned on my back patio light to see if I could tell what was going on. The figure had waded into the water and appeared to be digging in the reeds. At the blaze of light, the figure crouched down farther as though trying to be inconspicuous.

Hoping to scare whomever it was away, I opened the sliding glass door to yell out a warning just as Seedy appeared at my feet. When she began to bark, the figure crouched low, sloshed across the shallow end to the other side, and disappeared from view.

I phoned Marco immediately to tell him what I'd seen.

"You opened the sliding door? Abby, what were you thinking?"

"There's a good twenty yards between our house and the pond. If the person had started toward me, I had plenty of time to lock the door and drop the security bar."

"Do you see anyone out there now?"

I peered out the back window. "No."

"Good. Promise me that you won't take any more chances."

I had just hung up with Marco when I heard a noise coming from outside, but it wasn't in the back this time. I went to the side bedroom window and saw Theda, wearing a dark-colored coat, entering her house through her front door.

Surely that hadn't been her out in the water.

CHAPTER TWENTY-ONE

Friday

While we were having breakfast and making plans for the day, our doorbell rang and Marco went to answer it. Hearing Rye's voice, my curiosity prompted me to join my husband at the door.

"Morning, Mrs. Salvare," Rye said with his shy smile, twisting his baseball cap in his hands. "I was just saying I hope I'm not disturbing you so early, but I wanted you to know that I got my missing wrench back—if you still need to borrow it."

"Where did you find it?" I asked.

"I kinda hate to admit it—you know what they say about speaking ill of the dead—but since you asked, Dirk had it. His wife dropped it off here this morning. She said she found it among her husband's tools in the back of his truck."

"Did Dirk borrow it from you?" I asked.

"No, ma'am."

"How did Jane know it was yours?" Marco asked.

"I etched my name into the handle. It's hard to miss. Anyway, if you want to borrow it, I got it right out there." He hitched his thumb toward his pickup.

"Thanks, man," Marco said. "How soon would you need it back?"

"No rush. I bought a new one because I didn't think I'd ever see this one again."

"Perfect." Marco stepped outside and clapped him on the back. "Let's go get it."

When Marco returned, he was holding the jumbo wrench between his thumb and index finger at the very tip of the handle, which, as Rye had said, was etched with his name. Marco wrapped it carefully in newspaper and put it in a paper sack by the door.

"This is going to the police for testing. I just hope it hasn't been soaking in the pond all this time because any trace evidence could be gone."

"So it appears Dirk was also a tool thief," I said, rinsing off my plate at the sink.

Marco poured the last of the coffee into his cup. "Maybe, maybe not. I find it a little coincidental that right after you saw someone digging in the pond where Dirk was found, Rye showed up with the wrench."

"That's a *big* coincidence. But why would he bring Jane into the picture?"

"He can't very well say he pulled it out of the water. He wouldn't have known it was in the water unless he'd dropped it there. But if he says the widow brought it back, that adds another theft to Dirk's crimes and takes the heat off Rye—in his mind, at least."

Marco propped his foot on the barstool at the island. "Here's something else to consider. If it's true that Jane found the wrench in Dirk's truck bed, we need to know whether the police conducted a search of that truck. Because if they did, they'd undoubtedly have seen the wrench and confiscated it. Therefore how would Jane have it to give back unless she's been hiding it?"

"Why on earth would Jane bring Rye's wrench back if she'd used it to kill Dirk?"

"It gets the murder weapon out of her hands and into Rye's. She wouldn't know that he'd bring it straight to us. And don't forget the other possibility: that Rye planted the wrench in Dirk's truck after it was returned to Jane, and she just came across it. Remember, she told us the truck was parked behind the garage."

"Why wouldn't she give the wrench to the cops, then?"

"She could've assumed that whatever was left in the truck had been cleared."

"I see a fourth possibility, Marco: that the figure I spotted in the pond last night was Mitzi, and she planted Rye's wrench in Dirk's pickup to throw suspicion on Rye."

"Valid argument. And here's a counterargument. Theda was in the pond and she planted the wrench in Dirk's truck."

A sudden image of a shadowy figure in the pond and then Theda in her raincoat afterward ran through my mind, and I said halfheartedly, "That's ridiculous."

"Just as ridiculous as Mitzi planting it."

How could I argue otherwise without telling Marco what I'd seen?

"I'll give Lisa Wells a call and see what she'll tell me." Marco checked his watch. "It's almost eight. We've got to get you to Bloomers. Come on, Seedy. Let's put your leash on. We're going for a ride."

Business was brisk all morning, with a parlor full of customers, a spindle full of yellow slips, and more orders coming in every few minutes. We were so busy we skipped our midmorning break and worked straight through the noon hour as well.

I finally sent Rosa to lunch at one thirty and continued whittling down the orders while nibbling on peanuts. I wasn't complaining, however. Doing what I loved wasn't a burden; it was a joy, and I didn't mind one minute of it.

I was humming happily as I stowed a funeral spray in cooler number two when I heard Francesca Salvare call, "Abby?" I looked out to see her peering around the room as though checking for spies. She spotted me and said, "Is Marco here?"

I stepped out and shut the insulated door behind me. "Not unless he snuck in while I was in the cooler."

Marco's mom had on red dangling earrings, a red blouse beneath a black-and-white houndstooth jacket, flowing black slacks, and black ballet slippers. Giving me a kiss on both cheeks, she said, "*Bella*, how are you?

"I'm fine. Did you *want* to talk to Marco?"

"No." She put her black patent leather purse on the table and sat on a stool. "It's you I need to talk to, but in private, please."

"We're alone. Rosa is at lunch and Lottie is working up front."

"Good." She patted the stool beside her then took my hands in hers. "I have to tell you something very personal, but you must not breathe a word to Marco."

"Francesca, I really don't think you should be telling me—"

"I can't tell anyone else, Abby, and someone needs to know."

I was starting to feel apprehensive. "Are you okay?"

"More than okay." She squeezed my hands, her face

aglow with excitement. "I'm going away with Alfie on Sunday. He's taking me to his lake cottage."

In light of what Marco had learned about Alfred, I wasn't sure what to do. Should I add my own word of caution to Marco's or keep my mouth shut?

"Have I shocked you?"

I scoffed. "No, not at all!"

Francesca waited.

"Okay, to be honest, Marco told me about the restraining order Alfie's fourth wife took out, so I have to admit I'm a little concerned for your safety."

Francesca let go of my hands. "Let me tell you the other half of the story, which, if Marco had not been such a hothead, I would have told *him*. Alfie's fourth wife had a severe alcohol problem that she managed to hide until after they were married. Poor Alfie tried everything to help her get sober, and when his own health began to fail from the stress of living with her, he told her he wanted a divorce.

"This woman was so furious that she went to the police and accused him of hitting her. She claimed to be afraid he would hit her again, so the order was filed. What my son did not uncover in his investigation was that Alfred had to get a restraining order against *her* because after she was served the divorce papers, she tried to stab him and then made threatening calls to his office."

"Why didn't Alfie tell Marco that?"

Francesca picked up a stray rose petal and began to fold it. "Male pride, perhaps. He was shocked to find out that Marco was still investigating him."

"Francesca, Marco needs to know. He thinks Alfie is going to hurt you."

"Do you honestly believe that knowing about the

fourth wife's drinking will change Marco's mind?" She brushed the flower petal aside. "I know my son, *bella*, so please say nothing. I just want someone to know where I will be for the next few days, and you're the only one who has even tried to understand my side. My children seem to share the opinion that a massive influx of sex hormones has caused me to lose my mind."

That was way too much information.

She opened her purse and took out a tiny silver gift bag. "The lake cottage address is inside this bag, but it is *only* to be opened in case of an emergency. You must not reveal my plans or the address unless it becomes a dire necessity."

"I don't know, Francesca. You're asking me to keep a secret from my husband."

"Yes, I am, and do not forget he's also my son. I, his mother, am keeping this from him, too. But I give you my word that when I return, I will tell Marco everything, and then he will see that his worries are unfounded. Alfie is a good man, *bella*. Marco needs to trust that I know a good man from a bad one."

Francesca was going to go with or without my approval. At least if I agreed to help her, I would know where she was. With a nod of acceptance, I held out my hand.

"Do I have your promise?" she asked.

"Yes, as long as you keep your end of the bargain."

"I never go back on my word." She pressed the little bag in my hand. "Thank you, Abby. I knew I could count on you."

"*Hola,*" Rosa called, coming into the workroom.

"*Hola* and *arrivederci*, Rosa," Francesca said with a laugh. "I was just on my way out." At the curtain she turned to give me a wink, then, leaving a trail of light lemon scent in her wake, was gone.

Leaving me holding the bag.

Rosa, Lottie, and I finished the last three orders at seven o'clock that evening, exhausted, hungry, but glowing with satisfaction, all side effects of working in the floral business. When I finally sat down with Marco and Seedy in our booth at Down the Hatch, Marco had his beer and my red wine waiting along with a plate of our favorite appetizer—banana peppers stuffed with goat cheese and sausage, topped with marinara sauce.

"These are delicious," I said. "Thank you. I was starving. Tell me what's new."

"I met with Lisa Wells today, and she confirmed that Dirk's truck was thoroughly searched and anything resembling a weapon was sent for testing. She was happy to take Rye's wrench off my hands."

"Is she still focused on Theda?"

"Primarily." Marco finished his stuffed pepper and wiped his mouth. "As I suspected, the cat collar is a sticking point. But because of the wrench, she said she'd take a second look at the interviews she did with both Jane and Rye to look for any discrepancies. She's eliminated Brandon Thorne for the same reasons we did."

"I'm encouraged that she's willing to consider other suspects."

"You'll be happy to know she doesn't have any concrete evidence against Theda. It's all circumstantial at this point, but we know how that goes. If the DA wants to build a case against Theda, he will."

"At least you got Lisa thinking. Shall we order dinner?"

Marco motioned for Gert and we put in our orders, then sat back to enjoy our drinks. "Tell me what's new on your end," he said.

"We were crazy busy all day. I didn't even take a break for lunch. And then you'll never guess . . ." I stopped, realizing that I had nearly told him about his mom's visit. "Never mind. It wasn't important."

Marco said nothing, just studied me, so I dipped my finger in the leftover marinara sauce and stuck it in my mouth. "This is so good."

"Are you still having problems with Rosa?"

"Not today, why?"

"I thought you were about to tell me a Rosa story."

I really disliked keeping secrets from him. "I was going to say that we stayed an extra hour to finish, but I already told you that. I'm so tired I'm repeating myself."

Marco reached for my hand. "I'll be here late tonight, Sunshine, so after we finish dinner, go home and get a good night's rest."

If my conscience would let me.

Shortly before sunset as I was sacked out on the old sofa watching TV with Seedy, my doorbell rang. Seedy jumped off the sofa and squeezed beneath it as I tiptoed up the hallway to look through the peephole. There stood Spring, one of Reagan's book club members, with a pie in her hands.

"Oh, hi, Abby," she said when I opened the door. "I was beginning to think you weren't home."

"Sorry. I was half-asleep on the sofa." I held the door open. "Come in."

"I can't stay. I just wanted to drop this off." She stepped up to put a warm cherry pie in my hands. With her face close to mine, she whispered quickly, "The neighbors on the other side of Mitzi—the Reynoldses—have video surveillance of their front and back yards. Ask to see their tape from the night of the murder."

"What's on it?" I whispered back.

"So enjoy!" she said brightly. Casting a quick look around, she hurried away, her long braid swinging like a pendulum across her back.

"Thanks," I called. "We love cherry."

I was just about to shut the door when I saw the curtain in Theda's window drop. Was she the reason for Spring's caution?

CHAPTER TWENTY-TWO

Saturday

"Look who finally rolled out of bed, Seedy," Marco said, holding out a cup of coffee for me.

I patted the dog on the head, took the steaming cup, and sat at the kitchen island in my pajamas, still groggy from sleeping past my normal waking hour. "Thanks for letting me sleep in."

Marco poured himself some coffee and sat on a stool beside me. "I figured you needed it. You tossed and turned a lot last night."

"I had a nightmare."

Marco smiled. "That explains why you were muttering my mother's name."

I forced myself to smile with him even though the dream had been anything but funny: Francesca had been at the cottage, gagged and bound, while I desperately searched for the gift bag with the address in it so we could save her.

Where *had* I put the gift bag?

In your underwear drawer, Miss Memory, the little voice in my head whispered.

Nearly giddy with relief, I took a big drink of coffee

and scalded my throat. What I needed was one of Grace's quotes about soothing a guilty conscience, but the only saying that sprang to mind was *Liar, liar, pants on fire.*

Marco patted my shoulder. "I'm sure you had the dream because you're as concerned about her welfare as I am."

"Of course I'm concerned. I wouldn't want anything to happen to her."

That came out a lot sharper than I'd intended. Luckily, Marco didn't seem to notice. "I hope she took what I told her seriously," he said, "and doesn't entertain any thoughts of going to Alfred's cottage alone with him."

I suddenly couldn't swallow. Pushing my cup aside, I turned to face my husband. "Okay, Marco, I need to tell you something. Your mom came to see me yesterday."

And then in a case of perfect timing, one of Grace's quotes popped into my mind. I could even picture her delivering it, standing with fingers locked together, posture ramrod straight, and chin up. *As William Shakespeare wrote, "The better part of valour is discretion."*

In other words, I had to keep my promise to Francesca. The only thing I could do was give Marco something to chew on.

Marco swiveled the stool toward me. "What did she want?"

"Well . . . to tell me that she *did* take what you said to heart. She questioned Alfred about the restraining order. In a nutshell, he explained that his wife was a severe alcoholic, and when he filed for divorce, she went crazy and attacked him with a knife. He took out a restraining order, so she countered with her own. You can probably find it if you search. In fact, I hope you will."

"I've got a fellow private eye in Michigan working

on Alfred right now. For all we know, he made up the story to con my mom. It happens all the time to widows. They're easy prey."

I reached for my coffee again. There wasn't any point in arguing. Marco simply didn't want to believe anything good about Alfie.

He sat at the counter with his chin in his palm, thinking. "I'll bet she's still planning on going to the cottage with him, so we'll have to keep our eyes on her."

"Marco, it's her life. You have to trust her to know what to do."

"It's Alfred I don't trust."

"No, it's your mom you don't trust to make a smart decision."

"A woman in love doesn't think rationally."

"Wow. I can't believe you said that." I left him sitting there and went to get dressed.

Half an hour later, freshly showered, dressed, and groomed, I emerged from the bathroom to smell bacon frying. I walked into the kitchen and found my husband serving up a plate of eggs and turkey bacon, my favorite kind, with whole-grain toast on the side. He'd even buttered it.

He put it on the island and placed a fork and napkin beside it. "For you."

I waited with my arms folded.

Marco came over and put his arms around me. "As soon as the words were out of my mouth, I heard how rude it sounded. Forgive me. I never meant to imply that you ever thought irrationally. Please eat. I know you're hungry."

With an apology like that and a delicious plate of steaming hot eggs and crispy bacon in front of me, I couldn't stay angry. I sat down and dug in. "Your mom isn't irrational, either, Marco."

"Let's not argue about it. Enjoy your breakfast. I'm going to take Seedy to the park."

"Before you go, listen to this. One of the women from Reagan's book club came over yesterday evening to deliver a cherry pie."

"I wondered where that came from."

I glanced at the pie on the kitchen counter and saw a big slice missing. "Anyway, she wanted us to know that the Reynoldses, who live on the other side of Mitzi, have security cameras on their front and back yards."

"You're kidding. Pie *and* information. When Seedy and I get back from our walk, let's pay the Reynoldses a visit."

An hour later, Marco, Seedy, and I took a stroll down our street, where we spotted Mrs. Reynolds in front of her house watering her flower bed. She wore a blue visor in her permed gray hair, a sweatshirt that said *World's Best Grandma*, jeans, and white sneakers.

Marco handed me Seedy's leash. "Do your thing, babe."

"Let's go meet our neighbor, Seedy," I said loudly, causing the woman to look over. I waved and started across the lawn toward her, only to have Seedy balk and try to hide behind me, just as I'd expected.

"It's okay, sweetie," I said, crouching down. "This nice woman won't hurt you."

Mrs. Reynolds shut off the water and walked over to where I was petting my nervous mutt. "Oh, my! The poor little thing has some issues, doesn't she?"

Marco joined me as I rose, cradling my shivering dog in my arms. "Seedy was badly abused before we rescued her. She's getting better, but she has a way to go. I'm Abby, by the way, and this is my husband, Marco."

"Yes, I've heard all about you," Mrs. Reynolds said, shaking Marco's hand. "You're famous in this neighborhood. I'm Deloris Reynolds. My husband, Jim, is inside watching golf. Come on in and meet him. He loves dogs."

Marco and I exchanged glances. This was going exactly as planned.

An hour later we returned home with a plate of cookies and surveillance DVDs of the Reynoldses' front and back yards from the week Dirk was killed. The backyard camera angle, we were told, was wide enough to capture half of their neighbors' yards on each side of theirs. That meant we should be able to tell whether Mitzi left her house from her back door or was down by the pond that Friday evening.

"We're going to have to start refusing these desserts," Marco said as he put the backyard disk in our DVD player. "My jeans are a little snug."

"I'll give the cookies and the rest of the cherry pie to Lottie for her sons."

Marco was fast-forwarding through the footage, so it took a moment for my statement to register. "Maybe not the pie."

He stopped the recording when he saw the Friday time stamp. Then we sat on the floor in front of the television and watched the grass grow, literally, because nothing else was happening.

"There!" I pointed at the TV as Marco hit *Pause*. "Did you see that?"

He rewound the DVD so we could watch a small figure, barely visible in the dusk of the evening, hurry toward the pond then disappear from view. "Time stamp says seven o'clock," Marco said so I could note it.

He sped forward until the figure reappeared later and headed toward a house.

"Time stamp at seven fifty-three," Marco said.

I wrote it down then leaned back on my elbows. "Now do you believe Mitzi is the murderer?"

"It's not conclusive, Abby. She might have been leaving to go to her spa appointment."

"Come on, Marco. She's hardly going to walk there. It's clear across town."

"Maybe she was just going to another neighbor's house."

"Why don't you want to believe Mitzi is guilty?"

"All I'm saying is that it's still too circumstantial to make that judgment call. We need to confront Mitzi with this information and let her explain it." He checked his watch. "Let's give her a call to see if she's home."

"Do you have to come *today*?" Mitzi whined when I phoned her. "I'm trying to clean house. My husband is due back this evening."

"We won't take long. We just need you to verify something."

She let out a huff. "Fine. But come now. I need to get busy."

Ten minutes later we were seated on the white leather sofa in her living room with the DVD playing on her TV. Mitzi, wearing a short, colorful print dress and silver sandals that laced up her calves, sat on a navy chair adjacent to us. Marco held the remote control and, at the critical moments, paused the player so Mitzi could recognize the importance of what she was seeing.

As soon as she saw herself scurry up to her back door, cast a furtive glance around, and then dart inside, she stood up and began pointing her finger at us. "You tricked me! You're trying to accuse me of murder!" Then she burst into tears, covering her face with both hands as she sank into the chair. "I didn't kill Dirk. I didn't! I didn't!" She stamped her foot for emphasis.

"Then explain what you were doing heading toward the water around the time he was killed," Marco said.

Sniffling back tears, she wiped beneath her eyes with her fingertips. "I was on my way to my friend's house on the other side of the pond."

"Were you going to swim there?" I asked dryly.

She shot me a look of disgust. "Of course not. I circle the pond to get there. But I saw someone crouched down in the reeds and got scared, so I went another way."

Marco and I exchanged dubious glances, and then Marco asked, "Do you know who it was?"

She shook her head, rubbing her arms as though chilled. "It was getting dark, and I don't see well at night." She thought a moment, then said, "And his hood was up. He was wearing a gray hooded jacket."

"Was he facing toward or away from you?" Marco asked.

"I couldn't see his face, so away. Actually, he was looking down and his arms were in the water." Her eyes grew enormous and in a hushed voice she asked, "Do you think—I mean—is it possible I saw the *killer*?"

Cue the ominous music. I almost rolled my eyes. Mitzi's acting skills left a lot to be desired.

"Did you tell the police?" Marco asked.

She picked at her thumbnail. "I totally forgot about it until now."

"Didn't it raise your suspicions at the time to see someone crouched in the water at dusk?" I asked.

"Sometimes people go down there to fish. We've got a lot of fish in the pond."

"But you said he had his hands in the water," I said.

At Mitzi's blank look, I said, "So even after you heard that Dirk was killed that night around that time, you still didn't let the cops know what you'd seen."

She rubbed her forehead as though her head hurt. "I've got a lot on my plate. I was robbed. And betrayed. I just wanted to put it all out of my mind."

"How are you certain it was a man if you didn't see his face?" Marco asked.

"Because of his shape. You know, bulky."

"Could some of that bulk have been because of the sweatshirt?"

She shrugged.

"Did you notice anyone else with him?" Marco asked.

"No."

"When you returned, did you look to see if the man was still there?"

"He was gone."

"Did you notice any unfamiliar cars parked in front of your house that evening?"

"I wasn't paying attention."

"Why didn't you drive to your friend's house?" I asked.

Mitzi shrugged. "It seemed silly to use my car for such a short distance."

I wasn't buying it. A woman frightened by a strange man behind her house wouldn't risk walking alone at dark, even going in the opposite direction.

"We'll need your friend's name and contact information," I said.

She sprang up again, her hands at her waist. "I can't give you that information. You have no right to violate my friend's privacy."

"You're right, we don't," Marco said, "but the police do, so who would you rather have them talk to your friend?"

Mitzi began to pace in front of the fireplace, rubbing her forehead as though thinking hard. "Couldn't I just sign a statement saying that's where I was? We could have it notarized. Or I could take a lie detector test."

"Neither one of those will work," I said.

She began to pace again, wringing her hands. "I can't believe this is happening to me. My life is falling apart before my eyes, and all because of that idiot Dirk. What can I do to get you to believe me?"

"Provide us with indisputable proof of where you were between seven and eight that Friday night," Marco said.

She sat down on the edge of the chair and folded her hands beseechingly. "Look, you have to listen to me. If you go see my friend you'll absolutely destroy Sa . . ." She caught herself before she finished the name, and changed it to "her."

"All she has to do is swear you were there that night," I said.

"That's the problem. She *can't* swear to it." Mitzi picked at her thumbnail again. "She wasn't there."

"Were you alone in her house?" Marco asked.

"Not exactly," she muttered, moving to another fingernail.

The dawn broke. I glanced at Marco and saw by his

expression that he got it, too. "Were you there with her husband?" I asked.

Mitzi gave us a pitiful glance. "You won't tell anyone, will you? I've broken it off—I swear I have."

"We'll need to verify your alibi with your friend's husband," Marco said.

She began to pace again and finally said, "Then let me arrange it. I'll have him come down to the bar. Promise you won't do anything before I set it up, okay? Please?" She was almost on her knees before us.

I'd never expected to see Mitzi Kole grovel. Could it be that she was actually concerned about hurting her lover's wife?

"It has to be this evening," Marco said as we rose. "If he doesn't show up, we'll be at your door tomorrow whether your husband is home or not."

She threw her arms around him and then around me. "Thank you! Oh, thank you both! I swear he'll be there and then you'll have your proof."

As we walked up the sidewalk past Theda's house, I spotted our energetic neighbor digging a sickly looking rosebush out of the mulch around her front porch. When she saw us she put down her shovel and came over to talk.

"I hear you're hot on someone's trail," she said, removing her gardening gloves. "Deloris Reynolds told me you borrowed their surveillance recording."

Word certainly got around fast at Brandywine.

"We have to investigate every avenue," Marco said. "I see you replaced your garden shovel."

"I needed something a bit larger anyway." She pointed toward our house. "Look who's waiting for you."

Seedy was in the front window yipping soundlessly and wagging her tail.

"She needs to go out," Marco said. "I'll take care of it."

As he strode away, I asked Theda, "How did it go at the police station the other day?"

"Smoothly, but only because of my wonderful attorney, whom I can't thank you enough for recommending. After I'd explained my theory about the cat collar to Detective Wells, she began asking the same questions I'd answered twice before, so Dave, bless his heart, called a halt to the interview. He told her not to bother us unless she had something new to discuss."

Almost as though she found the situation droll, Theda added with a wry smile, "That young gal is just bristling with frustration because she can't find any hard evidence against me."

I smiled back, although I wasn't sure what she found so amusing. I hadn't seen anything to smile about when the detectives were pursuing me as their prime suspect.

"You're quiet, Sunshine," Marco said as we walked Seedy out to the park. "What's on your mind?"

I'd been mulling over how much Theda's offhand attitude concerned me, but I didn't want Marco to know that. "Just what we learned from Mitzi today."

"What did we learn?"

"That she's a poor actress, for one thing. Did you really believe her sudden recall of seeing a man crouched in the reeds? And that she conveniently forgot to tell the police? I think she just wanted to take the heat off herself by pointing a finger at Rye. She knows he wears a gray hooded jacket."

Seedy was tugging on her leash, wanting to romp with one of her canine buddies, so Marco crouched down to unsnap the lead from her collar. For a moment he just watched her play, then said, "So you don't believe it's possible Mitzi saw the killer? It was certainly the right time and location for it."

"Certainly it's possible, but given all the police attention, is it logical that she would just now remember it?"

"Not at all. But if her boyfriend can verify her alibi, then there's a high probability that Mitzi is telling the truth. So until we know otherwise, we need to take her claim seriously. And we have to consider that this hooded figure could be a woman."

"It would've had to be a fairly large woman. Mitzi said the person was bulky."

As soon as the words were out of my mouth, I knew exactly what Marco would say next, and he didn't prove me wrong. "Theda fits that description."

"I just don't believe Theda would kill someone over moss in her yard."

"Unless moss wasn't her only issue with Dirk."

I could tell by the tone of his voice that he had more information. "What aren't you telling me, Salvare?"

"Lisa Wells told me something in full confidence, and I'll share it, but you can't say a word to Theda."

"You know I won't."

At that moment Seedy came hobbling over, ready to go home. Running on three legs took more energy than four, so she tired more quickly than other dogs. So it wasn't until we were on our way home that Marco said, "Theda is alleging that Dirk drowned a cat she was fostering shortly after he started working at Brandywine.

That was the theory she presented to Lisa of how the cat collar came to be in the pond."

It wasn't the story she'd told me, but all I said was, "That's awful."

"According to Theda, the cat took an instant disliking to Dirk, hissing whenever he came around. At one point she saw him kick the cat and reported it to Thorne, which got back to Dirk. There was strong animosity between her and Dirk after that."

"Poor Theda, to lose a cat in such a horrible fashion. She loves her cats."

"Yes, Abby. She does." Marco said nothing more, but he had me doubting my gut again, because Theda's motive had just gotten a whole lot stronger. The unfortunate result was that my reason for investigating had changed. Now I just wanted to make sure we didn't have a murderer in the neighborhood.

To get my mind off Theda, I asked, "Are we going to reinterview Rye?"

"I'd like to talk to Mitzi's boyfriend first."

"Are you sure you'll be able to trust anything he says? I'm sure she'll coach him."

"Yes, she probably will, so we'll have to play up his being a good citizen to help us catch a killer."

"You know who I feel sorry for? The man's wife. She probably believes Mitzi is a good friend. But Mitzi will cheat on anyone, including her girlfriends."

As we stepped into our house, with Seedy hobbling ahead of us, I asked, "Did you ever connect with Jane Singletary about Dirk's photos?"

"She never called back. It's early yet, so let's take a drive over to see her. And after that, we can canvass Rye's neighbors to see if we can find an alibi witness."

CHAPTER TWENTY-THREE

The dark clouds arrived after all, bringing with them a heavy rain just as we reached Jane Singletary's neighborhood. Because we were in my yellow car, we had to park around the corner from Jane's house so we could catch her by surprise, which meant Marco and I had to share the small yellow travel umbrella I kept under the seat.

"I can't get the umbrella any lower, Abby. It's hitting the top of my head now."

"Half of me is getting drenched."

He put the handle in my hand. "Take it. I'll be fine."

Didn't have to tell me twice. I tilted it down to keep the driving rain off my face, while Marco pulled the collar of his jacket up, huddling into it like a turtle.

"If we had an inconspicuous car, like, say, a gray Prius," I said, "we could park close."

Marco didn't reply, but I saw a muscle twitch in his jaw. He rang Jane's doorbell, and I heard one of her sons call, "I'll get it, Mom."

Her youngest son swung the front door open just as Jane came up behind him, smiling. She saw us and immediately scowled. "Go back to the kitchen," she told her son, then said to us through the screen door, "What do you want?" She sounded impatient.

"We're following up on the photos you were going to look for," Marco said.

"Oh." She unlocked the screen door and opened it. "I forgot about that. I did find some. Come in while I'll get them."

Moments later Jane came back with a manila envelope. "I could find only a few that he took at Brandywine. The quality isn't great, but it's the best I could do."

"Thanks," I said, tucking the envelope into my purse.

"Rye told us you found his wrench in your husband's truck," Marco said. "He was glad to get it back."

Jane lifted one shoulder carelessly. "I guess it's the least I could do since my husband apparently stole it from him."

"I'm amazed the police didn't keep it for evidence," Marco said.

"All I know is that it was lying in the truck bed when I went to clean it out."

Marco's phone beeped, so he said, "Excuse me," and stepped away.

"If you know anyone who needs a brand-new truck," Jane said to me, "I just put the Tundra up for sale."

"Are you selling your other vehicle, too?" I asked.

"Not my CR-V, but I'm sure I'll sell the Prius. I don't need it."

Number one, she didn't have a black Ford. Number two, was the universe answering my prayer? "We had a Prius," I told her, as Marco rejoined us. "It was a great car." To Marco I said, "Jane is selling her third car, a Prius."

Marco didn't comment.

"I've never even driven it," Jane said. "Dirk bought it a few months ago, but I prefer my Honda."

"How much are you asking for it?" I asked, ignoring Marco's disgruntled glance.

"I haven't figure that out yet. Are you interested?"

"We might be. What color is it?"

"Navy. I can let you know when I have a price."

The rain had subsided when we left, leaving a strong fishy smell in the air. "I think we can eliminate Jane," I said. "She doesn't own a black Ford."

"I caught that."

"Are you really not interested in her Prius?"

"Really not interested."

"Aren't you even a little curious to find out what she's asking for it?"

"We'll get a new car, Abby, don't worry."

"Sorry for asking."

He took my hand. "I didn't mean to snap at you. I'm just a little distracted. I've been trying to reach my mom all day, and she hasn't returned my calls or texts. She's not answering Rafe's calls, either."

"Is that who called?"

"Yes. He's concerned now, too."

"Maybe she's out shopping and left her phone at home."

Marco merely grunted. As he unlocked the Corvette, I tried not to think about any other possibility, such as that something bad had happened at Alfie's lake cottage, but of course now my brain seized upon it and refused to let go. "I'll try texting her. She might be simply avoiding both of you."

I dug for my phone but Jane's envelope of photos was in my way, so I stuck it between the seats. Then I took out my phone and sent a text message to Francesca.

Ten minutes later we'd reached Rye's street and still had no response from Francesca.

"Something's wrong," Marco said, pulling up to the curb. "I'm going to call my guy on the ground in Michigan to see if he's learned anything new."

Marco dialed his buddy's number and waited while it rang, but the call went to voice mail. He left a detailed message and then turned the car around and headed home. "Let's leave this for another day. I'm too distracted."

Seedy was waiting for us at the door, so I took her outside while Marco paced through the house again, trying to reach his colleague. When I returned, Marco had put his phone on the kitchen island with its speaker turned on so I could hear. Because of a bad connection, he was leaning in, trying to make out what his friend was saying.

"Stuart keeps cutting out," Marco said quietly. "The big storm we had is now moving across lower Michigan."

A burst of static made us both jump. Then we heard, "You still there, Mar—" And then there was another long interruption before we heard, ". . . not going to believe . . . found out . . . Donnerson is . . ."

For a long moment all we could hear was crackling, and then Stuart called out, "Did you get that?"

"No. Repeat it, please," Marco said.

". . . said Donnerson is . . . serial kil . . ."

"What?" Marco shouted. "Stuart, repeat that!"

More static filled the air. Marco turned to me. "Did he say *serial killer*? Is that what you heard?"

My heart was pounding so hard I could barely breathe. Had I let Francesca drive away with a killer? Was my nightmare coming true? "We must have heard wrong, Marco. The connection was terrible." *Please, God, let that be it.*

"Stuart!" Marco shook his phone in frustration. "Damn it, Abby, what if that's exactly what he said? Stuart, come in, please!"

After more crackling, the line went dead.

Marco began to scroll through his phone contacts. "I'll call Gina. Mom might have told her where she was going today."

That would put his sister in a panic. "Don't do that. I know where your mom is."

Ignoring Marco's stunned look, I ran to the bedroom, grabbed the silver bag, and hurried back. I removed the envelope, but before I could get it open Marco snatched it and ripped the top off, pulling out the memo inside. "This is a Michigan address."

"It's Alfie's cottage. Your mom made me swear not to tell you unless it was a dire emergency."

"I'd say this qualifies." He grabbed the car keys. "I'm going up there."

"Wait, Marco! I want to go. Let me take Seedy over to Theda's."

I grabbed Seedy's leash, scooped her up, and ran through the garage, across our yards, and pounded on Theda's door. When she opened it, I said, "Would you watch Seedy? We have an emergency with Marco's mom and—"

She opened her door and took the dog. "Don't waste time explaining. Go!"

"Thank you!" I called, just as Marco backed out the 'Vette.

I jumped in and we took off.

"Let's try to think this through rationally," I said, my fingers tucked under my armpits in a futile attempt to keep my hands from shaking. "If Alfie is a serial killer, wouldn't all his wives be dead? Wouldn't Stuart have phoned the local police to tell them what he discovered?"

"Maybe he did phone them, Abby. I'm still going up there."

I fell silent but my mind continued to race. *Please let Francesca be okay,* I prayed.

It was the longest and worst hour-and-a-half ride of my life. I couldn't begin to imagine what Marco was feeling inside. I hoped he wasn't thinking it was all my fault, because I sure was.

"This can't be the right place," Marco said. "The GPS must be wrong."

We were sitting in front of two massive wrought iron gates that separated us from an enormous three-story pink brick house with a lake behind it. Could this mansion possibly belong to Alfie or had he purposely given Francesca a bad address so we couldn't find her?

"There's a big *D* on the gate, Marco. *D* for *Donnerson.*"

"I see it. His name came up when I did a search on this address, too. I just don't believe it." He pulled the Corvette off to one side and got out of the car. "In any case, I'm not leaving here until I know whether my mom is inside."

We followed the wrought iron fence around a huge expanse of lawn to the back, where a lower stone fence enclosed a spacious white brick patio that held a seating area, fire pit, hot tub, and a magnificent infinity pool that went right up to the lake. Marco helped me up onto the flat stone top and then we jumped down into the courtyard. From there we crept up to the expanse of windows along the back of the house.

Staying low to the ground, Marco peeked in the first window, cupping his hands around his eyes, then moved on down the line until he came to a set of French doors, where he again cupped his eyes to stare inside. "No sign of anyone."

Trying both handles, he found the doors unlocked, so he opened one side and stepped in. He paused to listen then motioned for me to follow. I slipped through the open door and glanced around in awe. I was standing in a massive family room that had white marble floors covered with luxurious Oriental carpets and two separate living areas separated by a dual-sided stone fireplace.

"I think you were right, Marco. This can't be Alfie's house. We're breaking and entering an innocent person's home. We'd better leave before we get into big trouble."

He picked up a black patent leather handbag lying on a table. "Recognize this?"

It was Francesca's. The blood drained out of my head so rapidly I had to lean against a wall.

Marco held his index finger to his lips, warning me to be quiet, then moved soundlessly across the vast room heading toward a wide doorway. I followed behind, glancing over my shoulder at the door we'd left open, my internal radar on full alert.

When we reached the doorway, he peered around it then motioned for me to take a look. I moved to his side and saw a kitchen so enormous, a cooking show could have been produced there. He pointed to an object on the white countertop, and my stomach roiled. There, lying next to a gigantic stainless steel sink, was a bloody butcher knife.

I heard a person whistling in the distance and we both stepped back.

"Get ready to dial nine-one-one and stay out of sight," he whispered. And then he was down, moving toward the kitchen island as stealthily as a panther.

I stood on the other side of the doorway, unable to see what was happening, my heart beating so hard I thought it would break ribs. What if this *was* Alfie's house? What if he *had* been lying to Marco and Francesca this whole time? What if even now Marco's mom lay dead somewhere? How would I ever live with myself?

The whistling person was closer now, and then I heard the slap of bare feet on the marble floor. My fingers were trembling so hard against the phone's touch pad I feared I wouldn't be able to press the right buttons.

A refrigerator door opened on the other side of the wall. I closed my eyes and held my breath, afraid I'd give myself away. For a moment there was complete silence. Then I heard a surprised grunt and scuffling, and then Alfie Donnerson cried out, "Let me go! Help! Someone, help!"

A huge wave of relief washed over me. Marco had him.

I hurried into the kitchen to see Marco with one arm around Alfie's neck, the other pinning Alfie's arm behind his back, causing the unfortunate man's satin maroon lounging robe to come loose at the waist. I dropped my gaze to his hairy legs and bare feet, afraid to look up.

"Tell me where my mother is," Marco ground out.

"Ow! You're hurting me," Alfie gasped, tugging at Marco's arm. "Let me go. Abby, make him let me go! I can explain."

"Right. Abby, phone the police."

"Wait!" Alfie called. "Don't do that. You'll regret it."

Marco loosened his hold on Alfie's neck, but pulled the man's arm higher up his back. "Where is she?"

"*Ow!* Son, you've got to let me talk."

"I'm not your son," Marco said through gritted teeth. "Tell me what you did to my mother or I promise this won't end well."

Alfie stunned me by letting out a bark of laughter then immediately winced when Marco tightened his hold. "You find this funny, Alfred?"

"Not at all, but you're right. This isn't going to end well unless you let me explain."

Marco pulled him over to a kitchen chair and sat him down. "Abby, find something to tie his wrists."

"You're going to tie my wrists?" Alfie said, as I hunted through a kitchen drawer. "Now you're really scaring me. What are you planning to do to me?"

Marco kept both hands on Alfie's shoulders and had me use the cord from an electric mixer to bind his wrists. "I need to hear just one word come out of your mouth, Alfie. Is my mother safe? Yes or no?"

"Have you lost your mind?" Alfie cried as I tied the cord to the chair leg.

"Don't play innocent. I had a local investigator check you out. So we know all about your *proclivities*, Alfred Donnerson."

"Look, I never claimed to be innocent, and I'm not exactly sure what you mean by *proclivities*, but I can assure you I have the same needs as any normal man. And to answer your question, your mother is upstairs, but I'm warning you, don't go up there."

"Keep your eye on him, Abby. I'm going to find my mother."

"Marco, stop," Alfie pleaded. "If you do that, this will end badly for *everyone*."

"Nice try," Marco said.

"Okay, okay," Alfie said. "You don't trust me. I get it. At least take me upstairs with you."

Marco eyed Alfie for a second then untied the cord from the chair leg and pulled him to his feet. "If anything has happened to my mother," he said, pushing him up the hallway, "you will pay."

"Son, if I had any idea to what lengths you would go to protect your mother I would never have brought her up here."

He led us up a massive curving staircase at the front of the house, then up a second staircase to a set of double doors on the third floor. Alfie reached for the door latches, but Marco stopped him. "What's on the other side?"

"I believe it's the answer to what your friend meant by *my proclivities*."

Marco grabbed Alfie's arm. "I don't know what kind of sick game you're playing, but we're not falling for it. Abby, it's time to bring in the cops."

"No, Abby," Alfie said firmly. "Both of you take a look at my collection first. Then if you want to call the cops, go ahead."

A scene from *The Silence of the Lambs* sprang into my mind, and I wrinkled my nose in disgust. "You turned them into a collection?"

"I have a whole floor dedicated to them," Alfie said with some pride.

Marco and I exchanged horrified glances, and then Marco gestured toward the doors. "Open them slowly. Abby, move back."

I slid behind Marco as Alfie used both hands on the latches and gave them a shove. "This," he said expansively, as the doors swung open, "is my collection."

A feeling of dread washed over me as I peered around

Marco into a room that seemed to take up the entire third floor. Glass display cases lined the walls and freestanding cases filled much of the floor space. I followed Marco into the room, gazing around in shock. Every case contained the same thing, and it wasn't at all what I was expecting.

"Oh," I said to Marco on a long breath. "*Cereal collector*, not *serial killer*."

There must have been hundreds of cereal boxes, some old and faded, some bright and shiny, with cartoon characters on them I hadn't seen since I was small. There was even a display of toy prizes that came inside.

My eyes met Marco's. He was as stunned as I was.

"This is my museum," Alfie said proudly as Marco untied the cord around his wrists. "I owned a cereal company before I retired. I got interested in the boxes after I found some of the original ones from the nineteen fifties in a warehouse. So I started collecting them over the years, and somehow it turned into this."

He gestured around the room as though giving a guided tour, not as though he'd nearly been hauled off to jail for murder. "Magnificent, isn't it?"

"You still haven't told me where my mother is," Marco said.

Alfie blushed to the tips of his scraggly hair. "She should be getting out of the shower about now."

I exchanged a chagrined glance with Marco and then I rushed forward to grab the poor man's hands. "We are so deeply sorry, Alfie. We had a bad phone connection with Marco's PI friend and completely misunderstood what he was trying to tell us. Then we couldn't reach Francesca and feared the worst."

"I am truly sorry," Marco said humbly. "This isn't how I normally operate. But it was my mom, so—"

At the sound of a throat being cleared all three of us turned to see Francesca leaning against the doorframe, her hair still wet. She was wearing a red satin robe with a black sash and black lace trim, and little black mules with red fur trim. Her arms were folded and her eyes blazed with fury, the very image of righteous indignation.

"Here's our Franny now," Alfie said uncertainly.

"Mom," Marco began, "I'm . . ."

She turned on her heel and left.

I chortled nearly all the way home, my laughter like a steam valve releasing the pent-up stress on my overtaxed nerves. Marco, by contrast, stayed stone silent, that little muscle in his jaw twitching, clearly not enjoying my mirth. I tried to quiet myself for his benefit, but then I'd replay a scene in my mind and start giggling all over again.

The bloody knife on the counter (Alfie had carved a roast into steaks for a romantic dinner); Alfie with his hairy legs hanging out of his untidy maroon robe, his hands bound with a white electrical cord, his thinning hair in disarray, looking like anything but a serial killer; Alfie proudly showing us hundreds of cardboard cereal boxes and offering to tell us each one's history if we'd like to stay.

Alfred Donnerson truly was a kind—and very forgiving—man. No hard feelings, he'd told Marco. But we never saw Francesca after that one furious moment.

It wasn't until we'd pulled into the garage and Marco had shut off the engine that he finally said something.

"We will never speak of this again."

That started me laughing all over again.

CHAPTER TWENTY-FOUR

Marco and I sat at the Down the Hatch for over two hours that evening waiting for Mitzi's boyfriend to show. Maybe Mitzi was playing us, I said to Marco, or maybe she was stalling for time. But time to do what? Run? I finally called it a night and took Seedy home, leaving my husband to his bartending duties. It had been a long, emotionally taxing day. We decided to deal with Mitzi in the morning.

At home, I changed into pajamas and a robe and had just settled in to watch a mystery on the Hallmark Channel when Seedy began to paw at the sliding door in the dining room, wanting to go into the backyard. I turned on the patio porch light then stepped outside with her and waited while she took care of her business. As she sniffed out a spot at the bottom of the yard, her head suddenly came up and she stared fixedly toward the pond.

"What is it, Seedy? What do you see?" I called as though she could give me an answer.

Suddenly she went on alert, bracing her legs as though prepared for an attack. I searched the area with my eyes but didn't see anything move. Was it a snake? A muskrat? Or something on two legs? Whatever it was, it made Seedy whirl around and hobble as fast as she could back to the house.

I opened the door to let her in then quickly jumped in after her and shut the screen and sliding door, dropping the steel bar into place. Thoroughly spooked, I pulled the curtain and headed to the kitchen to calm my jitters with a cup of chamomile tea, while Seedy leaped onto the sofa and circled in her favorite spot, preparing for a nap.

"Enjoy it while you can," I called. "You won't be sitting on the new one."

As I leaned against the kitchen counter waiting for the kettle to heat, I jumped at a sudden tapping on the sliding glass door. Seedy immediately lifted her head, her big butterfly ears forward as she stared at the door. Then she hopped down from the sofa and wriggled underneath.

The tapping got louder and more frantic.

Holding my phone in one hand, I tiptoed to the door and moved the curtain aside a fraction of an inch. There stood Mitzi, shivering in a sleeveless dress, glancing over both shoulders as though afraid of being seen. She didn't have a purse or jacket with her, as though she'd just darted across our backyards on a whim.

"Abby?" she called. "Abby, Marco, are you there? I need to talk to you."

I blew out the breath I'd been holding and opened the curtain.

"Oh, thank God," she said, and then stood there as though expecting me to let her inside. But did I trust her enough to be alone with her in my house?

"What do you want, Mitzi?"

She rubbed her upper arms. "I need to explain what happened tonight."

"Go ahead," I called.

"Seriously? You're going to make me stand out here?" She shivered.

I debated for a moment. Would she really try to hurt me? She didn't know whether Marco was home. I finally lifted the security bar, keeping it in one hand, and slid both doors back. She stepped inside, eyed the piece of steel in my hand, then glanced around the room. "Isn't Marco here?"

"He's still waiting for your boyfriend at Down the Hatch."

"I was afraid of that." Mitzi glanced past me. "Your teapot is about to whistle."

I headed toward the kitchen and she followed. I propped the bar against the cabinets, turned off the burner, and then waited, my arms folded, my hip against the counter.

"So," she said with a wry twist of her lips, "no tea for Mitzi. I guess I'm persona non grata now."

"What did you expect? We waited for your boyfriend to show all evening."

She traced the pattern in the granite countertop. "His wife had plans. He couldn't get away."

"Right."

"I'm serious, Abby. He couldn't get away without tipping his hand. Don't you think I *want* him to clear my name?"

"I don't know what to think at this point."

"Then think this. Mitzi knows she's in hot water and will do everything she can to set up another meeting."

"When?"

"Tomorrow evening. I swear he'll be there at Down the Hatch."

"The bar is closed on Sunday, and Sunday evenings are bad for us anyway. We have family commitments. How about in the afternoon, right here?"

She looked doubtful. "I'll have to check with him."

"Marco is not a patient man, Mitzi. If your friend doesn't show up tomorrow afternoon, we'll go to the detectives with our information and they'll haul him in for questioning. I'm sure his wife won't like that one bit."

"Fine. Tomorrow afternoon. I'll find a way to make it happen."

I walked across the kitchen and through the dining room to the sliding door. "We'll be waiting for your call." I opened the slider and waited. She stared at me for a moment then turned and marched out into the night.

Sunday

"You *are* coming to dinner this evening," my mom said to us after church. "I'm making something special. Everyone will be there." She nodded toward the group around us.

All of the Knights—my parents, brothers, sisters-in-law, and niece—had gathered outside the sanctuary after the service, as was our habit. My sisters-in-law were deep in conversation about fashion and my brothers were sipping the coffee that was provided between services, discussing sports. Tara was checking her phone for messages.

"What's the occasion?" Marco asked.

"You'll have to wait and see," Mom said with a smile, patting his arm.

"Hey, you two," my dad said, rolling up in his wheelchair, "we've got a great meal planned for tonight. Rosa and her son are coming."

And there was the occasion.

"Awesome," Tara said, and gave my mom a high five, her gaze never leaving the phone's screen.

"What can we bring?" Marco asked.

My mom tweaked my chin. "Some enthusiasm, I hope."

As we got into the Corvette to head home, I said, "I'd really like to skip the family dinner tonight."

"Then you should've spoken up."

"And say what? *We'll pass—thanks. I see enough of Rosa all week*? I know my mom. She'd be hurt, and I don't want that."

"You don't think the frown you gave her hurt her feelings?"

"Was I that obvious?"

"Sunshine, you wear your emotions on your sleeve. If you don't want to go, we should stay home. Pretending to enjoy yourself this evening isn't going to make anyone's day brighter."

I sighed. He was right. All the same, if I didn't show up, Mom would take it as a snub and so would Rosa. And that wouldn't make anyone's day at Bloomers brighter, either.

That afternoon, Marco and I planted pink, purple, and white sweet peas in six white ceramic pineapple-shaped pots and lined them along our front walk. Then we sat on the porch swing with glasses of iced tea, Seedy snuggled in beside Marco, waiting for Mitzi to call.

"I'll bet her boyfriend is a no-show," I said. "Watch. She'll have another excuse."

"It's early yet. Let's give her the benefit of the doubt."

He was always giving Mitzi the benefit of the doubt.

Half an hour later, we were still swinging lazily back and forth when I spotted Theda striding up the street in a zip-front white hooded sweatshirt, gray sweatpants, and lilac sneakers. She waved to us, used her remote to open her garage door, and then disappeared inside. Five minutes later she stepped out onto her front porch with Kitty in her arms.

She put the harnessed cat down in the grass and tied the rope to the porch column, then started toward us, calling, "Have you heard the news? Mitzi's been in a car accident."

"Is it serious?" I called.

"I don't think so," Theda said, coming up to the porch. "Just a fender bender, from what I gathered, but she insisted on being taken to the ER anyway."

"I told you Mitzi would find another excuse," I whispered to Marco.

"Where did the accident happen?" Marco asked, ignoring me.

"In front of the Burnses' house on the other side of the pond. And under very odd circumstances, I might add. You may remember Sarah Burns, Abby. She's one of Mitzi's Bees. Apparently Sarah rammed Mitzi's Jaguar after she came home unexpectedly and discovered Mitzi there with Tom. Mitzi phoned the police and Sarah was arrested."

My shocked gaze met Marco's. *Sarah's* husband was Mitzi's boyfriend?

"How did you hear about the accident?" Marco asked.

"I was out for a walk and stopped to visit with Sarah Burns's next-door neighbor. This woman's a chatty sort, so I'm sure the news will be all over Brandywine by morning."

Kitty began to meow plaintively and strain at the end of his rope, twisting as though trying to get out of his harness so he could reach us. "I think he wants to come play with Seedy," Theda said.

As though she understood, Seedy hobbled down the porch steps and across both yards until she reached the Russian Blue. Kitty butted his head against Seedy and then the two began to romp like puppies. "I swear Kitty is more dog than cat," Theda said.

"Any luck finding him a home?" I asked.

"Not yet. He's not a kitten, and unfortunately, adult cats are hard to place."

"I hate to interrupt," Marco said, patting my knee, "but we need to get some errands done before we have to be at your folks' house for dinner."

Theda smiled, watching the two play together. "Why don't you leave Seedy with me? Then they can continue to enjoy their playtime."

"Are you sure you don't mind?" I asked, handing her Seedy's leash.

"I'll be outside doing yard work anyway. If I do go in, they'll come with me."

"What errands are you talking about?" I asked Marco when we were back inside.

"We're going to visit Mitzi at the hospital."

I called my best friend and former roommate Nikki, an X-ray tech at the hospital, and asked her to find out Mitzi's status. She reported back in a whisper that she'd just finished doing a series of X-rays on her and that Mitzi had just been admitted and was being taken to a private room.

"Is she that badly injured?" I asked.

"You know, I'm not supposed to be telling you this, but I'm betting it's nothing more than a case of whiplash," Nikki said. "I sure didn't see anything broken on the X-rays. In fact, the doctor on call wanted to release her with a neck brace, but your neighbor caused such a commotion, claiming she'd sue if anything happened while she was home alone, that he finally admitted her."

"Was anyone with Mitzi?"

"Not that I saw."

"Can you get us in to see her?"

"Tell me what time you'll be here."

For a woman who was supposedly injured, Mitzi looked amazing cheery—until she saw me peering around the corner at her. Wearing a blue print hospital gown, she had the bed in an upright position and the television on the wall tuned to a shopping channel. The moment she spotted me, however, she clicked it off and placed one hand on the white neck brace at her throat, the other on her forehead, her face screwed up as though in excruciating pain.

"You've heard the news already?" she asked in a scratchy voice as Marco and I came up to her bedside.

"Theda told us," Marco said.

"Of course she would," Mitzi rasped. "This is all her fault, you know."

"Tell us what happened," Marco said.

Mitzi swallowed several times then whispered, "I was on Emmett Lane, the street on the other side of the pond, when my phone rang. I pulled over to answer it and suddenly, *bam!* Sarah Burns drove straight into my rear bumper."

"Didn't she see that you'd stopped?" I asked.

"Of course she did. This was no accident, Abby. She rammed me three times." Mitzi put both hands on her brace. "My poor neck! The doctor says I have a terrible spinal injury, one of the worst cases he's seen in years. I can't even feel my toes. I'll probably have to spend months in rehab. I could've been paralyzed!"

"Why would Sarah ram your car?" I asked. "I thought you were friends."

"*Best* friends, Abby," Mitzi said in a hurt voice, "but who knows with Sarah? She can be mean. She's very unstable. She's been treated for depression before. I have my suspicions that she's bipolar."

"But for her to ram your car," I said, "knowing that she'd damage her own car, not to mention get in trouble with the law, means she must have felt justified."

"That's Sarah for you," Mitzi said, her gaze straying to the television screen.

"Doesn't your Jag have a built-in phone system?" Marco asked.

Mitzi gazed at him, blinking hard, clearly trying to think up a good response. "Silly me. I forgot about that. I should use it so I don't have to pull over to answer a call. Of course, most people don't mind if you stop in front of their house. Not Sarah, though. She was on Ambien for years—a terrible insomniac. I think that addled her brain."

"Still," I said, "a woman doesn't ram another woman's car unless she's extremely angry. And why would she be angry at you for stopping in front of her house?"

Mitzi kept her gaze on the TV. "Her father has dementia. She might be getting it."

"Mitzi," Marco said. He waited until she turned toward him, then asked in a gentle voice, "Were you at Sarah's house to convince her husband to come see us?"

At that Mitzi broke into sobs, covering her face with her hands. "I was pleading for his help, Marco."

I plucked a tissue from the box on her side table and shoved it in her hand. "What happened?"

She dabbed carefully beneath her eyes. "Sarah was supposed to be attending a baby shower, but she came home early and heard me talking to Tom. It was horrible, Abby. She screamed at me and threw things and then chased me out of the house. I ran to my car. Then she came after me in *her* car." Mitzi started sobbing again. "I could've been killed. As it is, I may be in a wheelchair for life."

"What did Sarah overhear?" Marco asked.

"Me pleading with Tom to see you this afternoon. I don't know why she reacted so strongly. I never said exactly why I wanted him to talk to you. It could have been for any reason . . . maybe to ask you how to mix the perfect martini. Sarah's crazy, that's all. She's on blood pressure medicine. She might have suffered a stroke."

I rolled my eyes at Marco.

"Is it possible Sarah heard you ask Tom to be your alibi witness?" Marco asked.

"Anything's possible," she replied with a childish pout.

"Mitzi," Marco said, "we need the truth."

Sniffling, she tried to reach for the box of tissues and couldn't, so I handed her a fresh one. She blew her nose then said, "Sarah might have heard something to that effect. But Sarah hears voices anyway. She used to see a therapist, so you really can't count on what she hears. Would a sane person ram another person's vehicle? Has anyone considered that I'm the victim here?"

"Sarah's husband isn't going to help you, is he?" I asked.

"My head hurts. I need a pain pill." She pressed the call button on her bed controls repeatedly. "You'd better leave. The doctor said I shouldn't have any stress. There's swelling in my brain, and stress makes it worse. I'm getting dizzy. *Where* is that *nurse*?"

"Will your husband be home to look after you when you're released?" I asked as we moved toward the door.

"He won't be home until Friday. Nurse? Nurse!" She hit the button with her fist. "Doesn't this thing work?"

"We'll send in a nurse," I said. "Who's looking after your dog?"

"Deloris Reynolds. The Reynoldses are good neighbors. Unlike my ex-friend Sarah Burns. Unlike Theda Coros. *She* killed Dirk. *She's* the one you need to question."

"One more thing," Marco said, as a nurse hurried in. "You mentioned earlier that this is Theda's fault. How so?"

"I'll tell you how so," Mitzi said indignantly. "She's the one who told Sarah to come home early."

CHAPTER TWENTY-FIVE

"It's unbelievable how Mitzi always makes herself out to be the victim," I said as we walked out of the hospital. "She cheated with her best friend's husband and will probably be responsible for breaking up their marriage, and yet she wants us to feel sorry for her."

"It takes two to cheat," Marco said. "Where were Tom Burns's brains?"

"I think we know that answer. I'm telling you, Marco, Mitzi is sneaky and devious. She lies as easily as she breathes. My radar was going crazy in her room."

"I'll agree about the sneaky and devious, but *my* gut still says she's not the killer."

I linked my arm through Marco's and said teasingly, "Like your gut said your mom was in danger?"

"I'm going to ignore that"—his mouth curved up at the corners—"for now."

Dropping my voice to a husky whisper, I ran my hand up Marco's arm. "We don't have to spend the evening at my folks' house, you know. We could stay home instead and explore this subject further."

"Don't tempt me, woman," he replied playfully, "or I'll take you home right now."

"I don't have a problem with that. Do *you* have a problem with that?"

"Yes." He locked my hand between his. "We have another stop to make."

"Where?"

"The jail. I'm going to phone Reilly and see if he can get us in to see Sarah. I'd like to hear her take on this while it's still fresh in her mind."

That wasn't the thought that was fresh in *my* mind, but I understood Marco's urgency.

"You know what puzzles me?" he asked. "Theda's involvement."

"We don't know that Theda was involved, Marco. You know how Mitzi lies."

"But just suppose Mitzi *is* telling the truth. What would've prompted Theda to make sure Sarah got home when she did? Is it possible she knew Mitzi and Tom were alone at his house?"

"This is why I think Mitzi is lying. I don't believe Theda would deliberately hurt Sarah."

"Don't be too quick to dismiss the idea, Sunshine. Theda told us she'd been on that side of the pond for a walk after the accident happened. Maybe she was there earlier, witnessed Mitzi sneaking into the house, and wanted to do something about it. This is why we need to talk to Sarah. Because if Theda *was* the instigator here, it makes me wonder what else she's been up to."

I said crossly, "You're sure making a case against her."

"I'm sorry if that bothers you, Abby, but consider this. Except for what we witnessed with our own eyes, nearly every incriminating detail we know about the crime has come from Theda, including the black Ford sedan she saw on the evening of the murder. Has anyone else in the neighborhood seen a car like that? No. Who said Dirk didn't make the meeting that Friday evening? Who reported that Dirk drowned a cat? Who told us Dirk wanted Rye fired? Who saw Dirk entering Mitzi's house with wine and candy? And now we have Theda sending Sarah home to conveniently discover her husband with Mitzi."

I had nothing to offer in Theda's defense except a gut feeling that was growing weaker by the day.

Marco punched in a number then put his phone to his ear. "Hey, Sean. How's it going, man? Yeah, same here. Listen, I need a favor."

While he was talking, I pulled out my phone and called Theda to tell her we'd be a little longer than I'd planned. What I didn't say was that it was mostly because of her.

We got lucky. Not only was Reilly able to get us access to Sarah, but Patty, my favorite jail matron, was on duty. She had been fond of my dad while he was on the force, and that fondness got transferred directly to me, so I'd been able to tap her for a favor or two in the past. Now she gave me a hug, then patted me down and did the same with Marco, chewing gum and talking nonstop the whole time.

"You are so lucky I came in to work today, kiddo, 'cause otherwise you would'a got Maxine, and she's got a stare so icy she can freeze fire. I'm telling ya."

She kept up the monologue until she put us into the visitation room and left to get Sarah. Ten minutes later, she delivered a shell-shocked young woman in shackles and wearing an orange jumpsuit. Her honey brown hair was in a fancy updo, quite at odds with the rest of her ensemble.

Patty directed her to a chair on the other side of a clear partition directly across from us. Sarah sat down and scooted the chair close to the white laminate counter. She looked pale and frightened. "Are you here to get me out?"

"Your lawyer will have to do that," Marco said.

"I don't have a lawyer. I don't even know a lawyer to call." She slapped her hands on the counter, her handcuffs rattling. "I can't believe this. I'm in jail and Mitzi is home free. She's the one who should be here, that lying, cheating bi—"

"Sarah, do you want me to phone my friend Dave Hammond?" I asked. "He's a good attorney."

"I guess so. It's very apparent I can't rely on Tom to do anything for me." Her tone was irate, but the hurt was evident in her voice.

"Has he been here to see you?" Marco asked.

She shook her head, her lower lip trembling.

"I'll phone Dave right now," I said, rising. I stepped away to make the call while Marco talked to Sarah. When I returned, I said, "Dave will be down here within the hour."

Sarah let out of sigh of relief. "Thank you."

"Sarah was just telling me what happened when she arrived home this afternoon," Marco said. He waited until I had the notebook ready then said, "Go ahead, Sarah. You had just pulled into your garage."

"Okay, then I went through the door into the kitchen and the minute I walked in I heard Mitzi's shrill voice berating Tom. I couldn't imagine what he'd done to deserve it, so I paused to listen. That's when I heard her tell him he had to go to your house to swear that she was with him *in my house* the Friday evening Dirk died. 'You have to go right now,' she told him, 'while Sarah's at the shower, or else the Salvares will have the cops come here to talk to you. Do you want that? Do you want Sarah to find out about us?'

"That's when I lost it. Mitzi is my best friend! Or *was*. What kind of debased person does that to her best friend? I'm telling you, *Mitzi* should be in jail, not me!" She folded her arms and sat back, a furious expression on her face.

"I'm sorry, Sarah," I said. "You must feel devastated."

"At the moment I just want to get out of here."

"If you don't mind," Marco said, "I have a few questions for you."

At her nod, he asked, "Where were you on the Friday evening of the murder?"

"At church, setting up for a fund-raiser." Sarah shook her head. "I was actually filling in for Mitzi because she claimed to have a migraine. How's that for irony? She's never had a migraine in her life. I've heard her brag about it."

"What happened after you heard the two talking in your kitchen?" Marco asked.

"I grabbed a throw pillow from the sofa and started hitting Tom. Then I turned toward Mitzi and she let out a scream like I'd smacked her with a brick. She ran out the door, and I was so furious I went to the garage, backed my car down the driveway, and drove into her Jaguar before she could get away. Tom pounded on my window, ordering me to stop, and then Mitzi backed into *my* car! Twice! I jumped out and ran up to the Jag and tried to open the door, but she locked it and sat there until the police came. And then she told them I rammed her car three times!

"And by the way, I didn't hit her car hard enough to cause her so-called whiplash injury because I wasn't going fast enough. If she has whiplash, she caused it herself."

"I didn't hear the first part of your story," I told her. "Did you leave the bridal shower early or was it over when you left?"

"Early, because I got a call from Theda saying I needed to get home."

I felt Marco's gaze shift my way, but I ignored him.

"Why did Theda want you to go home?" I asked.

"She was walking past our house and heard two loud bangs, like gunshots, coming from inside. She said she knocked and rang the doorbell, but Tom didn't answer. So I got worried and drove home."

"When Theda called you, did she say anything about Mitzi being at your house?" Marco asked.

"No."

"Did she mention seeing Mitzi's car out front?" Marco asked.

"No."

Marco glanced at me again and I knew he was thinking that Theda had lied to get Sarah home.

"After Theda said she heard two bangs, why didn't you call the police?" I asked.

Sarah shrugged. "My first inclination was to find out what had happened. I thought maybe Tom had knocked something over in the garage and just didn't hear Theda ringing the bell. Looking back now, I wish I had called the cops. I would've loved to see Mitzi and Tom's faces when the police arrived."

"Did you ever figure out what caused those sounds?" Marco asked.

"I never thought about it again, Marco. I was a little busy wanting to maim someone."

"Would you do me a favor?" Marco asked. "If you find out, would you let one of us know?"

"Why do you want to know about the noises?" I asked Marco as we drove home.

"I'm the curious type."

"You think Theda made them up to get Sarah home, don't you?"

"Don't *you*?"

I glanced at the passing scenery out my side window. "Yeah, I guess I do."

"Theda was clever, Sunshine. She didn't want Sarah to send the police so she found another way to get her home, banking on Sarah's natural curiosity. I wonder if Theda ever did knock and ring the doorbell." Marco glanced at me. "I'm betting she didn't, because my guess is there were no loud noises."

Instead of defending Theda, which was becoming increasingly more difficult, I kept my head turned toward my window.

After a protracted silence, Marco said, "So, what are we doing about your parents' dinner?"

I drew a frowny face on the glass. "We're going."

Dinner at my parents' house was normally a boisterous affair, with everybody trying to outdo everybody else's *You'll never believe* my *week* story. There was always plenty of food to go with the storytelling, along with a lot of laughter, so that by the end of dinner, we would all have full bellies and smiles on our faces.

Tonight was totally different. Tonight everyone was on

their best behavior, the stories absent, the jokes tame, the laughter subdued. Tonight Rosa was there, and she and my mom were in the limelight, talking about how much fun they'd had working on Mom's latest art project.

Rosa's son Petey had decided to stay with his grandmother so he could finish a school report due the next day. However, I was betting that he really hadn't wanted to sit around a table with a bunch of strangers all evening, and who could blame him? I felt like *I* was with a bunch of strangers, too.

"So when do we get to see this fantastic art project?" my brother Jordan asked.

"After dessert," Mom said, glancing at Rosa as she passed out slices of custard pie.

"And how come you won't tell us what it is?" my niece Tara asked. Her cell phone was in a basket by the front door with the rest of the family's—my dad's policy.

"We don't want to ruin the surprise," Mom said.

"Everyone hurry," Tara said, and shoveled a bite into her mouth. "I hate suspense."

And I was pretty sick of the whole art project subject.

As soon as we'd cleared the table, we gathered in the family room while Mom and Rosa left to go to Mom's art studio, a converted screened-in porch at the back of the house. Minutes later Rosa returned and clapped to get our attention, then asked Marco and me to come to the center of the room.

"What for?" I asked warily.

"Just come!" Rosa said, waving me forward. *"Vamos!"* Marco took my hand and led me there.

"Now close your eyes," Rosa said.

"This is silly," I grumbled to Marco.

He squeezed my hand.

I heard paper rattling, then a thud, and then Mom announced, "Open your eyes!"

I opened them and saw bright yellow wrapping paper covering a tower about five feet high and two feet wide.

"It's your housewarming present," Mom said. "Rosa helped me with it."

That explained the secrecy.

"Were we all supposed to bring housewarming gifts?" my brother Jonathan asked.

His wife patted his leg. "We already sent a gift, Jon."

"Open your present, Aunt Abby," Tara called.

Marco let go of my hand. "Go ahead. You do the honors."

I ripped open the paper and found a metal sculpture of a giant purple daisy with a yellow center on a long green stem punctuated near the bottom by two giant leaves. The flower sat in a big yellow bucket filled with brown-tinted plaster to keep it from tipping over. I liked the flower but still didn't understand why Rosa's help had been needed. Mom had worked with metal before.

I walked over to hug Mom. "Thank you. I love it."

"We thought it would look pretty on your front porch," Mom said, beaming.

Marco was right behind me and gave her a hug, too. "It'll look great there."

We thanked Dad next, who said, "I'd like to take credit for it, Abracadabra, but it was all their doing." He pointed to Mom and Rosa. "I was just their support team."

I walked over to Rosa and hugged her. "Thanks. It's perfect."

"I'm glad you like it." She leaned close to whisper,

"Your mother wanted to make you a giant chicken mailbox. That was when I volunteered to help."

Ah. *Now* it all made sense.

Monday

When Seedy and I arrived at Bloomers the next morning, I could hear Lottie's booming laughter coming from the back of the building, where she was probably preparing the Monday-morning breakfast. Seedy sniffed the air then hobbled ahead of me straight through to the kitchen. There, wearing an orange scoop-neck blouse and an orange print skirt, was Rosa entertaining Grace and Lottie with the details of our housewarming celebration.

"I did not think Abby would appreciate a giant yellow chicken in front of her house," Rosa said, and they all laughed.

"Nor would the neighbors," Grace added.

"Rosa to the rescue again," Lottie said as she stirred the eggs.

Again?

"Here is Abby now," Rosa exclaimed. "Did you put your big daisy on your porch?"

"It's on the back patio," I said. "I forgot we have rules about decorations for the front. Nothing over three feet high."

"That's too bad," Lottie said. "No one will see it in the back."

"I guess the chicken would have worked after all," Rosa said, causing another round of laughter.

At ten o'clock, Marco phoned with news on the

investigation. "The forensic results came back on the garden shovel, Abby, and I'm afraid they're not what you were hoping to hear. Dirk's DNA was found in the seam where the handle meets the spade, and Theda's was found on the handle itself."

"It is her shovel, Marco."

"But no one else's DNA showed up."

I rubbed my forehead, thinking. "Well, okay, so the killer wore gloves. It doesn't mean *Theda* killed Dirk."

"But it does mean she will be arrested today."

CHAPTER TWENTY-SIX

"They can't arrest Theda based on that. It's completely circumstantial."

"But taken with everything else, they have a woman with the means, motive, and opportunity."

"Mitzi has all that, too!"

"Abby, you know how the DA's office works. That doesn't mean Theda will be convicted, and it doesn't mean we stop investigating."

"But it does mean she'll be humiliated in front of the whole community. We can't let that happen."

"*We* don't have a say in it. All we can do is find evidence pointing to the true guilty party. Let's head out to Rye's neighborhood at noon and see what we hunt up in the way of alibi witnesses for him."

Poor Theda! I ended the call and tried to focus on the next order, but I was so distraught I finally told my staff I had to leave for a few minutes. Throwing my purse strap over my shoulder, I dashed out the door and practically jogged across the square to the police station.

"Hey, beautiful!"

I turned to see Connor MacKay, the crime reporter for the *New Chapel News*, coming up the walk behind me. "Hello, MacKay," I said with a curt nod.

"Looks like we've got ourselves a serial murderess. And to think you've been living next door to her."

I really didn't want to take the time to talk to Connor, but that statement had me seeing red. "You're one hundred percent wrong, MacKay. The DA is on a witch hunt, that's all. Do you want to know why they arrested Theda?"

"Can I quote you?"

"You bet."

He pulled out a minirecorder and clicked a button. "Start talking."

I gave him a story to print, ending with, "And put in your piece that Marco and I have collected proof and are almost ready to name the real killer—and it's not Theda."

"You know the DA won't be happy about this," he said with a grin.

"That's what I'm hoping. I want to shake him up. He's got the wrong person in jail, and we'll prove it."

"When?"

"By the end of the week." I don't know why I said that, but there it was. Marco would not be pleased when he read it in the paper.

"Thanks, freckles. This will be in tomorrow's edition of the *News*."

"I need to see Detective Wells," I told the officer behind the window in the small entryway. "It's an emergency. About a case she's working on."

"And you are?"

"Abby Knight Salvare. Salvare Detective Agency. You know me. I've been here before. My dad was Sergeant Jeffrey Knight. Please tell Detective Wells I need to see her right away."

"You just missed her," the officer said. "She went out on a call about three minutes ago."

Damn! "Do you know where she was going?"

"You know I can't give out that information."

I pushed the door open and stepped out into the sunshine. I had to warn Theda.

I phoned her as I hurried back across the square, but the call went to voice mail. That meant I'd have to leave a message and hope she got it in time—or had the police already been there?

"Theda, leave the house," I said into the phone. "Go somewhere, just don't stay home. The police want to arrest you. If you get this message in the next ten minutes, I'm on my way."

I rounded the corner onto Michigan Avenue where the parking lot was, only to see that my yellow Corvette wasn't there. In a panic, I dug out my phone again and called Marco. "Where are you? My car's not in the lot."

"I'm at the restaurant supply store. What's up?"

"I need my car, Marco. I. Need. My. Car."

"Whoa, slow down, sweetheart. What happened?"

"I need to get to Theda's house before Lisa Wells arrests her—and you have my car!"

"Abby, you're getting squeaky. Calm down. Do you really think you're going to convince Lisa not to arrest Theda? Based on your gut feeling that she's innocent? Lisa might arrest you, too, for interfering with police business."

But at least I could try—and I couldn't even do that because I didn't have transportation. I was so frustrated

I stamped my foot, causing a couple walking past to cast me curious looks. "I want my car back!"

"I'll be there in fifteen minutes, and then we'll go to Theda's together, okay?"

"Fine." I hung up and threw my phone into my purse. Then I remembered our rental van. I hurried back to Bloomers, only to find that Lottie hadn't returned from making deliveries. So I paced in front of the shop, waiting for Marco to show up, getting angrier by the second.

"Abby, are you all right?" Grace asked, stepping outside.

"I'm waiting for Marco. There's been an emergency with my neighbor."

"I'm sorry to hear that. Is there anything I can do?"

"Just manage the shop for me." My phone rang and I grabbed it. "Theda?"

"Guess again," my cousin said cheerily.

"Jillian, I need to keep my line open. I'm expecting an important call."

"You'll get a beep. Anyway, I've got great news for you."

"What?"

"You don't need to snap at me. Your living room suite is ready to be delivered. How about I schedule it for tomorrow while you're at work and you can be surprised when you get home?"

"Fine."

"Aren't you excited?"

I took a breath and blew it out. "Yes, I'm excited. I'm just in a little bit of a rush right now."

"You leave everything to me. I promise you'll be amazed when you get home tomorrow."

Amazed? I hoped that was the word I'd be using.

I saw Lisa Wells drive by in her green Volkswagen Beetle heading toward the police station—and no one was with her. Maybe she hadn't gone to arrest Theda after all. Maybe I could still prevent that from happening.

"Okay. Thanks, Jill. Gotta go." Stuffing my phone into my purse, I hurried after Lisa's car.

By the time I reached the station, Lisa was on her way to the back entrance. I called her name and she waited for me. She was not smiling.

"What is it, Abby?"

"Lisa," I said, trying to catch my breath, "you can't arrest Theda Coros."

"Can and did."

"She's in jail?"

"Being processed."

"You've got the wrong person, Lisa. Theda isn't the killer."

She folded her arms over her black blazer. "Is that so? Then who is?"

"I don't know yet, but Marco and I are this close to solving the case." I held up two fingers and made a pinching motion.

"Have you uncovered evidence proving Theda's innocence?"

"No, but—"

"No *buts*, Abby. The prosecutor believes he can make a case against Theda, so if you can prove otherwise, bring me the evidence right away."

"What happened to innocent until proven guilty?"

"That's for a jury to decide."

"You know that's a cop-out. I thought you were a better detective than that."

"And *you* know that telling a suspect to flee is

considered aiding and abetting." And with that, she pulled the door open and walked inside.

I stared at the door, debating what to do next, but I was stymied. So I turned and headed back to Bloomers, where I found Marco leaning against my yellow car, arms crossed as though *he* was the one who was put out.

"You're too late," I said. "Theda's at the jail right now being booked." Giving him a furious look, I walked around my car and straight up to Bloomers' door.

"Abby."

"I don't want to talk right now." I went inside, headed directly to my workroom, stepped into one of the coolers, knelt down among my flowers, put my hands over my face, and cried.

A few minutes later Lottie came in and crouched down in front of me, putting her hands on my shoulders. "Sweetie, what's wrong?"

I wiped my eyes and sniffed. "I'm frustrated, that's all."

"Frustrated about what?"

"It's too long to go into."

"This is Lottie you're talking to. Come on. Tell me what's causing these tears. This isn't like you."

It *wasn't* like me. I didn't cry when the going got tough. I merely got going.

Perhaps Lottie was right. Perhaps what I needed was to get everything off my chest. So I took a deep breath and let it out. "I wanted to spare my neighbor Theda the trauma and embarrassment of being arrested and hauled off in handcuffs, but I couldn't get to her in time because Marco had my car once again and you were out with the van. And I can't find evidence to prove Theda's innocence." I started crying again. "What if I'm wrong,

Lottie? What if Theda is the murderer and my gut instinct is wrong about everything?"

"There now, sweetie," Lottie said, holding me.

"I really want to enter the flower show, Lottie, but I don't have time. And I'm afraid my living room will be a disaster when Jillian finishes with it. And I'm tired of Rosa getting all the glory—"

I heard a muffled gasp and looked around to see Grace, Marco, and Rosa standing just outside the open door. Rosa turned and ran off, the back of her hand pressed against her lips.

"I never would have said anything about Rosa if I'd known she was here."

"Maybe it was something she needed to hear. I'll go talk to her." Lottie got up and traded places with Marco, who held out a hand to help me up.

I walked straight into his arms and wrapped mine around his solid rib cage, breathing in his familiar calming scent. "How much did you hear?"

"From 'Marco had my car once again.'"

I opened my mouth to speak, but he put his finger over my lips. "No. Don't apologize. Just come with me."

He led me outside to my car parked at the curb.

"We're not supposed to use up a customer parking space," I said.

"It'll only be for another few minutes. You apparently didn't notice that Toyota parked behind the 'Vette when you came across the street."

I turned just as Marco's brother Rafe got out of a silver Prius. My mouth dropped open. "You bought a car?"

"I wasn't at the restaurant store, Abby. Rafe and I were picking up my new ride." He dangled my car keys. "This one's all yours again, Fireball."

Practically jumping for joy, I threw my arms around him and gave him a big hug. Pocketing the keys, I ran my hand along the Corvette's shiny yellow trunk, over the black ragtop, and down the hood. I had my baby back.

Marco came up behind me and put his arms around me, kissing me on the cheek. So I turned and gave him a proper kiss. I glanced over at the shop and saw Grace and Lottie at the bay window, beaming. Standing far back was Rosa.

I put my keys back in Marco's hand. "Would you drive my car to the parking lot? I need to go apologize to Rosa."

"Anything for my Sunshine." He turned to call to his brother, "Take the Prius to the lot. I'll follow."

Rafe got inside and gunned the engine, causing Marco to yell, "Be careful!"

Rafe gave him a thumbs-up and pulled away from the curb. Marco got into my car and gunned the engine, then winked at me and drove after Rafe.

I watched them turn the corner. Then I headed back inside to have a talk with Rosa.

I found her in the first cooler, pulling stems for a new order. She came out and placed them on the table. "Congratulations on the new car," she said, forcing a smile.

"Rosa, I'm sorry for what I said earlier."

"It's okay. Lottie explained that you have been very stressed."

"Then we're good?"

She lifted one shoulder as she prepped a blue ceramic vase. "I suppose so."

"What does that mean?"

"I don't understand what you mean by *the glory*. What did I do to get all of it?"

How could I explain without offending her more? As I stood there pondering, she said, "It's okay. I will keep my nose out of your business from now on."

"That's not what I want."

She put down the green foam and faced me. "Then what do you want? I am very confused."

I opened my mouth to explain but couldn't find the right words.

She waited a moment, then went back to the vase. "Never mind. It will be fine." I opened my mouth again but still couldn't think of anything to say that wouldn't make the situation worse. So I plucked a new ticket and went to choose my blossoms. And that was how we finished the day.

If things weren't bad enough at the shop, I then had to face Theda's empty house when I got home. She had sent a message through Dave Hammond asking me to take care of Kitty for her and giving me her garage door code to get in. Poor Kitty was so distraught, meowing and searching all over the house for Theda, that I brought him and all his trappings back to my house. There, at least, he would have company. And Seedy was overjoyed to have her best friend there.

Because my morning had been disrupted and because we'd had a flood of funeral orders, I hadn't gone with Marco to canvass Rye's neighborhood, and had worked through my lunch hour instead. So when he got home, he filled me in as we ate turkey white bean chili at our new table.

"I found a neighbor willing to swear that Rye was at his son's soccer game that Friday evening at seven o'clock.

He said Rye never misses a game and in fact helps coach the team. He told me he could get at least six other parents to verify that, too."

"I don't understand why Rye didn't tell us that."

"I wish I had an answer for you."

"Then we're crossing him off the list?"

"I'll wait until the DNA tests come back from the wrench, but as far as I'm concerned, it doesn't make sense to focus on him now."

"At least we've managed to narrow down our list to Mitzi, Jane, and Maynard."

"And Theda." Marco held up his hand as though to ward off my protest. "Abby, don't say it."

Kitty reached up to pat my arm, wanting to be petted. "I wasn't going to," I said glumly, stroking his soft silver fur. But once Marco saw Connor's article in the paper, he was going to see that I already had.

Tuesday

I woke up groggy; I hadn't slept well, and it wasn't Kitty who'd kept me awake. He had curled up with Seedy in her doggy bed and hadn't made a sound all night. It was the image of Theda in that cold, depressing jail cell that was responsible. I didn't care how much circumstantial evidence there was against her, there was just as much against Mitzi and *she* wasn't in jail. If I could only find the one conclusive piece to prove Mitzi was the killer.

"I see we're days from solving the case," Marco said as I made my breakfast. He placed the newspaper on the counter, folded back to Connor's front-page story.

"Don't be angry. I was furious at the time and just let it all out."

"To a newspaper reporter."

"I shouldn't have given Connor a timeline, but I'm not sorry about the rest of it. The DA rushed to arrest someone and needs to be called out on it."

"But now the real killer, if it isn't Theda, thinks we have proof that will close the case. Tactical error, Abby. You may have put us both in jeopardy."

I met Marco at Down the Hatch after work. I hadn't had a chance to talk to him all day; once again we'd been jammed with orders. And now he was working the evening shift, which was why I was eating my dinner at the bar's counter and he was behind it. Fortunately it wasn't crowded. I had the end to myself.

"We've got to talk to Tom Burns privately," I told him.

Marco had been mopping up a water ring with a towel but paused to look up curiously. "For what reason?"

"Because I'm certain Mitzi coached Tom on what to say. If we could wear him down I'll bet he'd tell us exactly what time she was with him that Friday evening."

"With Sarah out of jail, we might not be able to get Tom to cooperate right now. He might be busy trying to patch his marriage."

I took a drink of my light beer and sat the mug down with a thud. "We can at least give it the old college try. I'll do some research on him this evening and find out where he works. Maybe we can waylay him before he goes home. Did you get a chance to talk to Dave about Theda's incarceration?"

"For just a few minutes. The judge set the bail so

ridiculously high, there's no way she can get out, so Dave is going to petition for a bond reduction hearing."

I sank my chin on my hand. "That could take a week—or longer. Poor Theda. She must be a nervous wreck. I'll go see her tomorrow and let her know Kitty is doing fine. I'd stop on my way home, but I probably can't get into the jail this late."

"Sunshine, after what you said in that newspaper article, you're not going anywhere this evening except straight home. Lock the doors and stay put."

I saluted. "Aye, aye, Captain."

"Don't pretend this hasn't happened before, Abby. You find ways to get yourself into trouble. You're just lucky I haven't run out of ways to rescue you."

"I'm trying to make light of it, Marco. I know I made a mistake and I promise I'll be careful."

He leaned toward me to say quietly, "Good, because I'd be devastated if anything happened to you. You know I love you to distraction."

I moved close enough for our lips to lock in a deep kiss.

"Sorry to interrupt, lovebirds," Rafe said. "I've got a question for you, bro."

As Marco turned away to talk to his brother, I couldn't help but smile at the sight of the two, their identical heads of dark wavy hair bent toward each other, as Rafe explained his dilemma and my husband solved it. Then Marco turned to me, his back against the counter, his arms crossed. "How did it go with Rosa today?"

"Strained. She isn't singing to the radio, and she makes only brief comments. Mostly she just works. And she sighs. A lot."

"That has to be awkward."

I stabbed my fork into the last bite of salad. "I don't know how to fix it."

"You know what my opinion is."

"I tried to have a heart-to-heart talk with her, but I couldn't think of a kind way to explain away what I'd said. She wanted to know how she was getting all the glory. What could I tell her? *You get it by being you, Rosa, the best at everything, the most talented, the golden girl of the flower shop, the rescuer*?"

"Yeah, I don't think that would do it."

"Exactly. So there you have it."

"On another topic"—Marco took my empty dish and set it aside—"are you ready to see your new living room?"

"Is today the big reveal? I completely forgot about it."

"I know, and Jillian wanted to keep it that way. I let her in the house at lunchtime and then got shooed out so you and I can be *amazed* together. Her words, not mine."

I pushed my beer mug away. "Now my stomach feels queasy."

"Join the club." Marco laid the towel on the counter. "I'll tell Rafe I'll be gone for half an hour. You might want to text your cousin to let her know we're on our way. Remind me to get my things out of your car when we get to the house."

When we arrived home, Jillian was standing in the front window with a big smile on her face. Marco drove his new Prius into the garage first and then I pulled in beside him. While he collected his belongings from the Corvette, I put my arms on the yellow hood and gave it a hug.

Marco held up an envelope. "This was between the seats."

"Those are Jane's photos. I forgot I put them there."

I had to start making lists. I was forgetting a lot lately.

"I'll take a look at them later." He put the envelope and his belongings into the Prius. Then, holding hands, we walked up to the inside door. "Take a deep breath," Marco instructed, reaching for the doorknob.

I pulled his arm back. "What do we do if it's horrible?"

"We tell her what she's waiting to hear, that she did an *amazing* job, and tomorrow we sell the whole suite on Craigslist."

"No, seriously, Marco. I've got a huge knot in my stomach."

"What can we do, Sunshine? Hurt *her* feelings, too? Our only option will be to live with the furniture for a while, then sell it and buy something else. But then we can never, ever invite her over again."

I thought it over. "That'll work."

"Okay. Let's go in and face the music."

Marco opened the door for me, but I made him go in first. He walked up the short hallway into the kitchen and peered around the corner, giving him a view of the living room and dining area.

"Well?" I whispered.

"Welcome to your new living room, Marco," I heard Jillian chirp.

Marco stepped all the way in and stood there for a long moment looking around. And then he said, "You did an *amazing* job, Jillian."

My stomach knotted in seven more places.

CHAPTER TWENTY-SEVEN

"Where's Abby?" Jillian asked.

"She's right behind me," Marco said. "Abby? Jillian is waiting."

I braced myself for the shock, then called blithely, "I'm coming." I walked around the corner, came face-to-face with my new living room, and couldn't prevent a gasp of surprise.

The room was completely transformed. Gone were the ugly tan sofa, plain white walls, worn side chairs, and old black recliner. In their place was a plump navy-and-white sofa in a geometric print accented with three bright yellow pillows, side chairs in a soft yellow accented by a solid navy pillow on one chair, a navy-and-white throw on the other, and walls in a soft dove gray. On the wall above the sofa was a large modern art print in bold colors of yellow, navy, orange, purple, red, and white. My primary colors!

The cocktail table was a clever modern design of silvery ash wood that slid apart in the center, providing storage inside. At the windows Jillian had hung side drapes in the pale yellow color of the chairs, with white fabric shades beneath that could be tilted open or closed. But what really set off the room was the area rug—a play of primary colors that interwove across a pale gray background.

It was contemporary; it was classy; it was bright and cheerful; it was me! And Marco hadn't been forgotten, either. In one corner sat his recliner, now reupholstered in supple navy leather. He headed straight for it, sitting down and lifting the footrest, sinking back into it with a happy sigh.

Jillian had nailed it, everything I'd dreamed my living room could be. I flopped onto my ultracomfy new sofa, picked up a pretty yellow pillow, and hugged it to my chest. I couldn't stop smiling.

Then reality hit.

"What do we owe for this?" Marco asked.

Jillian wrinkled her nose. "Do you really want to spoil the moment?"

"I really want to know how much we owe," he answered, getting up.

"How about I come up with a payment plan tomorrow? For now, just enjoy it." She checked the time on her phone then dropped it into her oversized purse. "I need to get home to put Harper to bed."

I jumped up to give her a hug. "Thanks again, Jill. The room is absolutely beautiful. All the colors I wanted, all the soft fabrics—everything is perfect. You did it."

"No, Abs. *We* did it."

Once Marco had headed back to the bar, Jillian had gone home, and I'd grown tired of taking photos of my new living room and sending them to Lottie, Grace, Mom, and Nikki, I logged onto Marco's favorite search engine and got some background information on Tom Burns. I found out that Tom was the manager of our local grocery store, which would make it easy to catch him at work during the day. In fact, Marco could go see him before lunch tomorrow. We had to speed this investigation up.

As I sat at the computer, Kitty jumped onto my lap and curled up contentedly, so I decided to stay there and see what I could dig up on Mitzi's past. There was one interesting newspaper account of Mitzi being ejected from a dog show when she got into a fight with another dog owner after the owner claimed Mitzi sabotaged her grooming supplies. The accompanying photo showed a champion shih tzu with pink fur.

An older article reported that Mitzi had been kicked off her college cheerleading squad for shoving the head cheerleader into the bleachers before a game. The other cheerleader hadn't been hurt physically but had claimed mental duress. Apparently Mitzi had been harassing the girl for winning the position that Mitzi had coveted. Even back then she was a person you didn't want to anger. I saved the links to show Marco later.

Kitty didn't seem inclined to move, so I did a search on Maynard Dell next and found a news clipping from four years ago about a road rage incident. According to the report, after leaving a bar in a nearby town, Maynard had gotten into a dispute with another patron, followed the man in his car, and run him off the road, resulting in an injury serious enough to warrant hospitalization. Maynard had been sent to jail for six months and fired from his job with a heating/air-conditioning company. So much for his story about taking an early retirement.

I was just starting a search on Jane Singletary when someone rapped on the patio door. Kitty sprang off my lap and ran to the closed drapes, arching his back and hissing at whoever was on the other side of it, while Seedy ran for cover. I approached the door quietly and pulled back the drape just a fraction.

It was Mitzi again, nervously glancing around. But instead of one of her usual glitzy outfits, she was wearing a black T-shirt and a pair of camouflage pants with black sneakers, almost blending into the night. Even her blond hair was different, pulled severely off her face into a bun at the nape of her neck. Absent was her neck brace.

My stomach felt fluttery, a sign that something wasn't right. I flipped on the light and opened the drape wider. "What do you want?"

"To talk to you. Could you let me in? I hear noises."

She seemed to hear a lot of noises. Picking up the metal bar for protection, I unlocked the sliding door. Before I could pull it back, Kitty began to make low growling sounds as though he wanted to attack Mitzi.

"Hold on," I said, and lifted Kitty up. I took him into the guest bedroom and shut the door, then went back.

Mitzi stepped inside and eyed the piece of metal in my hand. "Marco's not here again?"

"He's due any second. Why do you always come to the back of the house?"

"Because it's faster to cut across our backyards. What did you think? That I wanted to rob you?"

I felt silly then and leaned the bar against the door-jamb, still within reach.

"I see you have Theda's cat, so obviously you've heard the news about her arrest. And now I can say I told you so."

"Theda didn't kill Dirk."

Mitzi eyed me gamely. "Then why was she arrested?"

"Because both Dirk's and Theda's DNA was on her shovel."

"Well, see? Right there you know she did it."

"Is that why you came over? To accuse Theda? It was her shovel, Mitzi. Why wouldn't her DNA be on it?"

Mitzi folded her arms across her bosom. "So what are you saying? That the killer put on gloves before using the shovel?"

"I *didn't* say that, but it's interesting that *you* did. There's never been anything in the news about the murder weapon."

Her nostrils flared. "I can't believe it. You really think I killed Dirk."

I couldn't deny it, so I said nothing.

"Well, I can prove I didn't."

"How?"

"My gloves. You can test every pair I own for Dirk's DNA. *That'll* show you." She opened the door and walked out into the night.

It was an illogical argument, but I let it go. She wasn't worth wasting my breath.

Kitty was meowing and scratching at the bedroom door, so I let him out and went back to the computer. I resumed my search on Jane but found only reports of Dirk's murder and mentions of a few school functions she'd chaired. Seedy had finally crawled from beneath the sofa and was now whining at the sliding door, so I got up to take her outside. I was just about to pull back the drape when someone rapped on the glass again. Seedy scrambled for safety, Kitty hissed, and I grabbed the bar.

It was Mitzi.

"Here you go," she said, when I opened the drape.

She dropped a pile of gloves on the patio in front of the door. "Have at it." Then she turned and marched away.

Did Mitzi really think I was stupid enough to believe she'd provide me with a pair that had Dirk's DNA on them?

I got a broom and a paper grocery bag from the kitchen to put the gloves in, chased Kitty away from the door, then scooped up Seedy and took her outside with me. "Go do your business," I said to her. As she hobbled off the patio and onto the lawn, I swept the gloves—three pairs of garden and one pair of black knit—into the paper bag.

When I looked around, Seedy was near our property line abutting the park still looking for the perfect spot. She was in the section of yard not well illuminated by my patio light, so I set the bag and broom inside, then walked to the edge of the patio to wait for her. I spotted something at our border with Theda's yard that appeared pink in the moonlight and went to investigate. I kicked it with my shoe and realized it was a pair of women's knit gloves.

Had Mitzi dropped them on her way to my house? But why would she have been walking so close to the pond? It was yet another odd behavior that made me uneasy.

I had just gone back to the house to get the paper bag and broom when my cell phone rang. Keeping one eye on Seedy, who was sniffing her way toward Theda's yard, I glanced at the phone's screen and saw Marco's name.

"I'm on my way home, Abby. I was looking at Jane's photos—"

"Hold on, Marco. Seedy's way down by the pond, and I need to go get her before she gets muddy. I'll be right back." I left the phone on the dining room table so I could carry the broom, the bag, and probably Seedy, then stepped out onto the patio, calling, "Seedy, come here!"

She turned to look at me, then kept sniffing. Suddenly she paused, her big butterfly ears facing forward as she stared at the water. I strained to see what was causing her alarm, but Theda's yard was too dark to make out anything. Other than mine, Mitzi's was the only one with a back light on. She usually turned it on when she let Peanut out, but neither of them were anywhere to be seen.

"Come here," I called, feeling suddenly anxious. "Come, Seedy. Good girl."

When she started sniffing again, I ran back to the house, got the metal bar for protection, and started toward her. Seedy finally chose a location and squatted in her awkward, three-legged fashion. She was just turning to come back when she went on alert again, staring toward the pond with her ears forward.

"Come here now!" I called, snapping my fingers. I was still a good twenty feet away.

At a sudden rustling of the reeds, Seedy began to tremble, and the hairs on my neck rose. Holding the bar like a baseball bat, I cried, "Mitzi! If that's you, come out right now or I'll call the police."

My heart almost stopped when a dark figure rose from the reeds. I could hear water dripping from soaked clothing. "Identify yourself!" I called.

The figure began to wade toward the bank *and* my cowering dog. If that was Mitzi, why wasn't she answering?

"Seedy, come here!" I clapped my hands, but she seemed frozen in place. I didn't know whether to run down and grab her or leave her and head for the house.

"Hey!" the figure called. A man's voice. I'd heard it before. Was it Rye's? "I need to talk to you."

"Who are you?"

He stepped onto the bank, still only a dark shape. "Maynard Dell."

It didn't sound like the voice I remembered. But Maynard had been drinking both times we'd interviewed him. "What do you want?" I shifted the metal bar into my right hand and inched closer to my dog, whispering for her to come, but she wouldn't take her gaze off the dark figure.

"Looks like the pump is out again."

Trying not to betray my fear I said, "Why are *you* checking on it?"

"We think someone's been tampering with it. Have you seen anyone out here?"

The man was on my lawn now. Soon he'd be in the illuminated part of the yard. He was also getting closer to Seedy, who was crouched low, trembling all over.

But I was even closer still. "You didn't answer my question," I called, then bent low to whisper, "Seedy, look! Treats!"

"A building inspector works all hours of the day. I just have a few questions."

"I'll send Marco out. You can talk to him."

"Sure. That's fine."

With my heart thudding against my ribs, I ran to where Seedy sat, scooped her up, and made a dash for the house. With Seedy cradled in my left arm, the bar in my right hand, I crossed the patio and was almost to the door when I heard heavy boots hitting the ground behind me. He was after me!

I had to drop the bar to grab the handle and pull the

door open, and then I tossed Seedy inside. Before I could follow, heavy hands clamped around my upper arms and yanked me away from the house.

As I screamed for help, struggling to twist out of his grasp, the man shook me hard. "Where is it? What did you do with it?" And then I recognized Maynard's voice.

With my arms pinned to my sides I was unable to fight, so I landed a hard kick to his shin, taking him by surprise. I twisted free and made a grab for the metal bar, but he was quicker, catching a fistful of my hair and jerking me back. As I screamed again and dug my short fingernails into the hand locked around my hair, he picked up the bar and flung it toward the pond, then wrenched me backward by the hair with so much force, my feet flew out from under me.

The back of my head hit the concrete with a sickening thud, sending shock waves down my body. My vision danced and my stomach roiled as he knelt beside me, his breath sour in my face. "I know you found it. What did you do with it?"

Stunned by the blow, all I could do was stare up at him, unable to make sense of what was happening. In frustration he stood up and kicked my legs then took me by both feet and dragged me across the prickly grass. I felt as lifeless as a rag doll, unable to even form words to call for help.

From a distance I heard Seedy barking, and a detached part of my mind thought, *She didn't run and hide this time. I wonder why.* I gasped as icy water hit my skin and I realized Maynard was pulling me through the cold, smelly moss into the pond. I tried to grab onto something to stop him, but the moss slipped through my fingers.

Maynard stopped a few feet offshore where we were

hidden by the reeds. He straddled my body, baring his teeth as he leaned down to snarl words that seemed to be muffled in cotton. "Where did you put it? I left it behind the pump, and now it's gone."

My head fell from side to side as I attempted to answer. "I don't—know what—you're talking about."

"Liar!" He pressed me down until all but my nose was submerged and then pulled me up again. "You said you found out who killed Dirk, so you must have it!"

I wheezed, nearly out of air, and rasped weakly, "I don't know what you're—"

"The shovel!" he roared, then pushed me down again, and this time the dirty liquid filled my nostrils. In my dazed state I mistakenly opened my mouth to gulp air, and it, too, filled. As my lungs took on pond water, I reached out to Maynard in a panic, but he merely shoved me down deeper. I knew then that he intended for me to die.

Unable to draw in air, a heavy blackness closed in around me. I ceased struggling, and that little detached part of my brain thought, *I should've kissed Marco good-bye. People always regret not telling a loved one good-bye.*

A thunderous bellow from above jerked me back to consciousness—and suddenly I was free. As I pushed up on my elbows and dragged air into my starved lungs, I could hear Seedy's frenzied barking nearby accompanied by a long, unearthly shriek. Coughing, I rolled onto all fours and immediately vomited in the water.

Get up! If Seedy was trying to defend me, she'd be no match for Maynard. I rose to my feet and swayed dizzily, ignoring the pounding in my head as I struggled to focus my eyes. I spotted Seedy at the edge of the pond, a bobbing blur of white and brown in the moonlight, her barks coming fast and furious. But the cry of distress was coming from behind me. I turned to see Maynard flailing his arms and screaming in pain as someone attacked him from the rear.

Was it Mitzi?

As my vision cleared, I realized my rescuer wasn't human at all. It was a large silver-blue cat who had his back claws hooked into Maynard's flesh and was ripping his ears and neck with his front claws and biting his face and scalp with his razor-sharp teeth, Kitty's high-pitched screeches sounding like something from the underworld.

I knew the brave feline couldn't fend Maynard off forever, so I forced my trembling legs to wade through the moss to retrieve the metal bar from the lawn. But before I could reach the grass, I heard a loud splash and turned to see Maynard on his back, the cat effectively trapped beneath him.

"No! Kitty!" I cried and raced back toward them, yelling for Maynard to let him up. I grabbed the man's ears and twisted them hard, but he was intent on smothering the poor animal. Screaming for help, I tried to gouge Maynard's eyes only to have him knock me aside with one heavy arm. I fell into the water, my head throbbing so hard I thought I'd pass out.

As I struggled to my feet I heard shouts and loud splashing, and then Marco was yelling, "Get back, Abby."

I moved aside as Marco grabbed Maynard by his soaked shirt and landed a solid punch to his jaw. "I've got this," he called. "Get the cat."

I snatched the animal and carried his limp body to

shore, praying he would survive. I laid him gently on the grass and knelt beside him, ready to start CPR, while Seedy nudged his unresponsive body and began to lick Kitty's head.

Suddenly Kitty gave a gasp, and then another, and then began to gag. He crouched on the grass while his body heaved and heaved and finally brought up dirty water. My eyes filled with tears, all my terror and pain and relief spilling out in noisy sobs as I comforted the cat. He had saved my life. And Marco had saved his.

"Marco, stand down now!" someone shouted. "That's enough."

I glanced around and only then noticed that Reilly and half a dozen of his men were racing toward the pond. Then I saw my husband rise and hold up his hands, palms out, as Maynard spluttered and coughed in the water. Red and blue lights flashed all the way down to the pond, and sirens blared from the street in front. I hadn't even heard them.

Maynard labored to his feet and pointed at Marco as he massaged his jaw. "He tried to kill me!"

Marco would have lunged at him again, but Reilly caught his arm and held him back while two of his men escorted Maynard to shore and handcuffed him.

But my whole attention was on Kitty, who was breathing with difficulty and shaking so hard I feared he was going into shock. I held him against me as I hurried to the house, ignoring the stabbing pain in my head. With Seedy at my side, watching the cat with anxious eyes, I wrapped Kitty in a big bath towel and sat on the floor with him, talking softly, telling him he was going to be fine. Hoping I was right.

*   *   *

I was sitting in the back of an emergency rescue van wrapped in a blanket, still holding Kitty, with Seedy at my feet, and two EMTs fussing over me, when I heard Marco and Reilly approach.

"You want to be the next one going to jail?" Reilly was saying. "What were you thinking?"

"The bastard was trying to kill my wife. That's what I was thinking. What would you have done in my place?"

They came around the back of the van and stopped. With my hair in wet strands, mascara undoubtedly smudged beneath my eyes, a heavy blanket covering my body, and sodden shoes hanging out at the bottom, I'm sure I was a sight.

Reilly nudged Marco. "Just shut up and hug her."

Marco climbed into the van and sat on the bench beside me, his arm around my back. I laid my head on his shoulder while Seedy wagged her tail and yipped to get his attention.

"Are you okay, sweetheart?" Marco asked. "Maynard landed a pretty severe blow."

"That was his second blow. This was the first one." I showed him the lump on the back of my head.

Marco muttered something under his breath about what he should've done to Maynard, so I said, "It's over, Marco. We found the killer, and thanks to you and Kitty I'm alive." I unwrapped the blanket so they could see the Russian Blue purring on my lap. He squinted at the light, so I covered him again.

"And thanks to me," Reilly said, "your husband isn't in jail."

Ignoring Reilly's remark, Marco said, "Is Kitty going to be okay?"

"These nice EMTs checked him over and said he'd used up one of his nine lives but he'd recover."

One of the EMTs said, "You can go now, Mrs. Salvare. Everything checked out okay. Just keep an ice pack on your head, twenty minutes on, twenty minutes off."

Marco hugged me to him again. "Let's get you back to the house. I'll ready the ice pack. Reilly, care for a cup of coffee?"

"I don't want to be a bother," he said, looking at me.

"You won't be," I said. "I want to hear what happened after I left."

While Marco started the coffeemaker, I went to the bedroom to strip off my wet clothes and wrap myself in a bathrobe. Then we sat in the living room, Marco and me side by side on our new sofa and Reilly in Marco's recliner. As they drank their coffee, I described how Maynard had nearly drowned me.

"Seedy's barking must have alerted Kitty," I told them. "He ripped into Maynard like no one's business. Another minute and I'd have drowned. Thank God the sliding door was open so he could get out."

"Seedy alerted me, too," Marco said. "When I drove up she was waiting to lead me around back. It's almost like she was trained for it."

"She surprised me, too." I turned to look over into the kitchen, where both animals were eating from their bowls. "Looking at them now, you'd think nothing bad had happened."

"They live in the moment," Marco said.

Reilly commented with a chuckle, "A cat, a dog, and a husband. You've got your own rescue team, Abby."

"I'll claim the husband and dog, but the cat isn't mine," I said.

"And let's leave the word *rescue* out of the equation," Marco said, giving me a look that said, *There'd better not be a need for another rescue.*

If only I could give him that guarantee. "Why were you on your way home?"

"When I saw the photos Jane Singletary had given us, I knew the murderer was Maynard." Marco turned to me and gazed into my eyes. "I was afraid he might do something because of that newspaper article—and I was right."

Marco looked down, too emotional to go on, and I could only imagine what horrible thoughts were running through his mind as he raced home. I set the ice pack aside and slid my arms around him. "I'm sorry, Marco."

He stroked my hair. "The only thing that matters is that you're safe, sweetheart."

"And that Maynard will be spending a long time behind bars," Reilly added. "We got quite a confession from him, Abby. He was so angry—at the cat, at Dirk, at Brandon Thorne, and at both of you—that even after I read him his rights, he kept raging on."

"Why was he angry at Brandon Thorne?" I asked.

"It was Thorne's pump that needed repairing," Marco said, "and Dirk who ordered Maynard to fix it."

"Why would he send Maynard to fix it?" I asked.

"Maynard had been a plumber," Marco said, "which he conveniently forgot to tell us. Dirk was already using the photos to blackmail him, so when Dirk needed to get that pump fixed to get Brandon off his back, he had Maynard do it that evening."

"Maynard had been drinking with his buddies that night and was in a dark mood when he got to the pond," Reilly said. "He used a garden shovel he found lying nearby to deliver a blow to Dirk's head, then dragged him into the water and—"

"I know the rest," I said with a shudder. "So Rye's wrench wasn't involved?"

"Nope. It was tested and came out clean," Reilly said.

"Does this mean Theda can be released?" I asked.

"If we can get a judge to sign the order, she'll be home tonight, and I don't see a problem there. Detective Wells is on her way to one of the judges' homes now."

"So what was in the photos?" I asked Marco.

"Pictures of Maynard passed out in his black Ford sedan parked in front of a construction site, similar to what we witnessed with the city van. It seems Maynard also forgot to tell us that he had his own car."

I shivered and hugged Marco tighter. "It's a miracle that you looked at those photos when you did."

"I know. The odd part is that I was busy at the time. But something made me stop and open that envelope."

"Don't question it," Reilly said, taking his empty cup to the kitchen. "Just be grateful." He pointed to me. "Take care of yourself."

Marco showed his friend to the door then sat down with me again. "How's your head?"

"Not quite as painful. The ice helps."

Seedy came hobbling up to the sofa and yipped for me to pick her up. "Don't get used to this," I told my little mutt, perching her on my knees. "Tonight is special."

Kitty leaped up onto the back of the sofa, hopped

down beside Marco, and curled up in his lap. As Marco ran his hand down the purring cat's still-damp body, he said, "You know we can't give Kitty up now, Abby, not after he saved your life."

I lifted my hand to give Marco a high five. "We're on the same page again, my darling hubby. Theda will be thrilled."

Marco lifted my hand to his lips. "You were right about Theda, Sunshine. I'm sorry I doubted you."

"But I was wrong, too, Marco. I really believed Mitzi was the guilty one. Or maybe I was just hoping so hard I made myself think my gut instinct was behind it."

"Actually, you weren't that far off, Abby. She *is* guilty, just not of murder."

I lay my head against Marco's shoulder with a sigh, hugging Seedy to me. Then I turned my head to gaze at my husband, who was petting a very contented Russian Blue. "So we're keeping Kitty for sure?"

"On one condition. That we give him a decent boy's name."

"You're on, Salvare."

Marco smiled at me, then leaned toward me to give me a kiss. Team Salvare had just become a foursome.

Chapter Twenty-eight

Saturday

The morning of the Midwest Regional Flower Show dawned sunny and bright, the temperature feeling more like late May than April, the trees budding out with tiny green leaves and the daffodils around Theda's porch waving their yellow and white blossoms in the warm breeze. As I backed my Corvette out of the garage, I made a mental note to plant bulbs around my porch in the autumn.

I put the ragtop down, turned up the radio, and sang along as I headed for the town square. Everything was finally back to normal: I had my car and Marco had his; Theda was home; and Grace would be at the shop to help me while Rosa and Lottie attended the flower show.

The days since Maynard's capture had passed in a blur of activities, with sales at the flower shop brisk and plans for our backyard open house moving along. The timing wasn't great. I hadn't realized when we'd set the date to welcome family, friends, and neighbors that the flower show was on the same day, or that I'd be occupied at the shop until midafternoon. Fortunately, my mom, Marco's mom, and Jillian had been more than happy to take command. *Ecstatic* would be a better word.

Theda had been released the night of Maynard's arrest, but we weren't able to tell her what had happened until the next morning. She'd been appalled by what Maynard had done, but overjoyed that I was okay and that we'd decided to give Kitty a home.

On the Brandywine front, we'd had a huge number of *yes* replies to our party invitation and an equal number of thank-yous from relieved neighbors who'd read about Maynard's arrest in the newspaper. Not surprisingly, Mitzi had declined the invite. In fact, she hadn't been seen around the neighborhood at all since word had gotten out about her affair with Tom Burns. Rumor had it that Sarah was going to file for divorce.

On the Bloomers front, relations with Rosa remained strained. She tiptoed around as though afraid of offending me, and I pretended like I didn't notice. I hoped in time we'd be able to resume our former rapport.

When I arrived at Bloomers, Grace had coffee ready, so we sat in the parlor and chatted as usual. The shop seemed quieter because I no longer brought Seedy with me. She now had a playmate to keep her company, and Marco always made sure to get home midday to let her outside.

"You're coming to our open house, aren't you, Grace?"

"Of course I'll be there, love. I wouldn't miss it, although I must say that I've never heard of anyone throwing themselves a welcome-to-the-neighborhood party."

"It just seemed like a fun way to get to know the neighbors."

"It's a wonder you're even here today. I can't imagine the work involved in putting on such a big fete."

"I'd rather be here than at *party central*. I just hope Lottie and Rosa get back in time to attend. Those flower shows can last until late in the evening."

"Speaking of which," Grace said, "you should have seen Rosa when she and Lottie came to pick up her floral arrangement. She was so excited she kept slipping into Spanish. She worked so hard on her entry that I do hope she wins a trophy." Grace glanced at me sidelong. "Or is that a touchy subject?"

"Not touchy at all. I hope Rosa wins, too." Did that sound as flat as it felt? "Seriously, I *really* hope she wins."

Now it just sounded feigned—and I hadn't meant it to.

Grace artfully changed the subject. "How's Mr. Kitty adjusting to his new home?"

"Like he belongs there. We're trying to choose a name for him, but so far we haven't agreed on anything."

"The right one will come to you. Just watch for it."

The phone rang, and Grace went to answer it. She came back just as I was rinsing my cup in the sink. "That was Lottie. There's been an accident with the cooler at the venue, and Rosa's arrangement was ruined. Lottie is on her way back and asked us to gather the materials for her. She said their plan is on the computer."

We went straight to the workroom and got started. Grace pulled up Lottie's notes and then I went to cooler number one to pull stems. But as I looked around, I realized that the exotic blossoms Rosa needed were gone, and our fresh flower order hadn't come in yet.

I heard Lottie's voice and stepped out of the cooler. "I have bad news, Lottie. We don't have the flowers you need."

Lottie sat down on a stool with a heavy sigh and put

her head in her hands. "I was afraid of that. All the way back I kept praying I was wrong."

"Perhaps we can call around to other flower shops in the area," Grace said as I printed out the orders that had come in overnight.

"It's too late," Lottie said. "The live flower competition is set to start in an hour."

Grace put her hand on Lottie's shoulder. "I'm so sorry, Lottie, dear. And poor Rosa. She did have her heart set on winning the competition, didn't she?"

"She was just tickled to be in it," Lottie said. "She's never been a part of anything like this before. Her whole family is rooting for her."

Trying not to listen to their conversation—or to the little voice in my head that kept whispering, *Rosa's flowers may be gone, but yours aren't*—I went to the cooler to pull red roses and white spider mums for the first order. I had to reach around the white delphinium to get the mums . . . and there were the Casablanca lilies staring at me with big innocent eyes, and the white cymbium orchids, as well, along with the white dendrobium orchids, enough of each lovely white blossom to make a stunning display.

I heard Lottie sigh deeply then scoot back the stool. "Guess I'd better break the news to her."

"Wait, Lottie." I ran to my desk, opened the top drawer, and took out my design. "Rosa can use my plan. We'll put it together here."

For the next fifteen minutes, Lottie, Grace, and I worked together on my floral design, carefully cutting each flower to the perfect height, adding stems of curly willow and bear grass for accent, choosing just the right river rocks for the bottom of the tall glass vase. As it came together, I felt immense pride in my creation and couldn't help but think how wonderful it was to have my Bloomers crew together again, just like old times.

And yet it didn't feel quite as perfect as I remembered.

It wasn't until I stepped back to view the final product that I realized why. We had always been a great team, Lottie, Grace, and me, working as efficiently as a well-oiled machine. But we'd moved on, added a new member, and now, much to my surprise, it simply felt wrong without her.

We boxed the arrangement carefully. Then Grace and I helped Lottie get it into her car and stood at the curb, calling out, "Good luck!" as she drove away.

"It's in God's hands now," Grace said as we returned to the shop.

I closed Bloomers at two o'clock and headed home, nervous and excited about what I'd find when I got there. But I needn't have worried. With Jillian functioning as party director, Francesca as food coordinator, and my mom as head decorator, I walked into my house to find a kitchen setup worthy of a *Top Chef* prize and walked out through my sliding glass door to find my yard full of people and the party in full swing.

Tiki lanterns topped tall poles that ringed our yard, with bright multicolored streamers running between them. Rented folding chairs sat around five long banquet tables covered with bright yellow plastic tablecloths. Red, yellow, and orange helium balloon centerpieces graced each table, and a huge buffet loaded with platters of chicken and bratwurst, salads, fruit, and corn on the cob sat on the patio. A separate table held a selection of beverages, buckets of ice, and stacks of plastic glasses.

"Here she is," Marco called, bringing me a colorful plastic glass filled with punch. After a big round of applause, I called out, "Welcome to our home, everyone." And Marco added, "Please enjoy yourselves. We've got plenty of food and drinks, and luckily the weather is cooperating, because we forgot the tent."

Theda called out, "Here's to our Brandywine host and hostess heroes!" and everyone cheered as they raised their glasses to toast us.

I smiled at the sea of faces, picking out family members along with Nikki and Grace and even—

I turned to Marco in surprise. "You invited Alfie?"

"Just trying to appease my mom," he said quietly.

I saw women from the Books and Bottles Book Club laughing with the Bees as though they were old friends, and Betsy from across the street chatting with Theda, and many others I hadn't met. I was about to walk among them when Theda took me aside.

"I want to show you something."

I followed her around to the front, where she pointed out what I had failed to notice when I drove in: a FOR SALE sign in Mitzi's yard. And then I saw the scarlet woman herself standing at the window, her arms crossed, a scowl on her face as she glared at us. She saw us looking and turned away. I could almost hear her indignant huff.

"There's a *For Sale* sign in the Burnses' window, too," Theda said.

As we started back, I said, "I have to ask you something, Theda. Did you know Mitzi and Tom were having an affair when you sent Sarah home early?"

She looked shocked—sort of. "Whatever would make you think that? You may as well be asking if I knew Maynard Dell was being blackmailed, or if I had proof that Dirk had stolen my friends' jewelry, or, more important, whether I felt you and Marco were savvy enough to bring the true murderer to justice."

She put her arm around my shoulders and said sagely, "There isn't much around here that escapes my attention, Abby, dear. I wasn't always just an elderly woman who loves animals." Then she leaned close to say, "But what else does a retired CIA agent do in her old age?"

I stopped in my tracks to stare at her, and she gave me a wink that I took to mean she was kidding.

Or did it mean to keep that information to myself?

We returned to the backyard to see everyone chatting and filling their plates, safe in the knowledge that Dirk was no longer around, Mitzi Kole was moving on, and Maynard Dell was in jail. As I pondered that, Theda said, "Don't look too hard at the clues, Abby. Just be happy with the results. Welcome to the neighborhood."

Marco and I sat at the head of the center table with family members on both sides. Grace was at the end with seats saved for Rosa and Lottie. It wasn't until later, when Marco and I were up at the buffet about to cut into one of the two huge sheet cakes, that Lottie and Rosa came around the corner, big smiles on their faces.

"We won!" Lottie called in her booming voice, as Rosa raised the big Silver Rose trophy high in the air. Conversations ceased as everyone turned to see what was happening.

"We took first prize in the live floral competition,"

Lottie called. "Someone grab a camera! Abby and Grace, come over here."

A warm feeling radiated from my heart as I walked around the dessert table to stand with my staff. My all-white design had won. I knew it would. I knew it!

"I'll use my phone," Marco said, and stepped back so he could get a shot of the four of us. "Okay, Rosa, hold up your trophy again. Everyone smile."

"No, Marco, wait." Rosa turned to me. "The trophy belongs to you, Abby, not to me. It was your talent and design that won the competition. All I did was accept the award." Blinking back tears, she said, "I can never thank you enough for what you did. *Gracias*, Abby." Then she passed the Silver Rose to Lottie so she could throw her arms around me for a big hug.

"Speech!" my dad called, and then others joined in, applauding when I finally raised my hand for silence.

"First let me introduce these amazing women to you." I pointed at each woman in turn and gave a brief intro, then said, "And I appreciate Rosa's gesture, but the Silver Rose isn't mine. It belongs to all four of us. If an accident hadn't happened, I'm sure Rosa's arrangement would have won. We were just fortunate to have a backup plan."

"I learned something important from this," I continued. "It isn't about winning a trophy. It's about pulling together as a team." I glanced at the three women around me. "And we did that, didn't we?"

After the applause, Marco said, "Now all of you hold the award and smile for me one more time."

We posed and then Rosa said, "Take one more photo, Marco. This time get a shot of just Abby holding it."

The women stood behind me as I wrapped my fingers around that beautiful Silver Rose award and lifted it proudly above my head.

I smiled at Marco and he winked back as though he knew what I was thinking.

Maybe it was about winning the trophy—*just* a little.

ACKNOWLEDGMENTS

Imagination is the beginning of creation. You imagine what you desire, you will what you imagine, and at last you create what you will.
— George Bernard Shaw (1856–1950)

When I imagined Abby Knight, I never dreamed she and her team—her beloved Marco, best friend, Nikki, her zany family, and her cherished staff at Bloomers— would gain so many fans—and then be shared with a wider audience on TV. So my first thank-you is to everyone who took Abby & Company to heart.

My second thanks goes to *my* team, who helped turn my creation into a reality: my past editor, Ellen Edwards, who was with me from the very first plot eighteen books ago and always shared my vision of what the Flower Shop Mysteries could be; editor Laura Fazio, who took Abby Knight under her capable wing; my assistant, Jason Eberhardt, whose ingenious ideas and hilarious insights give the plot greater depth and suspense; my beloved daughter Julie for assisting and supporting my creative endeavors (much like "Mad Mo" Knight is supported by Abby); my author friends the Cozy Chicks; and my personal friends for reminding me to enjoy life.

A special shout-out to Pam Kutchey at Kutchey's Flowers, Key West, Florida, for designing the winning floral arrangement in this book. Thanks, Pam. I loved hanging out with you and your staff in such a marvelous environment surrounded by the lush beauty and exotic aromas of flowers.

Abby is back in the next installment of the
Flower Shop Mystery series by Kate Collins,

YEWS WITH CAUTION

Available in paperback and e-book in
April 2017 wherever Penguin books are sold
or at penguinrandomhouse.com. Read on
for a short, but exciting, excerpt.

Sharp-needled evergreen branches whipped against my face as I fought my way through the dark forested labyrinth. Thorny limbs of overgrown barberry snagged my jeans and scratched my hands deep enough to draw blood. Sweat beaded on my forehead and soaked the T-shirt beneath my jean jacket, even in the cool of the late April afternoon.

I caught a glimpse of a building through the thicket and pushed my way in deeper only to discover what appeared to be a small wooden shack with a steeply pitched roof, its faded candy-colored shutters and fancy gingerbread trim reminding me of the fairy-tale house in "Hansel and Gretel." Unsure of which way to go next, I turned in a circle, trying to remember the way I'd come in, but there was no trace of my path. Indeed, the massive shrubs seemed to be closing in on me, causing my claustrophobia to rear its bristly head.

I pressed my back against the little house and took deep breaths to calm my racing heart. Cupping my hands around my mouth, I yelled, "Marco!" but the only sounds I heard were the birds chirping in the tall overgrown yews.

"Marco! Help me!"

That time even the birds went silent. I sank to the ground, covering my ears with my hands to block out the world.

"Abby?" I heard as though through a tunnel.

"Marco." I jumped up. "I'm here!"

"I don't see you. Move toward my voice. I'll keep talking."

"I don't know where your voice is coming from."

"I'll whistle."

He began to whistle the tune for "Heigh-ho, heigh-ho. It's off to work I go." Under normal circumstances, I would've laughed at his attempt at silliness, but I was in no frame of mind for that now. I stumbled forward on trembling legs, the tall trees blotting out what little light made it through the storm clouds overhead.

The toe of one of my running shoes hit something hard and I fell forward, landing on a circle of old splintered wood, my head directly over the gaping mouth of an old well. A terrible stench arose from the well, as though some unlucky animal had fallen in and died. I scrambled to my feet and backed away, brushing splinters from my palms. Had I not tripped onto the cover, I would have fallen in, too.

"Abby? Talk to me, sweetheart."

"I'm trying to find you, Marco." I carefully sidestepped the well and continued along a narrow winding path between walls of evergreens, watching the ground so I didn't trip again. I heard the crunching of footsteps on dead leaves and the snapping of branches nearby—and then Marco stepped through two tall shrubs. I ran straight into his arms, holding him around his rib cage as my breathing slowed.

"You're trembling all over, Sunshine. What happened?"

"I'm never leaving your side again, Marco, not in a treacherous place like this."

Marco held me by the shoulders to study me. "Abby, we're at a landscape center."